RAVENFALL

YOUR NUMBERS CAME UP!

Donald Piasu

Published in Great Britain by
L.R. Price Publications Ltd, 2019
27 Old Gloucester Street,
London, WC1N 3AX
www.lrpricepublications.com

Cover artwork by L.R. Price Publications Ltd

ISBN-13: 9781916467941

DEDICATION

To Cynthia who always believed in me.

RAVENFALL

YOUR NUMBERS CAME UP!

Donald Piasu

Introduction

How do I do what I do?

It's the first question - the only question - everyone asks. As for the reason - the answer... I can never seem to give a satisfactory explanation.

Some people say: "It wasn't meant to be this way; if I could do it all over again, I would!" Well, sorry, but that's not me. Truth is, I am what I am. I do what I do because... if I didn't, someone else would.

Satisfied? Well, neither am I.

By the end, you'll probably know no more of who I am and where I'm from. But, all that matters is the outcome – one which came about by the actions of one man. You'll also know no less about the day to day actions of people like me, who handle certain affairs, for certain people willing to pay not to get their own hands stained with blood.

Though death is not always the solution, it certainly is final. Sometimes there are certain trade-offs which need to be made for the greater good!

"Whose?" you may ask. Well, that's not something I think too much about. But, maybe - just, maybe – by the end, you *might.*

I can't promise that you'll find any deep meaning to this story, and it certainly won't end the way you'd expect; it's not a tale of good against evil. I'm not the hero; I'm just a person, doing a job.

Those of you out there who think the rules of society and life don't apply to you, consider this a learning experience - you never know when, or where, someone like me might come calling...

CHAPTER 1

The actual matter of life or death is where a person finds the most relevance to how they choose to live, or how they choose to meet their own end. Living on your own terms, or dying for something you believe in, most strongly, is considered by many to be the only power an individual may possess for their whole life.

Most just naturally accept the fate of every human being on this planet: there is the beginning, which is birth, and there is the end, which is death - what happens in-between is our own choice.

Or, sometimes, certain decisions are made for us.

Sometimes free will is not given to us at birth - it is something we have to fight for. As we grow and develop, we come to covet what others have, but lack the means to earn it.

And, the world breeds those who take from others, but do not think to give in return.

Then, there are the lucky ones: those who are given a second chance, even when their own number finally comes up!

The strong odour of greasy food and long-lingering tobacco is always overwhelming to the senses, as one walks through the front door, into any local café – this one was no different.

The sound of a voice, from the small television mounted above the patrons' heads in one corner, boomed down officiously, deafening the conversation of an Indian couple, sat at a side table close to it. Still, other than this, it was quiet.

Which was always an advantage.

The target was seated at the back table, facing away from the counter, attention focused on his third cup of coffee. The meal on the plate before him was only half-consumed.

Aside from the man, there were only three other people, plus the owner: a thin, grey-haired woman, reading a newspaper; but, you could never be too sure who else might turn up.

First off, don't think that this is me confessing to my crimes; I'm not dying, so I'm not asking to pay any form of penance.

I know the people I've killed have families. One squeeze of the trigger - a cut of the blade - changes their lives forever; turns their world upside down. And, I know I'm responsible.

But, people die every day, from accidents and illnesses - that changes lives too; it is no different. At least I make it quick!

There are no guarantees how long you will stay in this world, and all you can hope for is that there is something to look forward to on the other side.

Usually it starts with an envelope containing a photograph and memo of instructions; and, most importantly, the down payment: half of what the job is paying. The instructions are always explicit, as to specifically what you are being paid to do - as long as you follow them to the letter, you can last in the business and make a good career for yourself.

The one thing you won't often find in that envelope is the reason.

But, that day, the reason was why I was there. And, on this particular job, I had a unique set of instructions.

Obviously what I am and what I do is illegal, so the locations, names, dates and circumstances cannot be mentioned, in order to protect certain people's anonymity. As the reader, why don't you just choose where in the world you fancy this story is set? I can't give away much, so I'll leave it to your imagination.

Remember, this could be happening anywhere and, though you may be reading this in your native tongue, books often get published in many languages.

I could be anywhere!

The chair opposite the target was free (let's call him "Martin"), so, ordering a mug of tea, I sat down, causing him to look up, with some interest.

"Mind if I sit here, Martin?" I asked, casually.

Traitors, drug-dealers and human-traffickers are the most common assignment I would usually be assigned to handle - all deserving what they had coming to them, I assure you. Though, I suppose this would depend on how you view justice.

I'm just the tool of the trade; the decision itself comes from those who want - sometimes need *- the job done.*

"Who are you?" he asked. He was dressed from head to toe in mud-stained clothes; his face was pale and tired.

"I'm an associate of a certain party, who has tasked me with reacquiring certain items, which you stole," I said, simply; "quite a lot, according to the manifest I was given."

Playing dumb or straight denial were the usual responses. But, this guy shifted his gaze over me, very carefully, as though he had been expecting my visit. He was a medium-sized man, with thin, dark hair and a fresh bruise on his face; he wasn't known for violent behaviour, but he was notorious when it came to making rash decisions.

"I should warn you: I'm armed," I told him: "there's a silenced Sig Sauer pistol aimed at your abdomen, right now, so I wouldn't get any foolish notions."

He took in the warning, but again looked me over, seeming unconvinced, and even somewhat amused.

"I may not look like much, but I'm quick when I have to be, and I'll be gone before anyone here knows what has happened." I pressed the weapon into his knee, making my point clear.

Martin settled back in his chair; the look of skepticism had now vanished.

"You're here to kill me, anyway," he placed both palms down on the table, "so, what's the difference whether or not I choose to make it easy for you?"

My index finger lightly pressed the trigger, but did not squeeze fully, yet. "If somebody just wanted you dead, I would have waited until you left this place." I allowed myself a little grin. "I'm also here to retrieve what you stole. Why don't you tell me where it is?"

Martin took a sip from his cup and carefully placed both hands back on the table. There was now the appearance of a mild sweat upon his brow; "Its gone. It's all gone."

The answer made my index twitch a little more - not out of rage, but anticipation; maybe this job was going to be over sooner than I had expected.

"You sold it? Pawned it all? Already?" I asked, with clear doubt in my tone.

When I have to ask questions, they try to stall – to delay things. But, in the end, I will do what I have to do; this is nothing personal to me, after all. I always make it quick and clean - anything more than that, I leave to others.

Still, never be in too much of a hurry; take a second to breathe, otherwise you might get sloppy, and miss important things. The screw-ups are what will catch up to you, in the end.

"It was taken from me, last night; some people jumped me, beat me and took it all," Martin reached up and touched the scar on his face, in an irritated manner. "They left me on the side of the road, unconscious. I woke up and the van was gone."

I listened to the words, but found myself doubting his story. "Who were *they*? Old friends… partners in your little scheme?" I looked into his eyes, which turned downward. "Decided on a larger cut, perhaps, leaving you to take the fall?"

It was ironic - to be *done over*, the way he had been - since it was he who had caused so much trouble, by his own actions.

"I guess I can bring this meeting of ours to a close, then, since you have nothing to…" I stopped, and looked at his wrist. The watch he wore was good quality, but it was not on my list. "Nice timepiece they left you with - that was very generous; I guess there is some honour amongst thieves."

Again, I watched his perspiration starting to build.

"You wouldn't be lying to me, Martin?"

The questioning was not my playing a bargaining role: there was no need to negotiate, because he had nothing to offer me now. There are those who offer to double the bounty, but few have the money to actually pay up – if they did *they* would be the ones paying me, to kill those who want *them* dead.

"Let me make one thing clear at this point: there are no compromises; no ways to try and find an understanding; no explanations - I'm not paid to listen, just to do my job."

Martin reached up to stifle a tiny smile, and looked back, defiantly. "I'm sure you're very good."

He looked around the small room; "Don't suppose it would do me any good to make some kind of a scene? You'd probably kill everyone in here, too?"

The sound of two muzzled gunshots would unlikely be heard, any more than the conversation between the couple behind; I'd be on my feet and out the door before anyone knew what had happened.

"It's never personal: its business. And, today… *you* are business. It's best to keep this between the two of us - die with some dignity," I said, with a little disdain. "How you go out is more important than how you came in."

The most anyone could do at this point - at the end - was reminisce over their achievements, family and loved ones, because soon it was all going to disappear; their last thought may as well be a pleasant one.

For reasons already previously stipulated, I can't go too deeply into Martin's personal life. Only so far as to say that from what he was about to leave behind - from his own life achievements - there was little of comfort he would be able to draw upon. Especially when considering that with his crime - that which had made him a wanted man - it was his own family and loved ones he had betrayed.

Slowly, he unfastened the watch from his wrist and slid it across to me. "I only had enough for the cost of this meal - as you can see, it wasn't even that good; this is all I have left - I won't need it now. If you're going kill me, then just do it," he said, uncaring.

At times like this, there is usually begging and pleading. Often, they want to cut a deal: split the money, when there is any, or try to appeal to my better nature.

The watch was nice - too nice for him - so it was something he had perhaps stolen, and maybe attempted to pawn somewhere. Regardless, now this was going to end up the same way it always did.

"Who sent you after me?" he asked.

A common question – amongst those targets who bother to ask - but one I can never answer; "I don't betray the confidence of my employers."

He was even more amused by my retort; "I'm going to die anyway. Whatever, I think I know. I'm glad, in a way, to be leaving this world, knowing that old man is returning to his old ways." He folded his arms, smugly. "Sending you is an especially nice touch."

There are, of course, those who, in the end, happily accept their fate.

They figure it is best just to let go – to leave this world in a manner different to that with which you came into it: kicking and screaming. This wasn't the first or last speech I would hear, and I decided it was only fair to let the man have his say; I knew none of it was personally aimed at me, so it was all just words, anyway.

"I knew he couldn't stay legitimate. Now, my death is going to forever keep him and…"

He suddenly stopped in his gloating, looking as though I had already fired a round, silencing him forever. But, my finger still only lightly pressed the trigger. His face had changed, also, as though some strange, deep, internal revelation had come over him, tightening around his throat, making him gape, as if in some form of shock.

His eyes had become locked to the television; his mouth had dropped wide open.

Suddenly he reached into his pocket, almost causing me to take a shot. Then, I saw it was merely a small piece of paper he was withdrawing, rather than a weapon. Looking over the crumpled sheet, he looked up once more, to the television behind me.

"I've won! I can't believe it! I don't fucking believe it!" he whispered, quietly.

Glancing suspiciously behind, I found that the programme currently showing was that evening's "Euro Millions" lottery draw. The numbers were displayed clearly on the screen, as the announcer read them out, once again:

"Main numbers: five, twenty-five, thirty, forty-five and fifty; 'Lucky Stars': eight and eleven."

When I turned back, he was still clutching the ticket between his fingers. A tiny smile was forming, and the initial look of disbelief was slowly fading, being replaced now by complete jubilation.

I suddenly realized I had been perhaps a little too optimistic; this ploy, however desperately cunning, wasn't going to fool me, much less anybody else in this café. "Thinking positive and being optimistic won't get you anywhere - just a faster bullet than intended."

Rising, he let out a loud cry of victory, almost ramming the edge of the table forcefully into my arm; the jolt nearly did send a bullet his way - only it wasn't now his gut that the barrel was aimed at! "I've just won a hundred-million euros!" he shrieked, causing everyone to look our way.

Each person's decisions can either benefit or betray their own beliefs. As a professional killer, I do not allow emotions to take control of my behavior; when actions are needed, they are requested by the client, with specific terms - I can only judge what action to take within the letter of those who employ me.

Do not mistake any of my gestures for weakness or kindness - behind every of my good intentions is a self-serving cause: not necessarily to get me through the gates of Heaven, but it will sure help keep me a safe distance from the wrath of Hell!

CHAPTER 2

There are two things you need to be a cold-blooded killer: (i) no conscience; (ii) no remorse.

Additionally, to be a professional hitman/assassin takes a very particular skill-set. Planning is of the greatest of importance: you need to know everything before you move in; everything has to be figured out. Deciding when it is right to go in for the kill, and when it is best to wait, is always of great importance, and best done with a cool, clear head. How you will get in and out is where any plan starts: you need to know where everyone is going to be at one time, and to be certain that they have dismissed you as quickly as they have seen you. It is best not to linger or get distracted - stay focused and remember your main objective is to act quickly, and to avoid any mistakes.

The actual act of killing should be done quickly, and without thought - justice or revenge will have been served for your client, then you can go home.

Well, some *jobs go that way.*

Walking hastily along the pavement, I was pulling Martin along by his jacket, until we reached a dark alleyway. Our departure from the café had been brisk.

Throwing him hard against the wall, I shoved the muzzle of the silencer against his chest; "If you speak again, I'll kill you right now!"

Martin just stood there, breathless and flustered.

You might now be thinking to yourself that I'm not the typically average, everyday thug – I could have just shot him and left. Well, you happen to be right.

The people I sometimes work for do not consider intelligence and prudence necessarily traits with which to hold in high regard people who do my type of work. But, for others, such as the one who is paying me for this job, discretion and judgement are important factors, which were specifically outlined in my instructions.

It is also important to know when you've been made; i.e. when a woman sitting in a café sees you holding a gun, it's time to leave, before everything blows up in your face!

"Give me the ticket!" I ordered, trying to keep my voice as low as possible.

Martin was reluctant to part with it at first, but a swift knee to the genitals soon loosened his grip, and caused him to bend over with a whine of pain.

Looking once more at the numbers, I took out my phone and visited to the Euro Millions lottery website, checking the euro jackpot draw - they were, indeed, the winning numbers.

"You are one lucky bastard!" I growled, through gritted teeth. Again came a whine - all Martin could manage at the moment.

I could have just put two in his gut underneath the table and then walked out… if only that girl sitting behind us hadn't been drawn to our table, from Martin's outburst, knocking my arm and fixing her eyes on the gun I was holding on him. My first thought, on instinct, had been to leave immediately, taking Martin with me. I found that nobody was following after us, fortunately for them.

Taking a moment to get my thoughts together, I dialled a number and waited, until the voice of my employer (let's call him "Harry") came onto the line.

At this moment, you might be thinking that writing a book about all of this might be a breach of some sort of code of conduct, but, believe it or not, it isn't, since I haven't told you that much to begin with, have I?

There are indeed rules when you work for the criminal underworld, but so far I have not broken any – so far this is just a story about a guy I'm about to kill, who, at his last moment, has just won a fucking fortune!

At the end of each job, or when complications arise, it is customary to keep those higher up informed of the current situation - this present, particularly unique situation was certainly something to report in.

I could have still just killed Martin and walked away. But, rules are rules. So, instead, I made a phone call to my employer.

How is it that I can make a decision like this?

Well, I'm the one holding the gun.

Besides, it wasn't me who wanted this man dead. It's never personal - always just business. It is not for me to decide who lives or dies, no matter what the circumstances; I am just a device. I don't take enjoyment from my work; I don't feel it gives me power. The power comes from those who wish the life to be taken - they just use others to enact their will.

"I've found the target. He says he was betrayed by his associates and lost everything," I said, into the phone. "Right now, we're standing in an alley; I've got my gun pointed at his head."

There was a brief silence - not another word for ages. Clearly, disappointment was starting to sink in at this news.

Then, Harry came back again. "So, why haven't you finished the job?" he asked, flatly.

It wasn't all good news, but it wasn't all bad, either!

"The main reason I'm calling you is because the target is in possession of a Euro Millions lottery ticket, which is worth a lot of money."

The voice went quiet again, then finally spoke: "What do you mean?"

I realized I wasn't coming across very clearly; considering I was trying to keep the situation under control and report in, my mind was focused on two things at once. "I'm holding the winning ticket…" I paused, looking it over more carefully. "Would you mind holding a moment?"

Putting my gun away, I lifted Martin's head by the jaw and held the back of the ticket up to his eyeline; "This isn't even signed - why haven't you signed it?"

Realization began to cover Martin's face, making his complexion turn even whiter. "I… I… didn't think I'd win." His eyes now became fearful - as would anybody's, in this situation.

I returned my attention to the phone, keeping Martin under control by the jaw: "Sorry about that – a slight technical error."

"How much money are we talking?" Harry asked, impatiently.

"It's the full winning jackpot: about a hundred-million."

As I should have expected, the line went quiet again; this wasn't the most typical of reports to give a client.

"Is this some sort of bloody joke?" Harry's voice returned, now with a slightly irate tone.

"I wouldn't phone you if I wasn't being serious," I countered, remaining respectful.

Martin's eyes were still watery, but now actively looking off to the side - to the alleyway's entrance. I gave his jaw a slight squeeze, warning him not to get any ideas about calling out, to anyone who might happen to pass by.

"I need some time to think about this. Standby where you are and I'll call you right back."

Harry hung up, and we were left standing in that dark alley. I'd never actually killed anybody in a place like this before: it was not really my style. If a killing had to be made in private, it was best to do it indoors - only kill outside if you're in an isolated area. On the streets - these days, full of people and C.C.T.V. - it's just not wise.

Nor is letting your attention slip for a moment!

Martin's forearm had come crashing down onto mine, breaking the grip from his face; he followed up with a hooked punch round to the side of my head.

Ducking underneath, I covered my head with my arms and, using a defence style known as the *pensador*, delivered a vertical elbow strike directly under Martin's chin, to stun. I ended the conflict with a double hammer-fist combo to the head and a forward crushing forearm strike - known as the *pensataq* - to his chest. The impact sent him flying back, hard, against the wall, before sliding down it to sit on the ground, his legs sticking out, either side of my feet, as he wheezed harshly through his throat.

I hated myself for allowing my guard to drop; I shouldn't have put the gun away. At least my keysi fighting skills were enough to overpower his feeble efforts.

It is a necessity to know how to handle oneself physically, as well as just to pull a trigger - you never know when it might come in handy.

I don't like violence, but I accept it to be a part of human nature; it is necessary, when you have to do what needs to be done. You may not have been the one to have started it, but be sure there is only one way it will end: not as the other person expects!

"Are you going to kill me?" Martin finally got his voice back.

Standing over him, I tried to return to my original composure, answering quietly: "That's not my call, now."

As though to clarify the statement, the phone rang in my pocket. This time taking out my gun and keeping it in play, I used my free hand to retrieve my mobile, once more.

Harry's voice came back onto the line: "Given the circumstances, he's worth more to us alive now, so we'll need to make an adjustment to the contract."

These were not the words I had wanted to hear, but had been expecting: it was a lot of money, and there was still a debt which needed to be paid.

"What are you going to do about sending one of your men to look after this guy?" I asked, hastily, looking around to check it was still all clear.

Harry's thoughts were already coming down the line and into my head, before he even spoke: "Well, I've got you there now, haven't I?" I immediately didn't like what Harry was implying.

"I'm an eliminator, not a babysitter!" I said, flatly. "You sent me up here to kill him and to get back what he stole." And, so far, neither task had been fully completed, which made me uncomfortable.

"Well, he doesn't have that any more. But, there is still the money." Harry's voice was firm and clearly decisive on the matter, which he was now placing on me.

"Which he doesn't have, right now," I protested, feeling the urge to put a boot into Martin's gut. "He won't be able to pay you for weeks. If you want, I can still settle the debt the other way."

"No, no - I need him alive! A big opportunity just dropped into my lap; this could be the answer to a lot of our problems." Insistently, Harry said: "So, I'm putting him in your charge - you are going to escort him to wherever you need to go and claim that money!"

Claim the money? Like they're going to just hand it over in suitcases, in large denominations? I wasn't even sure how you went about claiming such a prize.

This was something I didn't want to hear. Nor would any professional, for that matter. When the assignments get more dangerous – stranger - you begin to question your loyalty to them. But, speaking out of turn, to employers who have done right by you over the years, is not something you jump into rashly.

When you fail to meet your objective, and start questioning your orders, that's when they *start to question your abilities, and your dedication.*

There are weeks - even months - when business can be slow. Then, it's not like I can go handing out business cards to every casual acquaintance, or that I can set up my own website.

It's always best to put business first: dedication to the work will prove your worth, and that's all you have going for you.

Looking down, once again, at my feet, I saw that Martin was still sitting there, clutching his chest. If only it had been a more forceful edge-of-hand strike to his throat, I wouldn't be having this conversation right now.

I suspect that there are a lot of you questioning, right about now: why did I just stand there, with an unsigned lottery ticket worth a hundred-million? Why didn't I just take it, or kill him and take the ticket to Harry?

Yes, I could have put my own name on it, killed Martin and disappeared, but, for reasons I'm not prepared to explain, I'll simply say it wouldn't be right.

Yes, even a killer has morals, strange as it may seem. It's not my ticket, and I didn't pick the numbers.

Remember, this whole situation is nothing personal, nor anything to do with me. I'm a complete professional, just doing a job, and anybody out there who thinks differently, and who would have taken the money, shame on you!

I didn't mention to Harry that it had not been signed, because, at the time, I didn't think it relevant: my job was to find Martin and retrieve what he stole. One out of two was satisfactory, to my employer.

Reaching down and dragging Martin back onto his feet, I placed the barrel of the silencer under his jaw cavity and spoke, firmly: "You and I haven't started out on the best of terms." I emphasized this with a slight, threatening, upward dig. "Your actions make me question whether or not you're going to survive this unique opportunity you've just been handed!"

Martin kept quiet, listening to every word being spoken, and clearly glad he was still able to hear at all.

"Despite what you might think, I'm a reasonable person," I told him; "when they're needed, I give direct instructions, and I expect direct obedience - anything other than that and this all ends quickly!"

All Martin could do was let out another low moan.

We walked out of the alley, together. We had a little journey ahead of us - I just hoped it wasn't going to be too long. Then again, if Martin did something stupid along the way, maybe it wouldn't.

It wouldn't be my fault if I had to kill him - I was tasked with keeping him alive, but if he, himself, didn't value that enough, things could happen differently.

The basic fact of life is that we all die, sooner or later. But, if you're lucky, you might just find that the man upstairs has extended your credit, for just a little while longer.

Maybe that was how it was for Martin: at the last moment, divine intervention stepped in, to give him one last chance.

But, so far, he wasn't living up to certain expectations - not in my book, anyway.

CHAPTER 3

Do I believe in God?

That is the question I remember the most about this whole story. Not because Martin asked me, and not because I'm particularly that religious; I just happened to see it, written in a leaflet somebody left on a bench at the train station.

It read: "God is all powerful. He gives us the free will to choose our own paths; what we choose to do is our own choice. If we believe our actions are of service to society, and to those we call our neighbours, then, in God's eyes, our actions are just."

In truth, there isn't one person who hasn't thought that somebody deserves to die - mainly because they are a bad person, or they lived a life hurting others. It isn't evil to think that way: to wish somebody dead is a darkness which lives in all of us. Sometimes, people even pray to God, to take the life of another.

That is no different to hiring someone like me, because, like God, I have the power to take a life. I have the will to do what my employers cannot, or, for whatever reason, are unable.

Like God, using his avenging angels.

I'm no angel, but I have enacted vengeance for other people, on many occasions. Maybe even for one or two of you, out there reading this.

Are there, amongst you, those who find some correlation between what is being presented in these pages and your own lives?

Okay, perhaps you've never killed, or hired a killer. But, you may have won a fortune.

Tell me, what went through your mind when your lucky numbers came up?

Sitting next to me, in the waiting area, Martin kept quiet, while I looked through the rules and regulations for claiming the lottery prize money, on their website.

I was also able to look up a breakdown of the prize fund for that night, and was surprised to find that there were actually a lot more winners than I thought there would be. Most only won a very small proportion, of course, while the third largest winner received just over twenty-two thousand.

"How did you find me?" Martin finally spoke, surprising me.

"That's a trade secret," I replied, still looking through the denominations. The table showed only one winner of the top prize - that had to be Martin's ticket. It just didn't seem right to me: that whole jackpot going to one person.

"Nobody knew where I was, except… Did my… associates… turn me in, after they left me?"

I laughed, scrolling down the phone's screen; "You really do have a low opinion of human nature." Then, I glanced briefly at Martin: "Tell me: would you have done the same, if you had been in their shoes?"

He looked away, with the expression of a spiteful child.

"Suffice to say it took considerable effort and expense to track you down," I concluded.

This wasn't actually true. There had been, in fact, a tiny tracker on the van they had stolen and used to transport the goods. Nowadays, you only had to pop in a sim card and call it from a mobile phone. This detail had not been mentioned to the police, at Harry's request; it was town business, and in this town they took care of their own affairs.

So, that was when he called and charged me with finding Martin, and retrieving what he had taken. I had found the van, not too far away, in an abandoned garage. It was empty, so I asked around, showing the picture of Martin I had on my phone - I hit a break and found him at the café.

You might now be asking: "Why are you taking a train? Don't you have your own car?"

Well, because I came up to retrieve what Martin and his associates had stolen – which happened to include a van; since I work alone, I couldn't very well bring another vehicle up here, just to have to leave it here, while I drove the van back.

When I found the van, all the wheels and the engine had been removed - probably sold off to some garage, as spare parts. That would also need to be included on Martin's bill!

"You should consider yourself fortunate," I said, with complete sincerity: "I don't do this sort of work. I kill; I don't make deliveries."

He scowled at the thought of being referred to as nothing more than a parcel. "Why do you need me? You've got the ticket."

"Yes, but it's your ticket!" I said, reminding him that it was useless without the actual winner.

"So, why can't I keep it?" he argued, like a badly behaved child, who'd had his favourite toy taken away – a toy which was currently in my jacket's inner pocket, for safe keeping.

"As long as I am holding onto it, I know you're not going anywhere, are you?" I said, relishing the control I now possessed.

This made him a little angrier. "I could… I could leave… run away!" he threatened.

"With what?" I countered. "What have you got without this ticket? You're wanted by the police."

Without any money or means, and being a wanted man, we both knew Martin had no choice but to comply with my instructions, and those of my employer. He was actually getting off quite lightly, given the circumstances.

"I could still take it from you. I could smuggle myself aboard a ship, and take the ticket abroad." He was thinking fast, on his feet, but to no avail.

"Well, you *couldn't* go abroad with it: according to the rules it has to be claimed in the country in which the ticket was purchased," I said, smugly. "What other options did you have before you met me? Just that watch, and I'm not sure I even want to know where that came from. But, then, I'm not big on asking questions."

Martin's eyes now shied away and came to rest on his own fingers, interlocked between his knees. His situation was hopeless, even if he refused to admit it, if only to himself.

"The only reason you're not dead right now is because of this lottery ticket: my employer believes that now you just might be able to make up for all the damage you've done!" I added a slight judgement to my tone; "My understanding is that you hurt a lot of people; you owe them, too!"

He looked around again, now puzzled: "What did I do to you?"

"Nothing. Well, not until our meeting in the café, anyway," I said, glancing around to the display board, "and our little scrap in the alley."

At this, Martin again felt the throbbing pain in his chest; it had been a rash move to go up against a professional. "You're tougher than you look," he conceded; "I should have known better than to take on a cold-blooded killer-"

"I'm not cold-blooded," I quickly jumped in, almost offended by the accusation. "I've got nothing invested in this; I will be paid, whether you get the money or you don't. Whether you live or die, on the other hand, is all on you!"

Again, Martin bowed his head, with skepticism; "You think he's going to let me keep it?"

The answer to this question, again, was of no real concern to me, and involved no emotional involvement on my part. "He didn't say otherwise," I said; "perhaps you'll just have to pay what you owe, and maybe spend some time in jail."

Martin surprised me by chuckling, half-heartedly: "What good is money if-"

"That's down to you and your solicitor; I'm just doing my job." I was now growing tired of the conversation; it shouldn't be too much longer before our train arrived.

Martin leaned over, to whisper, quietly: "Your job was to kill me."

I gave the statement some short consideration, remembering how easy it would be to do just that, if not for my new obligation to my employer.

"That might still be a possibility." I looked him coldly in the eyes, before returning, once more, to my phone, and reading, yet again, the claim details outlined on the Lotto website.

I'm just going to quickly take you through how we made the claim, leaving out any of the winner's suspense - it's not that sort of story, and you already know that Martin was the sole, main winner.

Firstly, we had to contact Lotto Centre and arrange to have the prize money awarded. The telephone number was on the back of the ticket, which put us immediately through to a representative of the lottery team. She asked for the slip number on the ticket, and, of course the winning numbers, to check on their system if the ticket was indeed a winner.

Like I said: no dramatic suspense - it was indeed the winning ticket. What a lucky bastard!

We needed to make an appointment with the Winners' Advisor - the person who validated the ticket and gave out the prize. The meeting would take place at a designated location, chosen by the winner. This was usually the winner's home, but, considering Martin was in trouble with the law, it was the last place we could offer. There were, however, the regional Lotto Centres, which were staffed during the hours that tickets could be validated.

Over the weekend, these appointments were usually made for the Monday, so the banks were open to receive the winnings. It was now

Friday night, so we had three days to kill.

Well, hopefully not *kill*!

Now, I know there's at least one of you out there, asking: "Why didn't you just mail it?"

Really?! Would you put a hundred-million euro lottery ticket in an envelope and send it in the mail? Would you trust it not to get lost? Would you even trust it with a courier?

Well, maybe you *would...*

Still, I had my orders: to take Martin and claim the money, straight away!

We would need two forms of I.D., to fill out the claim forms. This was a problem: Martin didn't have the necessary, even though there was a variety of listed choices he could bring - he had left both his passport and his birth certificate at home, and thrown away his driver's licence, after he'd woken on the road, in case he was picked up by police. So, now we had a problem.

But, according to Martin, a call to Harry could fix that.

Well, at least now I no longer had to be discreet regarding the identity of my employer.

The situation between a client and the target is usually of no concern to people in my profession - it is just a financial arrangement, involving the payment of funds, to carry out a particular service. The kind you couldn't advertise in your local newspaper.

Moving off of the bench, I walked over to the ticket booth, keeping a cautious eye on my charge.

It looked like Martin had spent the last of his money on dinner and a

Euro Lotto ticket, so it was left to me to spring for the train tickets. This was just typical: I must have been stuck with the only multi-millionaire in the world who can't afford to buy his own train ticket!

As a hired killer, you get paid a certain sum, depending on the contract; the nature of the target - or "mark" - is the reason why some jobs are better paid than others.

That said, doing a job wasn't always about the money... certainly not Martin's millions, anyway. I'm not looking to be rich - I've seen how those people live: how they become so spoilt, they lose respect for the rest of humanity.

What do I know of humanity, you may question; someone who takes people's lives? Well, I only kill those who need killing. And, only at the request of another; it's never personal, and my particular craftwork is usually quick and painless.

I'm not lying when I say that killing brings me no pleasure. But, I know it can bring satisfaction to others - those who have been wronged.

In society, we all have to pay a price for our wrongdoings, and Martin's bill had now arrived. Only, through some miracle, he had found the capital necessary to pay the cheque!

CHAPTER 4

I'll warn you, right now: stories such as this tend to end with mixed results.

It's going to get complicated towards the end, because that's just the way life is: it rarely runs like a movie, unless it is scripted that way. Things happen, which are just out of our control.

A person who experiences much bad luck might think they were born cursed. They may blame their parents for their misfortunes, but how the fuck were Mum and Dad supposed to know the sort of things which were bound to happen.

Some people are just born unlucky.

Then, there are those who make their lives worse, with bad decisions.

Harry's office - and main premises of business - was situated on the outskirts of the town. His own private residence was right in the heart of the town, which, for the benefit of this story, I will call "Ravenfall".

Whilst "Ravenfall" is, of course, just an alias, in many ways it is appropriate, when considering the amount of – primarily passerine - species of bird which can be found around the area. Indeed, on his desk, Harry owned a very beautiful stuffed *corvus corax* – more commonly known as the northern raven, at twenty-five inches in length, with dark feathers and a thick bill. Its wings spread wide, as though preparing to take off.

Harry was admiring the raven, when there came a knock from outside. Shortly after, having not received a response, a small, blonde-haired girl entered through the front door; behind her followed one of Harry's associates: a broad-shouldered man, in a sharp suit. His name was Victor; he ran the security side of Harry's business operations - mainly the construction and development projects around Ravenfall.

"Laurie" was Martin's wife, and Harry's own illegitimate daughter. He had arranged to have her picked up from their house and, at his request, to join him here – her and the twins she carried in her belly.

Her mother had been an old flame of Harry's, but the relationship had been difficult, and had not gone very far, because Helena's father had not approved of their being a couple. Which was ironic, because Harry had never approved of Laurie marrying Martin.

His eyes immediately caught the bump of her belly - it was much larger than when he had last seen her, a couple of months ago; when Martin had still been with her, and had not yet run away.

With regards to Martin's disappearance, Laurie had already been to the local police station, and she had co-operated as best she could; but, in truth, there was really nothing she knew. Martin hadn't confided in her at all before he had left, two days earlier; he had not even left her a note! Harry knew that she was an innocent in all of this, and just as much of a victim as he.

More so, in fact, given the fact she was carrying his children.

Though, not everyone saw it this way. She looked a little queasy, so he offered her a seat.

"I'll stand - I don't really want to be here any longer than I need to," she said. "Just tell me what you know about Martin. I'm guessing you found him; that's why I'm here, right?"

She eyed him, carefully, through slightly red lids, with dark bags underneath. *All those sleepless nights, crying; what a waste of good mascara!*

Harry figured she wouldn't have been sleeping well, given the events of the past two days.

"Well, I have got some news to tell you, but I really do think you should take a seat," he motioned towards the chair: "what I have to tell you is a little complicated, and will probably come as something of a shock."

Laurie had assumed that when Harry found Martin, he would make him suffer, severely, for the harm he had caused. What she had not expected to hear was what Harry told her: that Martin was now a very rich man.

"I don't believe you!" was all she could manage, sitting down across from him, in disbelief. Why was he doing this to her: putting her through all this false hope?

"It's only natural that you would doubt what I'm telling you. But, I have it on good authority that your family is about to become very wealthy," he reassured her, with uncharacteristic tenderness.

The last thing that Laurie had expected when Harry's man – Victor; some ex-military thug - had turned up on her doorstep, was to be brought here and played like a fool.

"He's never won anything in his life," she said, sourly; "he's always had a problem with gambling, but it's never done him any good."

Harry had always known this was Martin's problem, and had done his best to warn her of it. "The same could be said of you; the worst gamble you ever made was marrying a man like that!" he said, catching Laurie's scowl of resentment.

"I suppose you sent one of your pit-bulls after him," she challenged, looking over to Victor, still standing by the door. "They must have beaten him so hard that he'd tell them anything!"

Harry had always accepted her resentment at having a gangster for a father, who only acknowledged his parental responsibilities privately; never in public. Not letting her temper bother him, he said, coolly: "It's a genuine lottery ticket, worth a hundred-million euros. By rights, half belongs to you."

Laurie's mind took in what he had said, and she was now feeling a shiver creep up her spine, as she began to realize that this was all real - it wasn't a hoax, or a trick, to test her. Martin was still alive, and for now, apparently, in good health.

"So, why don't you just bring him back with it?" she queried.

Harry was pleased that she was now calm. He began to fill his pipe with tobacco, then thought better of it. "I thought it was appropriate to get the money claimed as soon as possible. He has lost everything else that he took, so he has to pay us back in some way," he said, with justification.

While Laurie sat motionless, taking this all in, Harry spied the envelope in her hands: "You did bring what I asked you to?"

She rose from the seat and stepped forward, dropping the vanilla envelope onto the desk in front of him.

"Don't think the money is going to make me go soft on you; I still haven't forgotten what you intended to take from me... from my children..." she touched the bump of her midriff, sympathetically.

Harry knew he had been a ruthless man in his younger years, and it had cost him, greatly. But then, Martin was no saint, either: a lousy husband who abandoned his wife in moments like this; he would surely make a lousy father.

"I always swore to your mother that I would look after you, and that's exactly what I'm doing: I'm looking out for your interests-"

"Not to mention your own interests!" she cut him off, quickly. "Surely, you don't think that I don't know you're going after a share of that money?"

Harry didn't see any point in denying that he had a vested interest in getting the money claimed, as soon as possible; he did indeed have plans for it – ones which were in the interest of the whole community. "He owes me; he owes the community," he replied, flatly. "Martin has the opportunity to make things right - it's why I've decided to let him live."

Again, Laurie eyed him, carefully; "And, if he hadn't bought that ticket?"

Harry eyes became hard, as he once again began filling his pipe; "You and I wouldn't be talking now." He didn't even pretend to give it a moment of thought.

She made her way to the door, turning back to address him one last time: "How do I know I can trust you not to kill Martin, once you've got the money?"

The question hit a nerve, slightly; it was sad to hear it put that way, from her lips. "How do you know that you can trust Martin, not to run away again?" he countered. Trust was a funny thing, especially when it came to relationships… and money.

Laurie continued past Victor, and went through the door without another word. Harry looked on, after his daughter, from his throne.

The thing about power is that it has both a positive and a negative effect. Take electricity: it can provide comfort in life, yet, if you come too close to contact, it can take a life!

Despite such danger, both men and women struggle to obtain power, without truly grasping both concepts of it. Therefore, the pleasures it brings are only shallow, and naturally unfulfilling. Money and power mean nothing, if you've no one to share them with.

But, it is an easy option: there is no end of desperate people, who can be coerced or manipulated into desperate acts, just to keep themselves and their families alive.

Now that Harry had the documents, he had to get them to Martin, and the contractor who was with him.

A woman that Harry had known for some time had a son, who had recently quit college and was looking for manual labour; as a favour, Harry had offered him a position. Unfortunately, he had recently found out that the boy - "Laurence" - had been working for somebody else: carrying out security work at a city nightspot. This was misconduct: any other employment had to be disclosed on the employment application form, even if that employment was easy money from a night-time gig, which didn't interfere with the day job. However, since Harry was friends with Laurence's mother, he decided that a small disciplinary measure would suffice, and may even present the lad with a good opportunity to earn some real money.

Now, as Laurence – already well-built, at the age of eighteen - sat across from Harry, straight up, in the tiny chair, his face wore a somewhat sheepish expression.

"I wasn't making enough money," he explained, defensively; "the work from you was a little bit slow. I'm not ungrateful - I just saw an opportunity to earn a little more, for the house; to help my mum out with the bills."

Harry was always willing to give credit where it was due: the lad was ambitious and he was loyal to his family. But, if people needed money so badly, he wished they would talk it over with him first. "I told you the conditions when you first started working for me," he said: "independent jobs and freelancing are for private contractors; those with no ties to the firm or its members."

"Are you going to fire me?" Laurence asked, with concern.

Usually this was an instant sacking offence, but Harry spotted a chance for the lad to prove his reliability, and to earn his redemption in the process.

"Well, you're not exactly on my trust list at the moment, and you're not working for free, either. I know it's small, but you are just starting out; you have to work your way up in this world. I need to know that my people are reliable and loyal, and I look after my friends, as if they were family."

Laurence knew about Harry's friendship with his mother, but would never consider him to be family; at least, certainly not the type to replace his father, a man who may have been poor, but who, at least, was honest and hard-working.

"It's all a matter of authority," Harry continued: "certain things I cannot allow – that's how an organization such as mine remains respected."

He rose from his seat and went to look out of the window. "What we build here is for the good of this community. You're a good, strong lad; very talented in the boxing ring, from what I've seen at the school tournaments."

Laurence didn't remember seeing him there, though the town's people often supported many of the youth programs. Besides, he was well known at high school for being ranked number one. Perhaps, someday, he would get a shot at turning professional. But, first, he had his mother and the house to take care of, and he needed this job.

"So, what do I have to do?" he asked, clearly eager to make amends.

This pleased Harry, and proved to him that everyone indeed deserved a shot at redemption.

"A bit of courier-work - take a package to a certain location," he explained, picking up the vanilla envelope on his desk. "It's an important job, so you do it and you're back in my good books. I understand you've got an aunt up north - could be a chance to pay her a little visit."

Laurence was well aware of Harry's history, so felt it was best to know exactly what he was getting himself into: "What's in the package?"

Harry didn't like being asked such questions. "It's very important. That's all you need to know."

Laurence looked at the envelope in Harry's hand; it wasn't particularly big. He reached out to take it, then paused, hesitantly, withdrawing his hand. "No disrespect, Sir, but I'm the one carrying it - if I get stopped…" he hesitated, slightly, "…and there turns out to be something… not entirely kosher…" His words trailed off, as Harry's eyes turned to stone.

"Maybe I should find someone else." Harry withdrew his hand and the envelope, walking back to behind his desk.

Laurence knew he had hit a nerve, but there was no excuse for crime; he needed a job, but would do nothing that felt too cagey. "I'm sorry, Sir - I'll clear out my locker, immediately." He rose to leave.

"What about your mother?" Harry called after him. "Won't she be upset to hear that you've lost your job?"

Laurence stopped at the door, then turned to look back at Harry. "My mother raised me to be a man, not a boy, who would irresponsibly take anything on offer, without even questioning just what it is that only I can deliver, and the post office can't."

As he opened the door, Laurence tried to think of how he was going to explain the same thing to his mother, especially now that their rent had increased; the security work just wasn't going to be enough.

"Come back in and sit down, son," Harry called to him, again; "I think you and I need to work this out like men."

Laurence turned to see Harry smiling, showing a clear hint of his understanding and admiration. As he retook his seat, Harry moved his own chair from behind the desk, placing it directly in front of Laurence, so that they now sat face to face.

"Very few would've been willing to throw in the towel like that - so easily. Not the act of a champion, but good common sense, nevertheless." Harry beamed, in an uncharacteristic show of pride; "I think you remind me a lot of your mother, when she used to work for my father. I liked her a lot; I went out of my way to keep her good name untarnished."

Harry may have been a crook, but he was fair when it came to good, respectable people, and Laurence nodded. He was grateful to Harry; his mother had always said they should be.

"You didn't have to do what you did for her," Laurence said, honestly.

"You didn't have to come back in the room, but you did. Why?"

Laurence felt a little like he was back in school, before the headmaster; perhaps being patronized for not doing so well in his classes. He was smart, just probably not as much as others. "You've always shown my family respect," he replied, trying to reiterate his gratitude.

His mother had been accused of gross misconduct by the company, once, but Harry had been the one to save her job, which, at the time, she had so badly needed.

"And, your mother always showed hers to mine. It's why I took you on, and I haven't regretted it, up to now. There are many who have disappointed me: you know about my stepson, Martin - about what he has done to this town?"

A dark cloud came over the young man's face: "He stole my grandmother's jewellery." The bitterness in the boy's voice was strong, and slowly building, along with his rage. The day after the Martin incident, Harry had seen Laurence swinging a sledge-hammer so hard that the wooden handle had broken free from its head. If he didn't curb his temper in the ring, the opponent was going to lose more than just a title.

"I've managed to locate him, Laurence," Harry said, noticing a look of surprise and optimism appear across the boy's face. "I'm afraid, however, that everything he took is gone."

As Laurence took the news in, he couldn't fathom why he or his mother had not been told of this sooner; "The police haven't contacted us, or anyone…"

"They don't know, Laurence - I found him through an unofficial source. There is much more to all this, but I need to be discreet about it; something has occurred which will make up for all of it – of that I assure you. There is going to be a big project coming up, if we can get this deal done, and there'll be a lot of work available - big opportunities for a smart lad such as yourself."

Laurence didn't like Harry's tone – he still felt that he was being patronized. But then, by his age, he knew that was often how older people spoke to the young. This was particularly true when older people warned that there could be repercussions, if certain emotions were not controlled, which is exactly what Harry had done, after Laurence had broken the sledgehammer. He had only been trying to vent his anger, otherwise unable to console his mother about losing her own dear mother's jewellery. And, he knew the theft had been his fault, for not locking the door behind him, when he went to the gym that day. It was the one thing he had always been taught: the need to be cautious – but, that day, he had not taken heed.

Now, listening as Harry was telling him of Martin's good luck, he could once again could hear those warnings coming back to him. But, he also knew, deep down, that the town needed the money.

Taking the envelope, he made straight for home, packed a few things and told his mother he was going away for a short while; he left enough money to tide her over. As he made for his motorbike, he stopped, and a thought occurred to him; reaching into his jacket pocket, he took out his mobile phone and made a short call.

Then, fixing his helmet in place, he started off, making sure to stop off at the nearest petrol station - one could never be too careful, and he had been given money for expenses.

Caution is what keeps you safe. It keeps you on the straight and narrow. It is your one true friend – one that you never want to lose. The questions that you ask, and the answers you receive, are all vital aids to your survival.

Some jobs you take on freely, because they seem simple; others require some thought, perhaps because they are a little too much for a person of your limited talents. But, listening very carefully to that little voice in your head, you can begin to weigh up the pros and cons. And, somewhere in between, you have to decide whether to stay where you are, or to take a chance.

Whatever the outcome, you accept that you are easily disposable.

CHAPTER 5

The innocent die, while the guilty live on - that's just how it sometimes goes. It is not a world of innocence that we live in.

We start out innocent, but, as we grow, we begin to see just how horrid the world can be.

Some say that it is not people who make it this way; that is just how it was created.

But, they also say that God made man in his own image; therefore, the terrible things that we say and do have been imprinted into our nature, presumably in order to do His dirty work.

So, what is *His excuse for this world?*

There are those, unhappy with the way things are, who try to do something about it. Not necessarily for the good of the world, or the people in it, don't get me wrong: they just know that self-serving ideals are the cornerstone of making your way in the big leagues; stepping over others, to get to the top, creates a staircase – one built from skeletons.

Mr. Braddock had a reputation for getting what he wanted.

He knew that people have a habit of saying "yes" only until they get what they want, and then "no", when they're no longer interested in what you have to offer. "Hard Ball" is a common term in business, and

Braddock knew that, at times, if you wanted to hear “yes” coming out of somebody’s mouth, there was no choice but to be ruthless and uncompromising.

Many welcomed Braddock, publicly, but despised him privately, due to his harsh business methods. But, he didn’t doubt that every corporation - however big or small - was into something *slightly* non-legitimate; you can’t make it in this world, just by an honest buck.

Not everyone, however, was able to see that same logic – thus, they became a liability. And, just how much of their concern they had already shared was a key factor in maintaining the company’s image; when it came to confidential company information, discretion was always required. In business, you have to do more, to go that little bit further; those who choose not to see your way of thinking have to be made to see reason.

Hostile negotiations involve a civil tongue, yet a rock-hard heart.

The heavy-handed work he left to others, such as the large man before him, panting slightly with exertion. In front of the large man was a small man, currently receiving a savage beating.

Awkward silences in business meetings often required certain pressures to be applied, in order to loosen tongues – though, those words were not necessarily always audible, or comprising full sentences. For Timothy, the metallic taste of blood, mixed with the saliva which dripped from the corners of the mouth – not to mention the odd broken tooth - made speaking particularly difficult.

Tied to his own kitchen chair, he looked up into the hard-set eyes of a man who had at one time been his business partner, as well as to the man's associate – Gavins - who was already nursing bruised knuckles.

Gavins was a brute, who had been unable to find regular work after leaving the forces, and whom Braddock had taken on as his head foreman. He wasn't the first, when it came to knowing anything about construction, but he had unique means of ensuring discipline amongst the work crew.

Following a snap of the fingers, at the request of his master, he stopped his playful exercise. He didn't like being treated like a dog, unless he had a nice bone to chew coming his way.

At first sight Braddock didn't seem the sort who would commission another person's death – but, beneath the false exterior, one would quickly find that he stood outside the moral laws of civilization. His supposed dealings with misfits like Gavins – a man who would cut someone's throat, without the slightest suggestion of moral conduct - had dubbed Braddock the "merchant of death".

Being thought of as no better than any hired gun actually made him unhappy; he preferred to refrain from taking a life, unless it was very personal, or occurred at short notice.

There was, however, always plenty of time for small-talk; it wasn't as if there wasn't plenty of that to go round – just like the treatment being dished out by Gavins.

Greed, force and might were the key ingredients to making a company thrive - if one didn't have the sense or the stomach to apply these things, it was time to exit this business; to take early retirement.

"I wish you would reconsider my proposal, Tim; I don't enjoy this as much as my associate, here. But, in the harsh realities of business, you just have to knuckle down," Braddock quipped. His tone was not that of a tough-spoken man - more that of a snake, talking to its prey. One with thick scales and a look in the eyes which read like the rest of his persona: cold and bloodless.

"I've read through the report you sent to the local council. As thorough and accurate as it is, it does cause the company a setback for this particular project, which is unacceptable."

Timothy couldn't speak: his throat was swelling badly from all the blood he had swallowed, during the meeting's past half-hour.

"I think you've been pushing yourself too hard, with all the fine work you've been doing; you're looking a little worse for wear. Some time off - on a permanent basis - would be in your best interests now." Braddock added: "But, I have to say, I'm proud of your tolerance towards the heavy caseload being piled onto you."

In the corner, Gavins chuckled; his master shot him a disapproving glare.

Moving over to the desk, Braddock picked up a sheet of paper, which he displayed before Timothy's eyes; they were as swollen and cut as the rest of his face, and Timothy was unable to make out the wording, through his blurred vision.

Braddock explained for him: "I've taken the incentive to draw up this letter of resignation, on your behalf - all it needs is your signature. I will then contact the company solicitor, who will follow up shortly with your settlement package."

It would take a lot more than a settlement to repair the harm that had been done to Timothy, but he knew that if he held out any longer, there would be no need for him to sign anything; there was no use in holding out - all he could do was nod in surrender. Immediately, he found one of his arms being cut loose, and could feel a pen being placed between his fingers. He scribbled his signature, as best he could, and hoped that this meeting was finally over.

Braddock's satisfied smile, and a nod in Gavins's direction, made relief wash over Timothy, as he welcomed release from his suffering.

The feel of a plastic bag forced over one's head, and the sudden deprivation of oxygen to the lungs, always makes the victim struggle, fiercely, despite his hopeless predicament.

When the struggle was finally over, and Timothy finally rested, the grip was released from around his neck; plastic sheeting was laid out on the floor, in preparation.

The meeting was a success, as were all of Braddock's business conferences. He knew the only time they would ever go awry is the occasion that he would one day be the one sitting in the victim's chair.

Carrying the wrapped corpse out to the car, Gavins placed it in the trunk and made his way round to the passenger's side.

Braddock always liked to drive himself - it was a luxury he enjoyed, ever since he had first driven his father's car - without permission – and caused a little bit of damage to its fender. It had been such a fancy car that, in his father's eyes, it was only fair that his son's face receive the same misfortune – albeit an impact with a fist, rather than a gate.

Still, family looked after its own, even after death, and when Braddock's inheritance finally came through, he set about taking over his father's company, in order to sell it, so he could go into business for himself.

As Gavins unlocked the gate, Braddock drove onto a building site, featuring his company's logo on the front fencing; what was soon to be Braddock's new place of residence. As they reached fresh, open ground, he stopped.

Gavin offloaded the parcel, pulled it away from the car and rolled it over the mud, into a freshly dug hole.

These days, it was easy to get fingered by D.N.A., so it was vitally important that the body never show up again. Kenton, the assistant foreman, was waiting nearby, next to the cement mixer, ready to pour what were going to be the foundations of Braddock's new mansion.

Kenton had been rather cranky lately, pushing his men to all hours, repeatedly going through files in his office and setting strict deadlines. Those who worked for him had to think quickly and efficiently on their feet; for those who didn't think so quickly, he had other work which needed attending. It wasn't difficult, nowadays, finding any thug willing to kill. Some used muscle, while others used more scientific methods - Gavins was all muscle; the only science he was capable of was switching on a light-bulb.

Of course, there was always the question of loyalty to be considered: too often employees could not be counted on, if anything were to ever be uncovered. The only way to be sure of true devotion to the firm was by genuine sacrifice. Approaching Gavins, Kenton extended his hand in congratulations. It was followed in an instant by a blade, slicing vertically upward, into the lung.

The penetrating wound caused a wheezing noise to expel through

Gavins's parted lips, as his large body fell into the foundation trench, alongside that of Timothy.

One could not be betrayed, if there was nobody to betray him.

Kenton crossed himself, out of respect to his predecessor and his new, permanent companion, whilst beside him, Braddock lit a fresh cigar; there were no words from the Bible spoken - at least, not from Braddock, and certainly not out loud.

As the cement mixture started to pour, Braddock turned to address Kenton, for the first time: "By the way, I'm promoting you immediately. Congratulations." Braddock always needed somebody responsible and expendable beside him.

Then, he waved goodbye and left.

Kenton crossed himself again, looking down into the slowly filling cement tomb. At least Timothy and Gavins now had a relationship they could build on.

As Braddock was settling back into the driver's seat, his mobile phone sounded. As he pressed the answer button, he heard the voice of his wife:

"Mother wants to know what time she can expect us for the Christening, tomorrow; I've already brought your new suit back from the dry-cleaners."

"We'll have to meet them at the church – I need to stop off in town first," he answered, hanging up before she could respond with some pithy argument. Family occasions were not the top priority on his list at the moment; Braddock was a man who liked to stick to his own agenda.

He had to make it to the bank by early afternoon, the following day, to confirm the transfer of funds which should have been placed in his account, in order to finance his upcoming property purchase: an acre of land, currently up for sale by the local council, all ready to undergo excavation, and a new stage of construction and marketing. There was a lot of undeveloped property in Ravenfall.

Thankfully, property values were down; you could buy for very little, and sell for a lot, as long as you had something worthwhile.

All other competitive buyers had been quickly neutralized, especially as, as far as Braddock was concerned, he had already placed the winning bid. The only other interested party had pulled out, due to an "investor withdrawal"; word was, though, it was due to a family member losing their temper and... well, domestics these days - you never know where they might lead.

Still, talking about people behind their back was considered by some the height of bad manners.

Laughing to himself, he yawned, tired, hoping to finish the day on a good note.

Then, almost as if on cue, his business phone rang again – he recognized the number as that of one of his employees, and one of his most resourceful sources, regarding current events at Ravenfall.

In this sort of business, you need ears and information, and these come at a price - there are no favours; just services rendered. An organization looking to grow needs people - lots of people - both on the inside and outside, working everyday jobs, but keeping their ears open, for any useful information, and making it possible to move in or out of situations at the drop of a hat, when needed. In return, they receive a generous reward, without having to worry about paying any extra tax in the process.

As he listened carefully, Braddock eyes began to focus less on the road and more on his fingers, now clasping the steering wheel with considerable force; his knuckles had begun to turn white. He could feel his foot pressing harder on the pedal, as the car increased speed and started to swerve when he turned corners. Only when the call was over, did he finally ease up on the pedal and uncurl his fingers.

He needed a moment to chill, so he went to a spot on the outskirts of town.

There had once stood an old meat factory here, which had burnt down, mysteriously, just after the first world war. It had been derelict for many years, and was now closed off by fences; the land it was on, however, was still usable.

It was going to be the base for his new project: a grand casino, much larger than the big one in the city, nearby. Once the casino was built, it wasn't going to be difficult finding a buyer; Braddock was already preparing for the big moment, when that sizeable sum would land in his bank account. It would give him the means to finish off his new home.

And, also, to settle a score with an old friend.

His excitement was not shared by everyone in town, many of whom were opposed to the gambling institution. Even his old friend, and once-trusted partner, had challenged the notion with the council.

The sudden news he now received from his source advised that it looked as if his opposition had managed to come by another form of investment – big enough that it would destroy all of Braddock's plans:

Harry was counting on some newfound wealth, recently won by his son-in-law, which would put him back in the running for the land. Apparently, he wanted to build a shopping mall on it.

The outcome of this was dependent on Martin following through with his obligation. And, he had not yet claimed the money.

Braddock had heard the news about Martin skipping town. He hadn't any problem with that, since Martin hadn't taken anything which belonged to him; on that account, at least, he had been smart. It was just unfortunate that Martin's associates had left him alive - a mistake Braddock would not have made.

As long as Martin never claimed that money, Harry couldn't interfere with what Braddock now believed was rightfully his. There were such scenarios in the past, which he had taken care of. He knew that this matter had to be dealt with swiftly, and with the utmost urgency.

He had only one counter-measure, which he knew could resolve this new situation; fortunately, a man in his position knew people – people with certain resources. Braddock didn't care who he had to deal with, or what needed to be done: Martin was a dead man. After what he had done, nobody would give a damn about him.

The fact that a professional was now guarding him made no difference: one person wouldn't be enough to protect him, no matter how good they were; bodyguard, or assassin - they were still flesh and blood. When the barrel of a gun talked, it was *always* one-sided, and its word was final.

This world is not for the weak, or for men of conscience, or those with souls. You have to be that which keeps the strong on top, and all the others down, beneath your feet; either you walked over them, or you got walked over - there is no other choice in-between.

CHAPTER 6

Don't ask me how I became what I am.

Murder and violence is conditioned in some, but, to others, it just comes naturally. I won't kid myself - go on with my life, pretending that everything about me is normal - so I don't even try.

I didn't invent it: being an assassin... a killer; it's the second oldest profession in the world.

I don't take the expensive contracts, because one has to ask oneself who would pay so much for such a simple hit. No government jobs, either: too many complications and not enough money!

Nothing in a contract is as easy as it seems, or is as it is advertised. As you, yourself, have seen, from my own predicament!

There would never be enough money to fill the pockets of some people; and, some had so much they didn't know what to do with it, happily giving it away, like an unwanted newspaper.

I'm talking about the rich, naturally; those who have so much they don't appreciate how much good can come from its use, instead, frittering it away, so easily, on disposable pleasures and unsentimental trinkets.

To others, the simplest of possessions can mean so much. When it took such hard work to achieve them, they last a lifetime, and they hold more value than any gold or diamond.

Martin's own feelings of what was held dear to his own heart clearly did not include marriage. No matter how badly one wanted to cover up the bad stuff, by replacing it with the good, there was always some reminder left over – his was what had been removed from his finger.

Sitting in the train carriage, as I looked up, I found him looking at me, intriguingly… knowingly.

Could it be that he was starting to feel he knew me?

What could he know about my life? He wouldn't even know about the lives he had ruined.

We were on our way to claim the prize money, which would, hopefully, make up for all that Martin had taken and lost, but there remained some things which were just irreplaceable: certain family sentimentalities.

Sitting across from Martin on the train, now, I found myself wondering just how badly he would be willing to try getting away from me; perhaps even throwing himself from a speeding train. It was something only an idiot would try - still, it was best I kept a close watch.

"I don't even know your name," he said, looking me over, as though for the first time.

"You know who hired me - that should be sufficient for you," I said, looking out of the window. Night had fallen; there was no moon to be seen in the dark sky.

"What do I call you?" he persisted.

"I'm sure you've already come up with your own ideas, on that account. If you feel it does matter you can call me 'redeemer' for now, and, maybe later, 'executioner'."

I decided it was best not to stir the pot too much, seeing that he was – now, at least - co-operative: "Right now, me killing you is the last thing you have to worry about: you're a wanted man; you have a lot to face, when I take you back."

Martin stifled a laugh; "You know what's going to happen if I go back. Do you actually think he's going to give me a chance to make it up?"

"That's not really my concern."

"You're just doing your job," he said, reiterating my own statement, from earlier.

"That's right," I said, coldly.

He leaned in, to whisper, despite the fact that we were alone: "What is he paying you? I can pay more."

This caused me a minor fit of laughing.

"Is my newfound wealth no good to you, then?" he said, retracting quickly, as though kicked away.

"It comes with risk - something I'm not fond of." *Nor any professional in this business.*

"Isn't that a part of your profession? Killing people must be a risky business." As he spoke, Martin was trying to unfasten the top window, which was apparently stuck.

"The higher the risk, the bigger the pay." I glanced over his clothes: they were a terrible sight. As if it wasn't bad enough that his associates left him exposed, but to leave him covered in mud, like they had, was sheer insult added to injury!

"Are you saying that you can't be bought? That you haven't ever been bought? Money's money - what does it matter to you?"

I took a moment to consider this, then shrugged: "There's no such thing as easy money – there is always a price to pay."

I never question how long I will be able to keep doing this sort of work. All I know is that when you start out in it, you have to always remember that there is a code – rules – which you can't break.

I was trained to be the best. I don't break or hesitate; I take hold of what's been given to me, both in work and in life. I am always thankful for having something, rather than having nothing - being *nothing - in life. It's the little things in life which keep us human, and sometimes everything comes down to that one, single thing which keeps us alive; which puts a roof over our heads, and clothes on our backs. It's the reason we all go to our crummy jobs, day after day. I'm really no different to you, except my work isn't legal or socially acceptable.*

It's not like I can look for another job: I've never seen an advertisement for people with my sort of skills; not even the Army would take me!

Let's get back to the story...

"You said you don't do this sort of work. So, how much more money will he be paying you for it?"

I looked at him harshly, as though his question were a rude one: that was a matter between Harry and I; client confidence was a privilege. But, then I decided it was best to keep the conversation and atmosphere light; besides, I supposed that Martin was just bored and looking for a way to help the time pass.

"You actually disappoint me," I told him: "to think that you'd actually try something as petty as bribery. At least, when we were in that café, I actually had a little respect for you."

Martin peaked a little, at hearing this; "Well, back then I didn't have as much of a bargaining chip as I do now."

"You still don't," I retorted, quickly. "If you must know, this arrangement is only a slight adjustment to the contract – I will get paid the same."

Martin looked surprised. "Which is peanuts, compared to what I can offer you." He glanced at my jacket's inside pocket, where I had placed the lottery ticket: "Seriously, you can name your price."

The fact that Martin thought that money could buy anything - or *anyone* – sickened me worse than salmonella. I shook my head, but he didn't let up.

"We can do what Harry wants: go to claim the money – and, I'll arrange for a chunk of it to be transferred into any account of your choice," he orated this as though silently rehearsed, giving the performance of his life. "Then we leave; both go our separate ways. Harry would be none the wiser; just tell him you lost me."

He made it sound so simple. I supposed it was, really. Still, I had ethics to consider.

Martin was now gleeful: "Better yet, tell him you did the job! We could get another body; burn it beyond recognition." Now he was throwing me a pitch from some T.V. movie!

"The autopsy would show, in an instant, that it isn't you, just by your dental records," I told him, matter of fact. "To pull something like that off takes a lot of work, not to mention a lot of money up front. Besides, I've never failed at a job, and I'm not about to start now."

Martin slumped back in his seat, glumly, crossing his arms in the manner of a sulking child; "You're a fucking idiot."

Though they didn't rile me, these were harsh words – particularly coming from a man who had left his pregnant wife, for friends who had ditched him, alone, on a muddy-puddled road.

"I would recommend your not falling out with me - you wouldn't like me when I'm angry," I told him, sternly. "Remember, also, that I'll always be watching you – so don't get any more clever ideas."

"I wish everything was as easy as that," he brightened up, nodding toward my coat pocket.

I knew that he wanted to hold the ticket just once more, as though it were a comfort blanket.

People know very little about me, but I know a lot about them - even from their lives before we met; their files and reports paint a pretty graphic picture.

It's no wonder why some people end up the way they are. You know the quote from the Bible: "Deliver me from evil"? This too often applies to our own families.

All Martin had ever done was suffer brutality, at the hands of his own father, almost driving him to the point where Martin would be willing to thrust a kitchen knife into the man's chest, while he slept soundly, next to Martin's mother. She had been weak and unable to help, or go to the authorities - mainly because he was a respected police sergeant. So, they were trapped in Hell, enduring the same pain.

The big always used the small as punching bags. As the victim, a child would soon get so bent out of shape, he would become unrecognizable – nothing left but a bruised, contaminated piece of meat, hanging in the freezer. If left alone for too long, it would become cold, hard and so rotten on the inside, the "best before" date was long since irrelevant.

The thoughts which ran through his head - the messed-up childhood - was where it all started for Martin: his first steps to resentment towards the whole world. Life had not been fair to him, or his mother, so he decided *fuck life!* That was when he started getting into trouble.

Got himself into so much trouble, in fact, that it proved the last straw for his father, who geared up to give him the hiding of his life.

That was when Henry – Martin's older brother, visiting at the time – intervened; right in front of Martin's eyes, Henry took a blade to his father.

Watching the man bleed to death was a welcome release.

Even though Henry was locked up for ten years, the boys and their mother had, at least, found peace.

Word spreads quickly. Mouths run a little too freely and harshly, and, before you know it, a fist has plugged the hole of one of them. Martin almost beat a drunk man to death in his local supermarket, for spouting off about Henry doing away with his old man, and how the boy should have been put on death row. Being underage, Martin was sent to a young offenders' centre, where he received counselling.

During his time there, Martin only received two visits from his mother. Then, she stopped coming. He received no mail, nor any other visitors from his home town, to keep up with the news. On the day of his release, Martin arrived home to find that his mother had moved away, and not left a forwarding address.

He did not receive a warm welcome, either; the looks he received told him that the town's residents all knew who he was. Now his mother was gone, there was nothing here for him, worth staying for.

Society is cruel to the weak; those who band together make it in their design, stepping over those who are alone – those who have nobody, and whom nobody wants. But, if one is lucky - which was always a rarity, in Martin's case – even the weak and alone can find somebody to team with.

There had been no real affection in Martin's life, until Laurie had come along, and they started seeing each other.

Since her own mother had passed away, Harry had never seen Laurie smile. He took Martin on for no other reason than Laurie's sake, seeing that she had found some happiness.

But, as it turned out, only those privileged, and the truly loved, live long, happy lives. Soon, starting to tire of the boring sex, Martin suspected that their love wasn't going to last.

He hated his job and, even more, hated being under Harry's thumb, even going as far as to tell him this to his face, one night, at a business dinner, taking a swing and accidentally punching a prominent investor in the face.

Following that, Harry lost an investor, and Martin lost his job.

Soon, desperation had driven Martin to drinking and gambling.

Though not a gambler myself, it was very clear to me that Martin was a man who made many serious lapses, when it came to making judgements. Instead of cutting his losses, he would take out markers, hoping that the cards would change in his favour. But, courage was no match for an unfriendly shoe - quite a few of which he would be feeling, a short time after (mainly to his ribs and in the face). There had also been a trip onto the casino roof, for a little chat with the manager, who subsequently had Martin thrown off of it. Fortunately, it was a one-storey building, and Martin had only broken his arm.

This, of course, laid him up for a while, leaving the sole responsibility of the debt to Laurie, with whom he had finally come clean about everything.

He had put himself into a corner; there was only one way out.

To get on in this world, one really needs to choose a side. Still, often, we choose to be on our own, whatever the cost.

Loading up whatever he could scrounge from Harry's construction site, and making a few house calls, he had managed, with the help of his double-crossing associates, to gather together a fine collection of expensive family heirlooms, in the back of the van, before skipping town.

Martin's biggest failure here was his choice not to be overly cautious when selecting colleagues he could trust. This is the reason why when I am doing a job, I keep, mostly, to myself. I need to concentrate on my work at all times, and I do so better without any distractions.

I never get flashbacks or visions, like those sentimental hitmen you see in the movies. Yes, I have memories - fond memories of my family, but do not expect to get the full story, or even a glimpse into my family or my childhood.

I don't have a wife, a husband, a son, or a daughter... or a fucking dog, which wags its tail when I come home; not even a goldfish called "Nemo". And, don't bother asking about a girlfriend; the only love I have is the kind which you pay for - once a week, and always a different selection.

Relationships, for me, haven't been a bed of roses - not the sweet kind, anyway; you'll only find a cluster of thorns underneath my sheets.

We leave no room for attachments - simple as that.

And, that's all you're getting, right?

CHAPTER 7

In this business I'm in, I meet a lot of dangerous, violent people.

If I receive any requests to torture, I leave the contract to others, who specialize in that sort of thing. The people who do that sort of work should only get half the fee, because they get so much pleasure out of it! Although, there are a few who take the job, and carry it out with a bit of finesse.

There are some which start out thinking that they can make a difference in the world, by getting rid of its undesirables; the people who make the world a bad place: those who sell drugs to children, in schools; those who steal from vulnerable, weak and old people. You get the idea.

But, that wasn't how it was for Mr. X.

The act of killing is easy; living with the memories of your actions is the most difficult part – though, not necessarily for everyone.

It was always his philosophy that you could never outrun the inevitable; sooner or later, death catches up to everyone.

Mr. X was a tall, dark, athletic-built man, with a moustache - at least, that was the description of him on the grapevine. Personally, I'd never met him, but his rep was well-deserved.

They say his very best shots were first achieved on the basketball court; a good eye and a good aim was all it took - no different to using a gun. He wasn't known to be a big player but, like the rest of us, he liked the distraction; standing alone, looking up at the hoop, helped him to focus more on other things.

Even as the phone in his bag rang, on this occasion, his complete focus didn't waiver in the slightest: *swoosh* – didn't even touch the hoop!

After such a perfect performance, the last thing you want is bad news. He'd been waiting for this call for a few hours now and, listening carefully, he kept the ball by the goal in sight.

After hanging up, he didn't sit and quietly ponder; instead, he did a few laps, bouncing the ball up and down the court, without taking shots - not quite yet.

When he finally did, he aimed for the headboard's square, taking a point, then changing direction, as he moved to take another shot, followed by another, then another, hitting dead-centre, every time.

Finally, he made a miss, and as the ball rolled off the side of the court, he just stood there, his breathing controlled and his mind focused – only now no longer on the solo game he was playing.

His focus was now the face of an old acquaintance - one of another particular profession.

Leaving the courts, he headed inside to the changing room and took a shower, then dressed into a white blazer, dark pants and boots. After exiting the leisure centre, he walked to his car and drove off into town, listening to the radio. Stopping off at a news-stand, he was handed the evening edition, before continuing on his journey.

Driving onto a rocky coastal road, on the outskirts of town, he turned down a private road, before arriving at a large, metal gate, to the front of a private estate.

He was approached by a large, well-dressed man in a tuxedo, who smiled pleasantly. Mr. X rolled down the driver's side window.

"May I see your invitation?" he was asked.

Reaching inside the newspaper, Mr. X produced an envelope and passed it through the window.

As he drove up to the large house, he was greeted once more, by other security personnel, all equally as courteous - opening the door and handing him a ticket stub for his car.

Walking up the steps, between two large pillars, he was met at the door by a young hostess, who took his coat and showed him through the hall, to where all the other guests were mingling.

The men present certainly seemed to be enjoying themselves, talking to pretty maidens dressed in skimpy, colourful lingerie and bikinis, whilst drinking fine wine, as loud music filled the place. Some of the girls wore expensive jewellery, and many appeared of eastern European nationality; all were very friendly towards the men present.

The men were all important business associates; most had political connections. They attended social occasions like this on a regular basis, if only to allow them to forget about their occupations, family, home lives and personal problems. They clearly had their pick of what was on offer here; there were no limits on the number.

Taking a glass of Champagne from one of the waitresses, Mr. X's eyes scanned the room, until he found his purpose for being there: at the back of the room sat two patrons, comfortably watching, as two blonde girls danced seductively together.

Time-limited contracts were always worth substantially more than the usual, because they were often the most complex or difficult; they very likely involved higher risk targets.

She was one of the best looking women in the room, and was usually quite expensive. He watched her dance.

The advantage of using a whore is that they leave straight after; gone from your life, in the blink of an eye. It is always better to avoid a woman you haven't already had to pay for: this is the only real way to ensure that she is only there for the money, and no more.

Sex is a service, and you are a customer; there is no need for a woman to get into your private affairs. Those who ask too many questions are a risk, if not an immediate danger.

Of course, becoming attached is always a possibility, which is why you can never let them get too comfortable or, even worse, close enough that you *become vulnerable to them.*

Retiring to one of the guest rooms, she turned down the lights and started to place her hands over Mr. X's finely toned torso, her eyes smiling, as he ran his fingers through her long strands. As they moved over to the bed, their fingers caressed, and their mouths sampled each other's body.

It may sound old-fashioned - as people these days don't seem to think beds are adventurous enough - but a bed really is the best way to get the most pleasure from a woman: when she is lying beneath you.

Besides, when having sex with the intended target, you want to be at least 97% in control!

The only one sure way to truly catch a person off-guard is when they are at their weakest and most vulnerable: underneath you, receiving what is making them happy.

Unless, of course, they have been trained to spot deception, even during what seems their most sincere expression of physical affection.

Under the covers, they both finally rested. With one last kiss, she turned away and closed her eyes to rest.

A little while later, as he watched her dream, peacefully, he carefully pulled back the sheet, away from her shoulders, revealing the artery in her neck; in his coat pocket, the syringe was ready.

Poison can be fast, or painfully slow, depending on the client's needs. Mr. X never asked questions, or took an interest why the client wanted a person dead, and he never worked for the same person more than once.

In this line of business, it is necessary not to get too personal, because there may be a time when you are called upon to eliminate someone you know. As professionals, sentimentality is a weakness we cannot afford; we are paid to simply do a job, without thinking about it, or second-guessing our actions.

Killing someone in their sleep is the easiest and best method, as long as they don't wake up while you're doing it.

Slipping out of bed, carefully, Mr. X took the syringe from his blazer pocket, as well as a small bottle, tipping its contents onto a handkerchief.

As he slid quietly back onto the bed, she stirred, ever so slightly.

Placing the cloth, gently, over her nose and mouth; he held it for a few seconds, until the body fell fully limp. Then, removing the cap from the needle, he worked quickly, but efficiently, without leaving a mark.

Quickly putting on his clothes, he moved over to the dresser, where he left a small, cellophane bag, containing what was to be the supposed cause of the poor girl's sudden demise: overdoses were not uncommon, particular when cocaine had been poorly cut.

He slipped quietly down the stairs, retrieved his coat and handed the parking stub back to one of the valets, who quickly went to get his car. As he waited, he lit a cigarette, without looking around him, or back at the house: when there was no familiarity, there was no fear of anyone coming too close. Of course, there was occasionally that one exception to this.

Living a double life can be awkward, whether you're a criminal or a hired killer; some assignments are urgent and unexpected, and you might have to be gone at a moment's notice, without any reason given.

The stories you make up, for the benefit of others, and the lies you tell yourself, can come back to haunt you at any time. Those you love the most always know you're lying - holding back something dark about your life.

Of course, they can never know the truth. It's so bad – so devastating, to them - that you can't share it freely. So, you spare them the pain. And, because you don't want your suffering to infect their life, you find yourselves growing apart – you and your loved ones.

They say that people aren't supposed to be alone, and that the heart can be so easily broken. But, it can just as easily be mended.

But, as for the soul...

Well, one would have to get past all my defences – to pull down the walls – in order to see, with open eyes, the truth behind. Who would even have the courage for that?

CHAPTER 8

You might ask if I come from a broken home, or how young did I start?

That's how it usually is in the movies, right? You always get those guys - or girls - questioning their morality, and whether they should retire, or try to lead a normal life. They take a moment to think about what they do for a living - then, what happens?

They fuck up!

Usually, they end up fighting against the very people they worked for; of course, they win, and go off to live a normal life... at least, that is, until the sequel.

That part the movies do get right: the best ones always come back. Not to sell movies, but because – as we all knew, deep down, when we last saw them - they are still the same person, and never really changed. They can't just walk away: they're betraying who they really are! And, they were good at what they did. They haven't changed their job, or their life - just their point of view.

I don't think like those guys do. If I did, I wouldn't be doing this in the first place. The job is what I do - it doesn't make up all that I am.

But, I can't really do anything else now, can I? Working at a supermarket: stacking shelves and taking money at a checkout? Sure, the retail industry is a big earner, but taking lives pays so much better!

Plus, I don't hate my job.

I don't question my own actions; I just do what I'm told, and I get paid for it, just like any other job.

Some people slaughter animals to make a living. Do you ever think about the meat you're eating, when you sit at the dinner table - meat that was once alive, and died by the hand of someone who was making a living, just like me? The abattoir staff don't hate themselves for what they do, any more than you hate yourself, for eating that meat; devouring the flesh of an animal – a true innocent.

I hear you ask: are all my victims guilty of something, then?

Well, really, who isn't?

Whilst it doesn't bring me any pleasure to kill those who some might argue don't deserve it, I take comfort that this decision was not my call to make. Why should I clutter my head with all of those thoughts?

So, could I stand behind the counter of McDonalds, serving fast food? Answer: only if I had a gun in the other hand, ready to put two in someone's head. After doing this job after a while, when it has become your life, it is everything else outside of it which seems distorted.

It's not that I think I'm in any way better than all of you good, hard-working people – it's just that I could never see myself in your shoes; I could not identify with any other profession. Probably for the best, because I could never put my C.V. on paper, either. They say that you have to quit sometime, but I can't see that in my future; there aren't a lot of jobs out there looking for someone like me, with my sort of skill-set.

Could I need a normal life?

This *is normal. It's my job; my family's professional legacy.*

Okay, I let that slip: yes, I do come from a family of killers. You've probably got an image of the Manson Family already, right? Well, you'd be far from right!

That's all you're getting, by the way - too much has already been said about that. Let's move on.

The train had pulled into a station and other passengers were boarding. We still had around six more stops to go, before we reached ours.

Our carriage was now completely empty of others, the only one of which had been a little old lady, who had briefly chattered, pleasantly, with Martin and myself. Old people like to talk while travelling - I guess it helps to pass the time.

Martin hadn't been very forthcoming, regarding our relationship, so I had taken it upon myself to concoct that we were siblings, travelling to our father's funeral. I chose such a story because they are sensitive in nature, and would not raise questions, amongst most, about a person's unusual behaviour, or the attire they chose to wear.

How a person chooses to dress says a lot about their character, I've always thought. My own was reasonably presentable, whilst Martin's was well-soiled. I told the old woman that he had accidently slipped and fell in a puddle. I also explained that we had lost our luggage, so he would have to wait until we got to our parents' house, to change.

An independent contractor has to work extremely hard at times, to maintain a cover story: without any prior preparation, people will usually see straight through you.

Just as I myself have a talent to do, and have so done on numerous occasions.

Particularly when I watched two young men enter our carriage, wearing heavy coats. Wasn't the temperature outside quite moderate? It wasn't summer, but they were surely perspiring, badly, underneath all that padding. Their choice of headwear was also questionable – thickly woolen and gathered toward the back of the head. Balaclavas?

Self-awareness is the key to personal survival, and small things like this can and should raise suspicion. Personally, I get a real bad feeling in my guts when I see people who don't belong, or who stand out from the crowd.

While most individuals sit with their arms between their legs, on their knees or crossed before them - commonly defensive postures - both of these guys had a hand positioned near or just under the inside of their coat.

This was a clear warning to me that they were strapped.

On my guard, my open and laid back demeanour suggested I was relaxed. Acting soft and distracted gave an impression I was vulnerable, when, in reality, I was a coiled spring, ready to bounce.

People don't need to know who you are or why you are there, but they would soon know if events suddenly became about them! Sometimes, death comes when you least expect it; in my opinion, it is always best to be on your guard.

There are always those moments, in the movies, when somebody screams and gives out a warning, before the pace slows down and everything happens in slow motion - well, that just doesn't happen in the real world.

Your enemies think that just because you're not expecting it, you're not prepared for conflict. But, as a person in my profession, this is something that never gives me rest; like a well-trained bodyguard, I am always looking for the little things which stand out - if I believe something poses an immediate threat, my mind is already going through either an escape plan or an active opposing scenario, based on the environment I am in at the time.

I moved over, whispering to Martin: "When I tell you to move, hit the floor."

He just looked at me, quizzically.

"If you don't want to die, do as I say."

He now realized now that something was imminently going down; he wasn't expecting that something to be a long, sharp blade swinging straight at his head. I had already grabbed hold of him, by the jacket, and managed to pull him clear, as the blade missed his head and struck the seat's arm-rest.

The assailants' masks had now come down to cover their faces, which I thought a little futile, considering I'd already seen them, as had the copious C.C.T.V. present. I then realized that the balaclavas were for intimidation: they were costume, resembling skulls; the machetes looked a lot more real.

As with any self-preservation defence, it is entirely ethical and legal to take the pre-emptive course of action, rather than waiting for the attack to kill you. It is also easier: the adrenalin is already being released, giving you the necessary advantage; the speed, combined with a clear vision of the precision and technique you intend to execute, will overpower most opponents - even when there are more than one. When, of course, those opponents are armed, heavily, with large cutting tools, it does present rather a challenge not to lose a limb, or your head, in the process.

Here is a quick lesson in close-quarter combat:

A direct punch to the solar plexus will quickly neutralize an assailant where he stands. Quickly following this with a ridge-hand or an edge-hand strike to the throat will cause immediate and severe damage, and the swelling can result in suffocation.

If you are armed, withdraw a concealed blade at the right moment, cutting into the artery of the second assailant's neck; this will end an aggression very quickly.

In the event that, by chance, you find yourself surprised by a third party, who proceeds to knock the weapon from your hand, it is wise to have a form of backup.

Being in an enclosed space, it wasn't appropriate to draw my gun, so I turned my attention to another means: deflecting the attack, I used another flexible form of cutting tool, namely a cheese-wire - concealed in my retractable key fob – which I wrapped around the third attacker's neck, tightly.

Being very sharp, and if pulled with sufficiently considerable force, a wire will slice just as deeply into flesh, and even bone, as a knife. You may have seen similar devices used in spy movies, often concealed in the assailant's watch. Whilst convenient and a good idea, the watch-wire has become a bit of an obvious weapon to look for in an assassin, these days.

If using hands, crushing someone's throat is a very passionate way to kill, which is why I settle for the wire – it is messy, but involves none of the emotional effort.

When it was all over, all I could hear was Martin's heavy breathing, as he lay on the floor at my feet, looking directly up at me, his complexion a pale white, and confusion on his face.

"Why did these people attack us?"

Staring at him incredulously, I allowed the question to hang in the air, before doing what any professional would do in such a circumstance: I chuckled, with the rocking of the train.

I started rifling the men's pockets, checking their phones, until I found what I was looking for.

"Because people will do anything for money." I showed him the screen of one of the phones: "They have your name and photograph; they came for you."

Martin looked, ashen, at his own face on the tablet phone's screen; "They're assassins, like you."

His suggestion was sickening: I would never use such weapons or tactics to kill someone. "No, they're just cheap hoods trying to make easy money." I placed one of the machetes on the seat. "They obviously weren't given the full story: namely, who you are with. If they had, they'd still be alive."

The last thing we needed was this sort of heat coming upon us; we had to move quickly, out of this carriage, and get off the train at the next station.

But, first, it was important to confirm the kill: so often, the wounded play dead.

The third of them was still twitching; maybe I could get something out of him.

When getting information, always get it face to face; I pulled back the mask. And, I received a shock.

The face was young - much more so than usual; a kid. He couldn't have been more than fifteen or sixteen years old. He was trying to speak, but the wire had complete severed his larynx.

If you look in their eyes, you will see a person's fear, then you will see all the strength drain from their face, as it comes to rest in peace.

They say that every time you kill a person you go a little more numb, until you don't feel anything. Well, that's not the case with me. I feel it all: the loss of that person's life, and the sudden realization that it's over.

They say that it's better to think of it as taking someone where they haven't been before, just like a mystery tour: you never know where it's headed, or how long it will take to get there.

I know that when my time comes, nobody will be taking me to a mystery place – or even a place I haven't already been! I know exactly where I'm headed, and my torment will last forever, if that's what the Lord wishes.

CHAPTER 9

You might well ask: do I have a conscience?

Well, a conscience is all well and good for the redeemable, but to others, like me, it's pointless: an unacceptable burden, which costs you a heavy price. I choose not to pay it. That is the reason I'm still alive.

After all, one more doesn't really make a difference to me, since my soul is my own; I choose how I keep it, and how to live with myself.

Sleeping at night is never a problem for me. I have no bad dreams, because I know I'm not alone.

Feel free to judge. But remember, in the end, there are more and more like me, being created every day.

We had to find a place to hide away for the night, and our journey had to be put on hold, while I found out what exactly was going on.

Finding a local bed-and-breakfast wasn't difficult. In a situation like this, it was best to find somewhere which took cash and didn't ask too many questions.

Even though, at that moment, I had a lot of my own of those, going through my mind.

If it was a contracted kill, who had hired those youngsters on the train to kill Martin?

I had recognized a tattoo on one of the thugs which had attacked us. Not that I'm a pushover - as you've just seen – but, in my profession, it is always advisable to know about the competition, because you never know when they might make an official call.

I don't blame them: I know it's nothing personal - just business – and that everybody's got to make a living; that's what you learn in my trade. But, it does make me wonder how some screw-ups actually manage to make anything of themselves - just dumb luck, I guess.

It was almost criminal - practically an insult – by whoever had sent guys like that after me and Martin. They're usually fodder; the type who usually buy it quite early in their careers, usually from their employers, who might be in need of tying up loose ends. As you have seen, what goes around comes around.

"You're pretty good with a blade; I've never seen anyone that fast," Martin said, flopping down on his bed, kicking off his shoes and looking around him, at the meagre surroundings. If he had thought I was about to spring for anywhere fancy to sleep, he was sadly mistaken.

"Seen a lot of knife fights, then?"

Martin shuddered, recalling again the fight on the train. "Just trying to make conversation."

A smile broke through my lips.

"You are pretty lethal… for someone…"

I regarded his unfinished statement, questioningly, then sighed: "Wouldn't you rather just sit there in your own thoughts?"

"I need to talk, because thinking is all I'm doing right now; I don't want to think about what just happened."

Assimilating the feeling of safety isn't easy when you are reliving a near-death experience. "Do you think that choice of conversation topic is going to help you?" I mused, making myself comfortable on the bed, opposite his. "Don't bother trying to forget it: you won't ever be able to. I can see that you're just overjoyed to still be alive."

"What do you want - a 'thank you'?" he spat.

Because of the pain and the horror he had just witnessed, Martin clearly needed a form of outlet; he wasn't accustomed to the level of violence he had just seen – at least, not since his father had died, all those years ago.

"Well, I did save your life!" I said, matter-of-factly; "You're alive, and… well, they're not!"

He knew well that I didn't really give a shit about his personal safety; I had simply been asked to escort him. I didn't put any value on his life: to me, he was nothing more than a package – one which, were it to get a little damaged in transit, I couldn't give a damn about… like any other courier.

"We're safe here now, aren't we?" he asked, tentatively. He didn't conceal the doubt in his voice, and the self-evident answer to his question was haunting him, like a bad smell, which would only desist if spoken aloud.

"You can consider this protective custody, if you like." Given his predicament - being with me, of all people: a killer - it was difficult to define this situation as "protective".

"You're not a cop. Only they could protect me," he said, though with little conviction; he immediately found difficulty finding peace of mind in that statement. "We should have just waited on the train for them."

Of course, he knew the answer to this, but quietly rationalized it to himself, anyway: "You couldn't have me talking to the cops; you'd be in it as much as I am."

I considered his point of view, briefly. "There are people out there who are still hunting us, and I'm not so keen on being in this situation, but don't be so quick to make assumptions."

Martin didn't like being patronized. He liked even less that he was tired and scared, and could find no obvious solution to his new predicament.

I continued: "Let's say we talked to the cops - what would you tell them? There's no crime been committed by myself: all I did was track you down and take you back home; wasn't my fault some guys jumped us."

Martin took up a serious and judgemental posture, folding his arms in front of himself; "You killed three people on that train - one was a kid! And then, you left without reporting it. That's a crime."

His words were those of a hypocrite, but they were true; I couldn't deny any of what he was saying.

"I killed in self defence; all I knew was that they were probably there to rob us, or maybe they're just crazies! But, it wasn't murder on my part. I'm unknown to the police, so they'll find nothing on me…" I looked him straight in the eye, now, equally judgementally; "You, on the other hand, are a wanted man, so going to the cops is not so smart for you. Remember, you haven't got your money yet."

Martin took this all in, dropped his arms and slumped forward, in annoyed defiance.

"I find your attitude ungrateful," I said, "but I'm not really bothered." I lifted myself off the bed, back onto my feet. "And, don't think my heart is in the right place; I'm not protecting you - I'm protecting my own interests. Now I need to go out for a while, to get some food and think."

Martin eyes returned to me, once more. "You're leaving me alone?"

"You'll be safe enough. Remember, just stay in this room; there are people out there who are willing to snuff you out, for what is probably a very large bounty on your head. I'm the only thing standing between you and them, so don't get any ideas about leaving; if you do, you're on your own, and I can promise you're no match for what might be coming next."

Even as Martin took the statement in, doubt began to darken his features again. "How do I know you'll come back, and not just leave me?"

He knew very well that I wanted out of this situation, and that I could have just walked, right then; this wasn't part of the contract I'd agreed with my employer.

"I take too much pride in my work to walk out on a job, just because I don't like the circumstances." I paused by the door, looking back. "Money is the most powerful motivating force in the world - that's why this is all happening."

Though he didn't like it, he knew that he really had no choice but to do this one smart thing, for the first time in his life. He didn't trust me, but he did need me.

"If you still have any doubts, why don't you keep this safe while I'm gone?" I took the lottery ticket from my pocket and left it on top of the cabinet, before leaving Martin alone in the room.

Now, I know you're probably asking: "was that wise?"

The trick to successfully being on the run for the rest of your life, is:

(i) *don't be found;*

(ii) *don't get caught; and*

(iii) *don't get killed!*

All this is not as easy as it sounds: you can very easily overestimate yourself and, before you even know it has happened, you're right back in the thick of it!

If you think Martin stands a better chance on his own, you obviously haven't been watching very hard. Yes, he can run, but I already found him once; I'll do it again, and that time the money won't matter.

As long as there is air in Martin's lungs this will never be over for him. And, I'm sure you know, by now, that he's nowhere near as strong as he puts on – at least, not in my world, anyway. A hundred-million euros can buy you a new life, but never enough to feel totally safe, ever again. In later years, he would live as though cursed: looking over his shoulder, for the rest of his life – it is the only way he could truly give himself the chance of safety. Every day above ground would be the ultimate payday for him; the money would be nothing more than a bonus.

Unfortunately, drawing a lifetime of violence and wrongdoing to a close is not something one can easily walk away from, and no amount of money can wash that dirt from their hands - the stain is under the skin, buried too deep. It is only with death that we leave it all behind.

CHAPTER 10

In modern business, in any enterprise, you will often find a chain. My line of work requires three particular factors, all of which are linked together, each equally as important as the other: first is the client; last is the contractor; and, between the two, you have the agent. This is the person you go to when you need something special – something you can't get from anyone else - or if you need somebody removed, but you don't have the resources to do it yourself.

Agents often present themselves as everyday businessmen, which is what they usually are; mostly entrepreneurs, with their fingers in many pies - not always legal; often borderline. They don't openly present this as part of their business, and it is not known to just anybody; usually, these requests come via referrals, from other satisfied clients. Discretion is an absolute necessity.

They are the closest approximation to vultures, feeding off of the bones of corpses, whose flesh and blood are still warm.

Those who don't use an agent are known as "freelancers", and thus waive the 10-15 percent commission fee, which ensures their full anonymity, not to mention that of their client - not that experienced professionals usually ask "who" or "why"; there is no mystery when somebody wants to kill, or to have somebody killed.

It usually starts with the client just thinking about wanting someone dead. The idea might hang around in that person's head, until, soon, they can no longer shake off the thought; it makes their palms itch and their blood boil.

It doesn't really matter how a person's name came to be on a contract - when their number comes up, that's it; that's just the way it works, in our world.

Is it a person's destiny to die by the hand of another? A question such as this is never the agent's concern. If you do something wrong, you are bound to pay, one way or another.

And, there are always people happy to pay to see another dead. The words "I'll see what I can arrange; it might be very expensive" are the first of the small cogs, which turn the very big wheel of fate, which is set up in an agent's office.

People are so squeamish, whenever the word "murder" is mentioned. They can act so much like children that he has to be able to take them by the hand and slowly walk them through it, step by step, until they are reassured. Often the client's mentality is all wrong, not to mention the stomach.

Why do they have to make it so hard for themselves? They're just the decision makers; no actions are carried out by their own hands.

Because it stains too deeply; because you can't wash it off.

People call for a professional because they can't do it themselves - no different to hiring a plumber, or a carpenter. Killing can be an art - a specialist field - and, because their art is so good, some are expensive.

As an agent, you have to be sure you send the right people, otherwise reputations die, along with the target.

Contract killing was a good business, from Mr. Lamoure's point of view; a route to the finer things. In Lamoure's case, a nice T-bone steak and a couple of dry martinis was his preferred choice, along with an attractive woman, seated by his side.

Sitting in a booth, in one of uptown's finest restaurants, he had just ordered coffee, when Mr. X dropped by, to pick up the balance of his payment.

So the men could talk business, the lady excused herself from the table; she went to the ladies' convenience to powder her nose - or, in her case, put powder *up* her nose.

Retrieving a large, wrapped package from his briefcase, Mr. Lamoure passed it over, along with a complementary belch, towards the purveyors of the meal he was consuming.

"Another job well done, I hear. My contact said there was little fuss; the body was discovered and taken away – a suspected overdose, just as the client requested." He raised his glass in salute.

Mr. X didn't bother to count it: a man like Lamoure knew better than to try cheating the people who put bread on his table, and into his fat belly.

"I have another job, recently come in, from the same source." He continued cutting up his steak. "The client didn't come to me immediately; his first choice was the 'Skulls', but the wannabe punks screwed it up." Sometimes, it was cheaper and faster to hire low-rate thugs, particularly if you wanted a job done quickly.

Mr. X took an immediate interest in this job, as the name of the hit squad had specific relevance.

"They nearly killed the target, but 'nearly' don't count," Lamoure continued, chewing on the meat. "They couldn't just keep it simple; they had to get creative: tooled up with fucking machetes. What do they think this is - Africa?" He laughed, causing himself a slight coughing fit.

Mr. X did not share the amusement. He moved around to sit closer, so they were less in earshot of the other diners. "They identify anyone?" he asked, somewhat eagerly.

"Only by their street names. These kids will go by anything these days - think it's cool to be called Griff, Rooker and Caleb."

Mr. X recognized the last name immediately.

"They didn't know that the target is travelling with a freelancer, much like yourself; heavy artillery, from what I gather - dispatched all three, single-handed."

Mr. X took a moment, to let the words sink in. "Who took the job?"

Lamoure smiled, as another woman passed by, but sobered as he recognized the growing impatience on his associate's face. "It's an independent contractor. No number on my phone," he said, with some regret, "so must not be local."

An out of town contractor?

How was it the boys hadn't known who they were dealing with? Either they hadn't bothered to ask, or certain omissions had been made. "Who is this contractor working for?" Mr. X pressed, a little harder.

"Probably a party who is interested in keeping the target alive. But, why that is, I have no idea," Lamoure said. "From what I hear, from a reliable source, it's unusual for a contractor of this type to take on a job of this nature. You're asking a lot more questions than usual."

Mr. X just sat quietly, now in his own thoughts. This wasn't much to go on, and he would need more answers before this evening was over.

"Do you want the job or not, or will I find someone else?" Lamoure asked, trying to keep his tone as respectful as possible, never forgetting whom he was currently addressing.

"You're going to have to: this particular situation just turned personal. I need to know who put the contract out," Mr. X said, with another hint of urgency.

Lamoure could tell this was something of an emotional complication, and it really had no business at this table. "Maybe I should get someone else. But, I wouldn't get involved if I were you - it may not be promising to your own health!" He dabbed at his mouth with a napkin.

"Is that a threat?" The voice was now challenging.

Lamoure raised both hands, in a calming, neutral manner; "Not from me, but the client is somebody you don't want to fuck with: a very important man, with a lot of connections." He said, in a serious tone: "The gang leader is no pushover, either."

Mr. X was not the type to be easily intimidated – especially not when this was about his own family. Not letting it drop, he asked: "Who put out the contract?"

Lamoure leant forward, speaking cautiously to his best contractor: "Don't go stepping on the wrong toes. Word is the man takes care of his friends the same as his enemies!"

Lamoure noticed that Mr. X's fingers were playfully touching the silverware. He grew nervous; he hadn't meant to be disrespectful, and he didn't want this news escalating into something unpleasant.

Besides, people usually paid a lot of money for his advice!

He swallowed that notion, when Mr. X started polishing the table knife with the serviette. "Just give me the name and address," he said, quietly.

Mr. Lamoure could see there was no way to dissuade his associate from interfering in this matter, but still there was the concern of his own involvement. "Just how personal does this get? This might have serious repercussions for me!"

Mr. X now looked at him, with hard-set eyes; "It most definitely will, if I don't leave here with that name and address."

Regretting every moment, Lamoure ruefully scribbled something on his napkin and passed it across the table. "Whatever this situation is, I have to consider any future business between us terminated; a man in my position has to watch his back, as he never knows when something uncomfortable might be stuck in it!"

Without another word, Mr. X got up from the table and left the restaurant. Lamoure watched him go, sorry to be losing such a fine talent.

He felt better when he saw that his dessert was making her way back to the table.

I've killed many people - that's who I am and what I do. It was the purpose that was given to me; without it, there is no purpose in my life.

The same could be said for Mr. X. He was, like me, part of a family-

run business, although it's not as common as I might be making it seem.

The purpose of our profession is to make things less complicated. I've never killed out of emotion – it is best to leave such things as that to others; those who make it personal, or emotional, tend to make mistakes. They start to question themselves, and promise themselves: "Once I've saved enough money, I will stop."

But, retirement is only possible when you have passed on the torch, or when you've been retired by another party. Mr. X's chance for the first option had now slipped away. As for the other... well, time would tell, one way or another.

CHAPTER 11

Waiters and waitresses work for minimum wage, plus tips. Bust their ass all day, carrying plates and serving food. Isn't it only right that they should get a little extra for their trouble?

They'll never earn as much as I do, in one shot; one cut.

It's not very often you'll find a little extra in the envelope - a little cherry on top. Yet, there's nothing wrong with a little show of appreciation from a satisfied client.

Until there's a catch, and you hear the words: "Nothing you can't handle."

There's nothing free in this world, and certainly not my services. Bullets cost money, knives need replacing, and my own life is now on the line.

As a professional it is wise not to take risks, nor usually to tolerate changes to a contract. When it compromises your own safety, you have every right to speak freely on the subject.

Finding a payphone, I called Harry, to check for updates and give a debriefing.

"We've had to hold up for the night. Martin's secure for now, but I'm not sure how co-operative he will remain; fear is the only thing keeping him attached to me at the moment."

Harry voice was calm and reassuring, as it came back from the other end: "I've taken care of the documents: they're on their way up to you now. Do you know anything about the guys who jumped you on the train?"

Harry was a man of complete control - taking it, as well as giving it.

"The tattoo on one of them is the symbol of a bunch of low-rent thugs who work locally," I said, feeling a chill blowing down my back. "Harry, just let me kill Martin, hide the body, and make arrangements to have it picked up and taken care of."

At times, when you shouldn't leave a trace, there were people you could call to clean up after you; they were so good that not even the slightest drop of D.N.A. would ever be found.

"I'll bring you the ticket. Get some false I.D. and we'll get somebody to stand in for Martin."

Harry voice came back, in total disagreement of the suggestion: "No, no, there isn't time. You're not that far from the nearest Lotto Centre - it's quickest if you go straight there, and I'll get the courier to bring the identification to you."

I didn't like the idea of babysitting Martin, but Harry was the boss, and I couldn't go back on the contract now. My obligation needed to remain firm; I couldn't afford to tarnish our relationship.

"I'm going to look into this matter personally. I just need you to keep Martin safe, for now." Harry finished and hung up, leaving the phone's dial-tone ringing in my ear.

Replacing the receiver, I suddenly, reflexively went for my gun.

For just a second I thought I had seen a shadow, out of the corner of my eye.

It turned out to be nothing, so I withdrew my hand, concealing the weapon beneath my jacket, once more.

I decided to get some food. Crossing the street to the local takeaway, I glanced at people as they passed me by - they looked back at me, no differently to anyone else.

But, every soul has slight darkness. You can smell it on most people - like a nasty stench - as they walk by you, lost in their thoughts; it follows them around, but they don't seem to notice.

Every time I hear a siren, not too far away, I don't feel my heart race, because I know they aren't coming for me. Standing at the food counter, I can smile pleasantly and, for those who bother, receive the same in return; perhaps, at most, a slight look of interest. In the land of the living, I feel quite at ease.

It's just the ghosts that are restless.

I don't believe in ghosts, so I know there are no unhappy spirits, looking to haunt me. When you die, you leave this world; where you go, who can say?

Many talk of a tunnel of light: the pathway to Heaven. Perhaps going to Hell is just the opposite: darkness - as though someone forgot to pay their utility bill. Perhaps you wander, blindly, in the dark, bumping into other souls, on the same journey.

I don't think about the afterlife too much; it's not a subject I need to worry about, at this moment in my life. Even if I had come close to it, that very night.

That had been the first time I'd killed in self-defence - the others had been in cold blood.

Where I was headed, when it came to my own end, I wasn't sure.

Funny: nobody wants to die, yet we're all happy to go to Heaven.

Returning to the bed-and-breakfast, I found that Martin was still there, laid comfortably on his bed, for the first time. Until I walked back in. I noticed that the ticket was where I had left it.

"This is the best I can do for dinner at the moment." I placed a wrapped burger and fries beside him, before returning to my own bed. "It's best we keep a low profile tonight; we don't want to go looking for trouble, and we don't want trouble finding us." This was the last situation anybody wanted to be in, but sometimes life just wasn't fair like that.

"Why are they going to all this trouble?" It was literally the hundred-million winning question, and he had probably been thinking about nothing else since I left him, not so long ago, to his own thoughts.

"Whoever it is that wants you dead, I'm guessing it's about the money." I took a bite and went to work, inspecting my firearm - in these moments of calm, it was always a good idea to check your arsenal. As, between bites, I stripped the weapon, I could see Martin watching me, with curiosity.

"You act tough, but I don't think you're so strong, underneath," he said, resting his back against the wall; "you're just as scared as I am, aren't you?"

Clearly, Martin was starting to get his self-confidence back - funny how food prompted such a change in a person's attitude.

"We all handle fear differently," I said, laying out all the parts of the pistol, on the bed's cover: "some people fold under pressure; others, like me, focus on our objectives."

"So, what exactly is the objective now? Kill me, or wait until somebody else comes to kill me?"

You're probably thinking that this particular ritual might have left me vulnerable.

I didn't think, by now, that he was particularly a threat to me, physically – I had handled myself well enough against him, in the alley. Yes, he was willing to fight, but only when he thought he could get the upper hand. Back then, he pissed me off, and I retaliated. By now, Martin had learnt that I wasn't a pushover; he wasn't going to try anything stupid again. And, he'd seen what I was capable of, even without my gun!

"I don't have much of a choice in killing you, or allowing other people to do it: I've been given my instructions - I intend to follow them to the letter."

He smirked, as he popped a French fry in his mouth, chewing and savouring, childishly.

"You should be grateful you're still alive," I said, working and cleaning the gun's mechanism: "they may be amateurs, but they're fully prepared to kill you."

His eyes began to edge, hard and sharp, towards me; "Just like you. I'm not so sure I find your company very comforting anymore - what's to stop you cutting a deal with those guys, to let you walk with that ticket?"

Martin was actually making a good point; there was a lot of money at stake. He guessed he was expendable, and that, as I had already mentioned to Harry, we could always find a willing stand-in. Who at Lotto Centre would be any the wiser? They only needed a glimpse of Martin's I.D.; the date of birth and nationality could all be fabricated, along with the name.

But, that suggestion had already been rejected by Harry, and it wasn't for me to decide otherwise. Martin was going to die, one way or the other, but it wasn't going to be at the expense of my own life.

"There are a lot of people going to be sending more bullets our way, so just remember to keep your head down," I said, quickly reassembling my weapon. "They're probably not as well trained as me, but will be just as prepared. So, don't get in my way!"

I replaced the weapon back into its holster, and screwed up the food wrapping, tossing it into a waste basket, in the far corner of the room.

Laying my head down on the pillow, I looked up at the ceiling. "We need to get some sleep - if we're not rested, we're going to get sloppy; then, we won't last long."

Martin said nothing more. He just put all his attention into consuming his meal, with greater urgency, as though it were going to be his last supper. Humans are greedy creatures, whether for money or food - it's in our nature.

Watching Martin eat, I could tell he was still minding me, cautiously, out of the corner of his eye. It was clear we still had an issue regarding trust.

Then again, in truth, some days you just don't know who to trust. Especially when you enter the criminal world.

Bringing other people in on your plan - telling them you'll do right by them - you would think would create such a thing as real trust; working it all out together, then pulling it off without a hitch. Until you find out, painfully, that they had their own plan: a blow to the back of the head, and you wake up in the mud. Everything he possessed had been taken, just as he had taken it from his neighbours. For that, he now had paid killers after him. Not to mention the one guarding him, for now.

He didn't want to die yet: there were things he hadn't seen and done, and now he had the opportunity to do them, with the money he had coming to him; a chance to restart his life over. But, Harry wasn't going to make it easy for him - not after what he had done.

What about Laurie? What could he possibly say to her, to make up for what he did? Was he to collapse onto his knees, and beg at her feet for forgiveness? He was a man of pride; and now, a man with a fortune.

Sure, he had made rash decisions, which had put him in harm's way, and maybe he had brought shame to her and her own, but at least something good had now come from all of this. He was a rich man, and should it please Laurie and her father, he would write a few cheques and hand them out on the street corner, like cookies, if it would give him a little leeway with the justice system. That way, if he was going to do a stint in prison, like his brother, it surely wasn't going to be for as long.

And, with his money, he could probably arrange things inside, so his time would pass by more comfortably. There were always those in prison - especially those of a certain stature - who could arrange specific luxuries, for a price. He'd seen enough prison movies to know that there was always one top man - the head of some syndicate, currently doing his own time - who had some sway with the penal system. Word spread quickly in the Big House, if you were affiliated to important people: you were untouchable, and free to do what you wanted. He wouldn't be a small fish. Well, perhaps at the start.

First, he would need to find out just who the Big Dog was, and arrange a meeting; propose a little business transaction, making him eligible for certain privileges.

And, if he was lucky enough to have some of his former associates join him inside, towards the end, he could perhaps arrange a special reunion! Unfinished business was something of a big issue, to a lot of people in jail, and there were many just looking for an excuse to take out their rage on other people; he could simply sit back and take his revenge, without even getting his hands dirty.

Suddenly, his future wasn't looking so bleak.

Once free and clear, he could leave the past behind him forever, and from then on it would be the good life; no more mistakes.

Truthfully, you can bury the mistakes of your past.

It's just the same as when you die: your body might be left behind, to rot in the earth, but the soul is free, to move on. The past can't be brought with you; it is left behind, too.

In our life, however, it is a different matter: some can't move on from their dark past; they relive it, every day.

I know where that leads: a fire, burning you up twenty-four/seven; a horrible fever, which drives you so crazy that you even think about doing away with yourself. That's what it comes to: the only real escape is death. The measure by which a person weighs their own life, is the reasons to live or die.

Just like one cannot change what is in his nature, so can only live by it, a dead man cannot change his decision, once that decision has been made for him.

CHAPTER 12

In this profession, there are very few people you can trust – not even those who give you the work! Those who may only ever see you as a paid asset.

Delayed payments, or the sudden need to ask questions, are normally signs which can make a person in our trade very nervous. When you start to feel this nervousness, it's time to follow your instincts and move on, tying up any loose ends.

But, before you do, there are questions you may need answering - the answers you get will determine whether or not you leave a dead body in your wake.

Then again, sometimes the answers don't make any difference to this.

Double-crossing, betrayal and treachery are hazards which can be found in any business, and they are hazards you must always expect in ours. Loyalty, honour and brotherhood are only for the movies.

In business there is always a danger of workers trading or leaking substantial information to competitors, leading to work contracts being stolen from under suppliers' noses.

Laurence's mother, Margaret, had worked as secretary for Harry's father once, when his company had befallen this very fate. An internal investigation was held and a lot of the men were questioned, but nothing came of it.

Then, Margaret was accused of accepting money; a bribe from a rival company. Harry's father had been sent some still shots by an unknown source, depicting Margaret being followed uptown, making certain deliveries and stopping off at a well-known public house, often frequented by the competition's staff.

To some, interpretations of photographs were obvious, particularly if those photographs were accompanied by a report from an unidentified source, clarifying what you might have already been suspecting.

To others, however, what you saw in a photo wasn't always the truth; the photographs could have come from anyone – perhaps even from the competition, to divert attention away from the imminent discovery of their real mole.

They might say that contacts in the opposition would hardly have let her be photographed in such an obvious manner, out in the wide open.

Still, the grumble from high - which is to say, Harry's father - was a demand that someone had to be held accountable. For this, they had to be sure; they hadn't actually caught her doing anything wrong.

He had been breathing hard down her neck, but no amount of heat would make her change her story. Still, one could only expect denial, or, on rare occasions, an admittance of guilt. She had taken certain packages and made the deliveries, but insisted she'd been told to go there and collect something, which she later reposted - the request had come from one of the workers, under orders from one of the foremen.

It was young Harry himself who had then asked the question: "Why would she have been sent uptown, if not asked to for business reasons?" Something didn't fit right, and Harry had been determined to get to the truth of the matter.

It was easy to make up the answers to your own questions, but then there would always be the doubt, lingering, somewhere in the back of your mind. Harry was, even then, old-fashioned enough to at least give people the benefit of the doubt; even in a court of law, evidence could be ruled as circumstantial, and nobody should be sentenced without a fair hearing. They had to know the truth: the organization's "firm but fair" reputation was riding on this, and they could not afford to make any mistakes.

The deliveries in question had been made to individuals with whom his father had had no previous or present dealings - not even on an unofficial basis. Nor did anybody in his father's company, or those associated, frequent that public house, or go near it to do any form of business transaction.

Carrying out his own investigation, Harry began to look into the head foreman's lifestyle, and found that he had been making some substantial purchases over the past few months - the kind he couldn't possibly make on his salary. He easily discovered that the foreman had been using his position to feed the competition information, from time to time - when somebody had started to ask questions, he had tried to avert suspicion, by framing Margaret. It had been he who had taken the photos and sent them to Harry's father, though he denied ever seeing them, despite his fingerprints being on them. In the end, it was always carelessness that caught out the stupid. Harry had sacked the foreman right off, and done his father proud.

Margaret kept her job until she got pregnant and became a housewife, marrying one of Harry's own men, in fact. It was always good to keep business in the family.

Now, because he had known Margaret for some time, Harry decided to take her into his confidence, explaining to her all about Martin and the money. She was surprised, just as Laurence had been.

Sitting in her kitchen, across from her, they drank a cup of coffee together, then Harry called Laurence on the mobile, asking if he had told anyone about the trip.

"I just told a girl I was seeing that I was going away for a few days, and where I was going," Laurence said, a little confused by the call. "She was interested in why I was delivering so far away."

"But I told you to use your discretion; to be careful not to talk to anyone," Harry said, reminding him of their previous conversation in his office.

Laurence had recalled this, but thought little of it, seeing as she wasn't local, nor a member of the community; he had just told her what Harry had told him. "She was very interested. It was a hell of a story, Harry."

It was indeed. And someone had caught wind of it, and passed it on to another party, who didn't like how the ending was going to play out.

"Listen carefully," Harry told him: "I need you to get rid of your phone after we're done speaking; only contact me by public payphone. There may be some other parties that are interested in those documents you have, and they may try to track you."

Laurence didn't like the sound of that; for a moment, he thought about coming back.

"This job means a lot to this community, so we're counting on you," Harry added, sensing Laurence's notion. "Don't worry: once you get to where you're going, just lie low until I contact you - I'll get your aunt's number from your mum." He paused, as he had a thought: "Does your girlfriend know where your aunt lives?"

"No, I just said what part of the country I was travelling to, not the exact location," Laurence said, starting to realize now how badly he had messed this up. Was his mother in danger now?

"Well, that's fine then," Harry said, with some relief. "Everything is going to work out just fine; I'm going to take care of everything at this end."

Hanging up, he turned to Margaret, who was clearly concerned, both for her son and for herself. Harry went over and took her shoulders, firmly, in his hands.

"I'm going to have someone watch over this place, to see that you're safe." He kissed her cheek, warmly. "What do you know about this new girl he's been seeing?"

The words "trust me", spoken to one's very face, can set us at war with ourselves; we have the option to believe or not to believe this phrase, when it is told to us so many times. But, it is difficult to know what side people are on, and easy to lose track of an employee's loyalty towards the firm.

Even if you give someone what they need, how do they repay you? History can often repeat itself and, as such, you learn from past experiences, just enough to give the benefit of the doubt. But, that didn't change the fact that it was difficult, at times, to find reliable people, whom one could truly trust.

Maybe he should have given the job to one of his other men, Harry pondered: Laurence had promised he wouldn't say anything.

But, when it comes to being young, it is so easy to allow the excitement of rare opportunities to cloud one's judgement. Particularly when looking to impress a pretty girl!

Stopping by one of the popular nightspots in the city, Harry did some asking around, and eventually found who he was looking for - the young woman - sat in a booth, with two other girls. They were drinking and enjoying themselves.

He couldn't fathom what the lad found so special about her. Perhaps she was one of those which bridged the two worlds: decency on one side, and on the other… well, you get the point. She definitely looked the sort of girl who travelled equally comfortably in both - some young, inexperienced boys found this exciting in a woman.

As though on cue, a young man, dressed in a blazer, came to sit on the edge of the seat next to her. She giggled, as he whispered something in her ear, whilst resting his hand on her thigh, slowly caressing, halfway up her skirt.

The old expression "good-time girl" was not one often heard these days, yet it sprang to mind. In Harry's generation, even the girls who liked a bit of fun acted in a respectable manner, at least - even when in the company of a suggestive gentleman. He wasn't quite able to ascertain the extent of the relationship between these two, until the boy pressed his mouth firmly onto that of the girl, who neither pulled away or resisted his sudden advances; the mutual temptation to indulge her hunger and his particular requirement was apparent. Harry was already starting to feel sorry for Laurence.

When the boy had left, he sauntered over to the table. The three girls looked up, quizzically.

"Evening, ladies. Can I partake of your lovely company for a moment?" he asked, inviting himself to sit next to her, as her friends looked on, with slight amusement.

"I believe we have a mutual friend," Harry spoke: "Laurence - he works here, in security, doesn't he?"

The girl took in the name, with little interest. "Yes, but he's off tonight," she replied. It was clearly making her feel uncomfortable: his sitting at their table, as other people passed by and looked at them.

"That's a shame: a nice girl like you, all alone on a night like this. He tells me you're his special *lady*," he almost choked on the last word. "I didn't catch your name."

The girls sitting across from them were watching the scene in clear hilarity, hearing her being hit on by an old man – almost as amusing as his insinuation about her relationship with Laurence.

"It's Debbie: Debbie Hatchard. But, we're not an item," she said, noting her friends still giggling uncontrollably, and hoping that the old guy would move on soon.

Hearing her surname suddenly added a large piece of the picture to the puzzle; everything was now becoming clearer. It seemed that history was, indeed, repeating itself.

"I remember your father, Danny; he worked for me." Harry then went on to introduce his full name to her, and she clearly recognized it. Why wouldn't she: Laurence had only spoken about his employer just before he left, a few hours ago.

"Yes. He found other work - same line," she said, nervously.

"With Braddock, I suppose?"

Her eyes shied away, and she didn't say any more. Harry knew straight away that she didn't have to: he had got the answer he needed.

She had told her father about Laurence leaving town, and why.

Danny Hatchard was still acting as Braddock's informant.

There is no mystery when it comes to any living creature; each has only one single interest - the one we all share: the instinct to survive, at any cost. Even the smallest organism, such as a parasite, has to evolve and adapt to its host. You don't even know it is there; it's only a matter of time before it grows strong.

It seems that even genes such as these can be passed on, through the generations.

The strongest impulse to self-preservation will allow us to carry out any atrocity – it seems that, with this lot, using or sacrificing others for their own self gain was a family trait.

Still, it was not Harry's place to question the girl's motives; he had the answer he needed.

Just in time, too, because the young man in the blazer, along with two others, returned to the table, a disapproving expression on his face.

"What you want, Grandad?" Then, he looked down at Debbie, and saw an immediate look of concern wash over her face.

With a parting glance at a relieved-looking Debbie, Harry got up and moved, hastily, away from the group. He was not intimidated by the youth; he just wanted to get back to his car. It was getting late and he needed to contact me, with this new information.

As he walked back through the crowds, watching as they danced, and snorted cocaine off of each other's bodies, it became apparent to him that people like this were beyond the realm of good and respectable social integration. Psychologically, they had been tweaked, from childhood, to be drones; sheep, grazing in a field as the lion passed through them, without even knowing enough as to bat an eyelid. If only they knew the things that people like him had done, at one time, to keep a hold of this country. Just so they could keep living their mundane lives.

He was no saint – nor, in the eyes of the law, was he a hero – but, he was no sheep, either.

Upon exiting the club, as Harry moved slowly across the road, he heard a voice, calling after him - the young man in the blazer was following, not far behind, flanked by his two friends.

"What's your business with Debbie and her old man?" he demanded.

All of them were buckling, slightly, at the knees, and he could assess their character in a heartbeat: they had no self-control; they just embraced the effects of alcohol and drugs, without the slightest concern for the consequences.

"Your smart move would be to go back in there and enjoy your evening with those girls. But, then, whoever said that your generation had the intellect to grasp good advice when it was given?"

The boy snarled and curled his fingers, tightly. "What the fuck did you just say to me, old man?"

It didn't matter what you wore, or which cologne you chose to apply, the rotten smell of street sewage still poured from every orifice.

"It would be a shame to ruin that suit: the only smart thing about you," Harry pressed, further. The truth was a terrible thing, but beautifully put, in an old-school manner.

These were just of the new generation of offenders, which society had no idea what to do with - Harry was not so ignorant when it came to incorrigible teenagers, who had no respect for their elders. Any modern human behavioural specialist will tell you that the young people of today are always looking to gain "rep", street cred and respect – these days, you can't survive the streets without it. In their own way, they think they can get things done with a harsh word, and they so easily rebel, when told what to do and what not to do. Despite the warnings they are given, they continue to choose their own path to destruction.

If this boy wanted to go face-to-face and toe-to-toe, he was happy to oblige. Although both of the boy's fists were large, and probably had the impact of a sledgehammer, Harry was severely spoilt for choice: this lad was big and unstable on his feet; Harry could pull the blade in his coat pocket or use the glass bottle by his foot. He finally decided that was a little unsporting; he would just settle this the old-school way.

As the fist came around, toward him, he took the full force on his forearms - it slightly unbalanced his footing, but he recovered fast enough to deliver a knee to the boy's testicles.

When you had to dip your hand into uncharted water, you had to be careful that something didn't bite it off. And, like a shark, Harry was looking to take a big mouthful! He clamped his jaws down hard on the youth's finger, until he felt the bone crunch and give way, in his mouth.

Withdrawing, all he could hear was the young man, screaming in agony, as he dropped to his knees; the boy's two friends just looked on in horror, from behind.

Then, allowing the tiny digit to drop from his mouth, onto the street, Harry took the hip-flask from his inside coat pocket, took a drag of the whisky and spat it back out. It was a wicked waste, but one could never be too careful!

Punks like this deserve no less; they know nothing about respect - laughing and spitting in people's faces.

It isn't at all like the old days - days long gone; the country has changed so much. Kids run wild, rioting in the streets, burning property and randomly beating people. What's worse is that the law is unable to get it under control; there is nothing to stop them doing it, over and over again.

Sometimes, you just have to meet chaos with a unique form of calm. Sometimes, the permanent kind, which comes out of the barrel of a gun, is too quick. Sometimes, slow, precise justice is better than no justice.

CHAPTER 13

When you open the door, into your memories, you inevitably remember the bad things you've done – those you have to live with, if you want to live with yourself.

You just have to try and justify that you did the best you could, with what life offered you - you'd go mad if you didn't.

We're all guilty of something; none of us have lived perfect lives. And, though we don't always say it out loud, we're all afraid that it will come back to haunt us, one day.

By the time Harry had got back to his car a lot of old memories had started to resurface.

As he drove back, through the streets, the familiar surroundings and the most mundane smells started to trigger emotions, long buried from years before. They were so incredibly powerful that he had to pull the car over for a moment.

A memory about his old firm had come back to Harry.

One night, they had all gone out together, dined and drank well. They were celebrating their retirement from an illicit life, and looking forward to their newly legitimized business venture.

Exiting the restaurant, onto the street, they had been met by a hail of automatic gunfire.

Harry had been hit, badly, but not badly enough to kill him.

Unlike most of his companions; all but one of the old firm had been wiped out.

As he writhed on the blood-stained pavement, Harry reached across to Helena, who lay still, her face at peace in the dim light.

People learn to cope with historical trauma in different ways. In times of guilt, some turn instead to thoughts of happiness or pleasure; this helps them let certain details fade away.

But, they're never truly gone, and you can't go back in time, to relive your past, hoping for a change in circumstances.

Harry had enjoyed a relatively happy childhood. His had been like that of any other child growing up in Ravenfall: not exactly one of privilege. But, whatever other guys had, he always had the same, and felt no less adequate for it.

There were, of course, others, who did not share this philosophy.

One was Braddock - a once-close friend, whom he had known since high school. Theirs had, at first, started out as a childish rivalry: sports; girls; anything there was to compete over, they did so. They were almost like brothers, though they did like to go at it in the boxing ring, from time to time, giving each other a bit of a tickle on the jaw; always standing toe-to-toe, and neither backing down. In the best of these bouts, the gym coach would always have to prise them apart; they would always settle down in the pub, later, over a few drinks.

Back in the day, they had been the leaders of a firm, which was made up of former schoolfriends; they were always out and about together, getting into some form of trouble or another. Most of the time, their misdeeds were overlooked, due to the status of Harry's father within the community; there were always bigger fish for the law to concern themselves with.

A certain big city organization, known as "The Syndicate", had started to come around, making threats and collecting protection money from local shops and businesses. They started to own a little piece of every part of the town.

To Braddock, this was a big issue: other firms muscling in on their turf, taking what didn't belong to them. The community and the police were clueless - most were just shit-scared - so, they would have to do something about it themselves.

There was one exception in the police - one with a little bit of knowledge of how to deal with these people – and, with his help, Braddock started to organize, and began to take the fight to the Syndicate, on enemy territory. The Ravenfall group were far from vigilantes, and were more than willing to cross the line, on occasions.

It started with a list of names: those who had crossed them, their friends, neighbours and businesses, were the first to come under attack. Then, Braddock got ambitious, and started going after the ringleaders; to him, attack was all about quality now, and not quantity; remove the big fish, and all the little fish will swim away, deserting the reef. The landscape became a war zone.

The public and even the police came to fear the firm's actions. But, not the residents of Ravenfall, who believed Braddock was merely fighting fire with fire, just as many of them had done, during the second world war. They were happy with Braddock's progress.

That was, until their own friends and neighbours started to become victimized by the firm.

Harry called a stop to the firm's activities: they were no longer what they had started out as; now, instead of heroes, they were no better than those they had successfully fought off, supposedly to protect the town.

But, Braddock disagreed, insisting that the place would turn into a shithole if they didn't continue what needed to be done; for the greater good, sacrifices needed to be made.

This was now turning into something more than just a pithy turf war, or power move; innocent lives were at stake, and Harry insisted they should not be thought of as mere chess pieces, to be sacrificed for the firm's gain, or even for that of the community.

Braddock had already walked away from them when the firm met its end, the following week.

The drive-by shooting incident made the morning papers. They reported the attack to be random, and perhaps a case of mistaken identity, but Harry knew the truth: they had been set up and double-crossed.

Lifestyle has long been known as a mortality factor but, in some cases, it can save a life. Being such a large man - neither weak or thin - the bullets which struck Harry had only inflicted flesh wounds; not a single organ had been damaged.

After his discharge from hospital, he tried to visit Laurie, but she blamed him for her mother's death, cursing the day he had come into her life. It was true: if he hadn't, Helena would still be alive today.

"But, then, neither would you," he could only retort, to his daughter.

It had been his decision, at the time, to let them both go.

The echo of the door slamming behind him still haunted him, even now.

Now, years later, he stood, once again, at that very front door.

He waited, patiently until the hall light had come on. When Laurie answered the door, he immediately read concern in her eyes.

She listened to what he had to say, and by the time he had finished, she could feel the nausea returning, just as she had felt it in his office. As if it wasn't bad enough that he had woken her up in the middle of the night, and that she had been losing sleep for the past few days over Martin, trying to figure out why had had left her in the first place, now Harry was telling her she had to come away with him, because Martin was on the run again, with one of his hoodlum friends, and people were after them.

"I can protect you better at my place," he insisted. "Now, go and pack what you need."

"This is my home; I don't want to go anywhere, and certainly not with you!"

He hadn't wanted it to come to this, but he had guessed that she would make it difficult. "I just want to keep you safe for the moment, until I can resolve all of this."

"Or, keep me as a bargaining chip, in case your guy loses Martin before you can get your money," she countered, aware that the thought must have been on his mind for some time.

It could very well be that he was playing her, just so she would go with him; perhaps Martin was being difficult, and Harry needed leverage, to keep him under control.

“You can’t force me to go with you!” She moved backward, to close the door. “If you try to make me, I’ll call the police!”

Harry wasn’t at all shaken by this; the girl, as always, had no idea what her husband had got her into; these people would go to any lengths to stop Martin from getting that money.

“The police still don’t know about the money, Laurie. If they ask, I might be forced to tell them, but then they’ll be after him even more.” Martin being dead or behind bars was going to help anyone - certainly not Laurie.

“Well, at least he would be in protective custody, away from them and away from you!” she argued.

Harry was surprised to see that she was still trying to protect Martin, despite all he had done. A wife’s loyalty to her husband was something Harry knew nothing about; he had to admire her integrity, at least. She was wrong, however: police were not the solution, particularly city cops, who could be paid off.

On the other, hand, Laurie didn’t think Harry was helping the situation much, either. She didn’t believe that any of this was about protecting Martin, or her; it was all about protecting his own interests: that damned building project, which Martin had stopped, accidentally.

“Well, I can’t let you stay here on your own, so I might just have to send one of my men around, to watch you here; protect you, until this is all over.”

The more she considered her options, the more fearful she was becoming. At this point there wasn’t anywhere she could go, or anyone she could rely on. "I don't want one of your hoodlums in this house! No one is coming after me; it's Martin who needs your protection, and whoever is after him isn't going to stop until they get to him. What are you going to do about it?" Laurie couldn't bear the thought of her husband being hunted by killers. How could Harry have let this happen? It was inexcusable.

"I can't afford to take that chance." He pressed a little harder: "I need you to think about this carefully; if you won't do it for me, think of your children."

It all seemed so wrong: him taking her out of her own house, because she might now be in danger - all because somebody had found out about Martin's lottery win.

Harry was never going to change: always trying to be in control; deciding what was best, with regard to other people's interests. What bothered her the most, though, was that she hadn't seen this coming. She should have: a man like Harry had enemies, who would stop at nothing to see his plans fail.

Finally, she conceded. Within ten minutes, she had packed a few things and was sitting quietly in Harry's car, on the drive back to his house.

Harry couldn't help but hate himself, for putting Laurie through all this, but it was for her own good and protection. Braddock had become even more a crazy bastard than before. He wanted to complete his revenge; to destroy all that Harry had.

But, the one thing about power is that it won't be given up without a fight; from its origins to its evolution, it is the one thing that we can never bear to part with. It is the legacy we so badly want to leave behind for our children, no matter what the cost, or self-sacrifice.

At that moment, Harry did not fear for his own life, but he did for that of the only true family he had left. He should really have taken care of all this years ago - sometimes it was better to take chances, than to live your whole life in fear.

He hadn't talked to Braddock in five years, but he had always known that someday his former partner would be looking to settle the old score; this made him fearful for Laurie.

There wasn't a day which went by that Harry hadn't wanted to kill Braddock; to go out to his house, drag him outside, onto the front lawn, and stick a gun in his mouth. He would make Braddock beg for his life, then, when satisfied that he was scared enough, would pull the trigger, with Braddock's family watching.

But, that would mean that he would then have to turn the gun on them; taking out Braddock would only lead to more bloodshed. The family - if he even had one - did not deserve to die for his actions; neither should they be haunted by such images, for the rest of their lives. Harry would not make unnecessary sacrifices anymore.

He was still human, despite his dark past. He felt that perhaps he had become the man he was never supposed to be. He hadn't been forced into this world, and now, finally, he had the chance to leave it all behind. Harry was trying to be a different man; to leave the past in the past.

But, still, he couldn't let it go. His head was still messed up, as though a thousand cockroaches were feeding on his brain. The itching of these pests is the reason that exterminators sometimes need to be called in, to deal with the problem.

Originally, the firm acted only as private assassins, when needed to keep the competition in line; on occasion, it was the best insurance people could buy. But, it wasn't always about revenge; it was about keeping order. As one of the last surviving members of the firm, he had felt it his duty to remain in the town which had meant so much to all of them; to ensure that all their deaths were not in vain. This new turn of events would, hopefully, go a long way to restoring reputation and honour to the family name, which had become tarnished.

Sometimes, of course, problems could never be solved; you eliminated one, and two more popped up to take its place. Sometimes, in the end, you just had to live with them.

Some people believe that the best way to cleanse evil from this world is to kill it. But, how do you judge what is truly evil; what does deserve to die?

As I have said, that is not my call; I'm just doing a job. I don't get emotional, attempt to justify, or any of that, no matter how much the person may sicken me, because, as a professional, this is all just another transaction to be completed. It's business - that's the way to look at it. If you take it personally, it goes beyond money. And, I will never walk away satisfied just because I made a profit.

My meeting with Martin was never fate; it was because of the choices he made.

If you don't think it is your destiny to suffer the wrath of God, for all the bad you've done in your life, why don't you take it up with the Big Man himself?

CHAPTER 14

What keeps me awake at night?

Well, like I already said, I do sleep normally. I just didn't that night. The vision of the door to our room bursting open and several masked thugs rushing in, with heavy hardware, is what kept me from a good night's rest.

Of course, it would take more than a lock-pick, shoulder or foot to get in, since I had wedged three door-stops underneath ours, to seal us both in. Still, sometimes there was just no place to hide; no real sanctuary; an undisclosed location and a locked door didn't always provide complete security.

Across the room, Martin was actually sleeping, quietly. He had eaten and washed, but said very little, since our last talk.

Now, as I lay there, looking up at the ceiling, I began to replay all my previous jobs, as though they were projecting out of my eyes, onto a giant screen.

You can be asked to do some pretty terrible things; things which will never permit you to sleep again. After a while, though, you get to live with them, because you grow not to care whether or not there is a just cause; right or wrong, sometimes killing is just unavoidable.

It's nothing to be proud of, particularly when taking those who are too young to have lived a full life. But, then, death has no age restriction.

You might be surprised to hear this, but there is no intense satisfaction in watching another person's body twitch, for the last time, before coming to lie still.

Especially that of a child.

They say that when you die your life flashes before your eyes. This is why I never look into the eyes of my prey, because a glimpse of the life I'm taking away could haunt me forever. A dead person's eyes can be a curse, so it is always important not to make a connection.

Their hopes and dreams shatter with one bullet. Voices and songs become silent, as the cord tightens around the throat; love pours and runs red, like a waterfall from the heart, as the blade digs deep...

That's what usually fucks up some guys: they let it get personal - under their skin - whereas I can usually wash the blood, very easily, from my hands, just like a butcher, after cutting up meat.

Sometimes, murder is justice. None of the people I've killed did I ever once consider innocent. Although, I had to really look at that kid, lying dead at my feet, but not as a target - and, not as an innocent bystander, either; sometimes, the people I kill are just victims of circumstance.

I don't mind the women, but I won't kill children. Those who will are not like me; I'll make that clear, right from the very start.

There have been only a few times when a young child was present, but I would always wait for a time when the child is gone - upstairs, at a friend's house, or maybe in the next room - making the kill quick and quiet; even, if necessary, abducting and terminating elsewhere. It isn't necessarily a matter of conscience; perhaps more about moral values.

You think my employers would blame me? No, they know the deal up front; they know my limitations, and no amount of money or loyalty will make me cross that line. It's not a good business, for them or for me.

It had never happened to me before: right then, something began to feel broken.

All of the lives I took previously had been paid for, but I killed that boy on the train because he was going to kill me, and the man which I had originally been sent to kill. At that moment, *I* had felt like the target, only I had seen it coming - it's the only reason I was still alive. Only amateurs end up dead or in prison.

But, what of us? How do we live on? What had once made us human can be replaced by a dark, empty shell, if we're not careful.

This new situation I found myself in had got me thinking about the other side to this business.

There are often two elements, when it comes to contract killing: the killer and the protector, one of which, so far, I had not previously encountered - all of my previous targets have been unprotected; which is to say: no security or bodyguards.

They were definitely a problem, though. Even my own father had often brought it up, saying that all security personnel had to be taken into serious consideration, if you intended to get close to the target.

In truth, I had always been curious about why somebody would choose to put their own life on the line for another. It couldn't just be about the money: what good was that if you were dead? Perhaps it could be explained by an element of duty, integrity and honour - I could understand that in respect of someone very important, but not just anybody. I guess that's what separates a person like that from someone like me.

Only, now here I was, responsible for protecting another person's life, rather than taking it away. I still didn't get it, especially considering I was still contemplating the act of killing my charge, right at that moment, as he slept - I could make up any reason, and nobody would be any the wiser.

Which just goes to show, of course, that I am neither courageous or heroic.

But, it was my job to keep Martin alive, despite the fact that I thought the guy to be the scum of the Earth, and I was doing so solely out of obligation to my employer. That I could remain honourable to my employer's wishes, and wait three more days, thereby prolonging the inevitable, I was starting to seriously doubt.

I looked at Martin, right there across from me, asleep and vulnerable. It would be so easy to just smother him, or to put one in his head, at least allowing him the grace to die in his sleep - it was more than I had offered any of my targets previously. Somehow, such a death didn't seem befitting of a person of such low moral and family values: this man had ruined so many lives, and betrayed loved ones.

He was even starting to push my buttons; making me wish I had just taken the ticket back to Harry and not made the call. I wouldn't have been on that train, ending up a target myself.

I shouldn't be thinking this, I shouldn't even be saying it, nor any of what I have been saying.

Just what the hell am I doing here?

This was supposed to be a simple story, but the more I get into its deep and personal facts, the more I want to stop holding back. Though, I don't know why this should be of any concern to you. You can choose to stop reading at any time, and just go back to your lives, with one close of the book, if you haven't already done so.

Strangely, so far, I've tried to be fair with the facts. But, the more I put words to paper, the less I seem able to stop the whole truth from pouring out. I honestly thought I wouldn't care about that - after all, you don't really know me.

Perhaps, if you are still there, it's because you're just being fair to me, or maybe you just like hearing me talk? Are you, like me, lying comfy in your bed, right now (well, technically on *it, but the mattress is still comfortable, and the room smells real nice - not like my own room back at home).*

Damn, I promised I wasn't going to do this, but since I can't sleep, and maybe you can't either, why don't I go into a few more details? I have to be careful - anonymity is still an important factor here – so, let's just keep it all simple.

Let me start by saying I'm probably not what you will have expected. By now, you've probably built an image in your mind of how you would picture me: you know, those guys who always wear black in the movies... Well, that is the first and biggest mistake: the single most important skill in this profession is to blend in; if you stand out, people will see you coming a mile off. The plainer you look, the more likely you are to walk by, without being noticed.

Everything I've told you, up until now, is more-or-less accurate, though perhaps there are a few omissions to straighten out.

I've never actually paid to sleep with a whore. I've never done this, because I'm not gay.

That's right: I am, in fact, a woman.

Sorry to all of you out there, who had the impression otherwise, but I never actually said I was a man; I said I could be any nationality, but omitted to mention that I could be either gender, too.

I won't bother describing myself - I'll leave that to your imagination – but, I assure you, I am quite a looker; in that respect I take after my mum, in fact.

There is good reason why people like me exist - you just won't like hear those reasons from me. I simply am what I am.

The question is: who are you? Are you the sort of person who would hire me to do a job? Perhaps, as you are reading this book, you have a particular interest in my work?

I don't mean any offence, but, like my own father says: there are always people who want another person dead, for any number of reasons. They want their pound of flesh, but they'll always expect the butcher to do the carving.

Okay, since I already mentioned it, I might as well come clean: that's my family's other business: meat. You see, we own a family-run butcher-shop, in our local home town.

Before you get any wild notions, we do not dispose of victims in our products, or cannibalize the people we kill - that would make us very sick people indeed, which we are not. I'm simply a fourth-generation butcher and a professional killer rolled into one, which is what makes me so good with a knife. But, I am far from insane, which, hopefully, you have already gathered.

My family is as respected for our meat as we are for our history as contract killers. Though, it has to be said that the second is not common knowledge around town; it would undoubtedly be bad for business – especially ours.

You may think that it is not possible to mix the life of an assassin with the life of a family; that attachments are usually forbidden. Well, that's only how it goes in the movies.

Another omission is that my family and I reside within the centre of Ravenfall, and have done now for at least five generations. It is quite a nice little community, our town of Ravenfall (I still can't give you the real name and address, naturally).

I know what you're thinking: that this doesn't read like the life of a professional killer; usually, they live alone. Well, sometimes they do, but what's wrong with being part of a family? What's wrong with living another life, as well as this job? You only have to be a creature of the shadows when you are working.

When in Ravenfall, there are never times I feel like a ghost; walking in Limbo, without people ever really seeing me - which is, of course, the whole point, when I am working; only then is it necessary to be as mysterious and flippant as déjà vu. The fact is that we never truly see a person when they are in plain sight.

Now, you're probably asking: if I live in Ravenfall, why doesn't Martin know me? Well, I wondered briefly myself – earlier, on the train - if he did recognize me, but my concerns have been put to rest: he obviously doesn't recollect. Can you honestly say that you know everyone in your home town? Or, know every person on your street by name? Are sociable with every family? Well if you are, lucky you!

Besides, Ravenfall isn't actually all that small; through the decades it has grown and developed. It survived two world wars, and even has a new supermarket, not far from where we live.

Coming from such a reclusive community, it isn't difficult not to know every resident: those who grow up usually leave, and only a few come from the city to visit. Sure, my family has a popular butchers' shop, but only a select number of clientele - most residents are nowadays content with meat from the supermarket. Neither Martin or Laurie have ever visited our shop.

They are not really church-goers either, unlike Harry, who we see about every Sunday; the couple didn't even get married in our own church. They certainly didn't invite Harry to the wedding! From what I understand, they pretty much kept to themselves, until Martin started getting into trouble, and lost his job, working for Harry.

We'd all heard that things had gone bad with Harry's project, and offered to help; when Martin stole from the community, we were only too happy to track him down. I'm just sorry I couldn't retrieve what he and his associates took. Still, at least the money should make up for some of that.

I'm just not too fond of being around the guy now, as you've no doubt gathered. I should have just shot him in that alley and gone back with the ticket; placed it in Harry's hands - at least he would be able to do great things with the money.

What will Martin do with it?

Well, you're just going have to wait and see; I don't want to give away the ending.

Laid there, on my bed, I closed my eyes and allowed my mind to drift, thinking of all the good things I would be going back to, once this was all over.

When it comes to family, not a lot of parents understand their children's motivations. As you grow up, it would be hard for them to imagine you saying: "I want to be a killer, too!"

It is only a family tradition by choice, as it has always been; nobody forced us into this profession. This is probably why I'm so good.

Being young, we all strive to make something of our career. Whatever it is, we want to make it successful and, hopefully, make our parents proud. Sure, there are always bad choices and wrong decisions along the way, but we all make them.

The only difference, in this business, is that the mistake can cost you your freedom… or your life!

CHAPTER 15

At some point during this you might have asked: "Do these people have any fear of death?"

That depends on your point of view, doesn't it? Each has their own insight, and some have their own beliefs; there are also those who supposedly cross over and come back.

Just, not the ones I kill.

To me, death is a way to make a living. Nobody can avoid it, whatever their circumstances – although, as you've borne witness, it can be delayed. But, sooner or later, we all have to pay the price for our lives.

Yes, death is a price, particularly to those who do bad things, or do not appreciate all of that which life had to offer. If they did, they wouldn't get greedy, want for more, and get themselves into debt, so people like me come knocking at their door.

On the other hand, wrong place, wrong time and bad circumstances are the only things that lead to people like myself becoming a target.

We all die, sooner or later, but if you're willing to fight, you might just find that the man upstairs has extended your credit, if just for a little while longer. The meeting may have been postponed, but we all have to keep that appointment, sometime.

*

It is never easy to hear that a family member has died. Especially one so young and, of all things, so violently.

Arriving at the local morgue, Mr. X was immediately greeted by the local police.

At times of such distressing news, it is natural for questions to be asked, particularly regarding the identity of the persons who have committed the murder.

"We can't exactly call it 'murder'," the police sergeant said: "he wasn't the victim, so to speak; the real intended victim actually got away."

They had managed to get a look at the train's C.C.T.V., and had seen the boy and his other two associates attacking two unidentified people, with machetes.

"We've had a lot in here, related to gang killing," said the officer, "but this particular one is different: whoever killed these boys knew what they were doing." He paused for a moment, as his colleague handed him the official report; "What I mean to say is that there was a certain skill involved; this person definitely had anatomical knowledge. The cuts were made by something sharp, but we don't think that just a knife was used. By the way this person used her hands, and the way she moved, it was clear that she was very well trained and extremely dangerous."

Mr. X simply nodded, as the sergeant continued with a monologue about the mindset of youngsters these days, and how strongly it was influenced by all those crazy video games, twisting their minds.

To say that Mr. X would have never thought the young lad capable of something like this would have been a lie: there are some people of which you always knew what they were capable, particularly when it ran in their blood.

"I'm sorry for your loss," the sergeant concluded, excusing himself and his colleague.

"I'm sorry." The two words most commonly used before a bullet leaves the chamber. If you listen carefully enough, you can often still hear them, echoing through the gunshot.

There is always a choice: be what you've always been, do what you've always done, or die as you choose to die. Being what you are, being who you are, and choosing what you mean to do are sure ways to meet your end, faster than even God intended. If you think it is someone's simple destiny to be taken out of this life in this way... well, you must be stranger than the rest of us all: no one takes up this role expecting to buy it in this way. But, it is not something you can fool yourself about, either.

There were only two other people in the room: one, a dark woman, in her late forties, wearing casual jeans and a red shirt; the other, the mortuary assistant, currently opening the door of one of the cold-storage units. A small figure was rolled out, on a tray covered with a white sheet, reminiscent of a left-over dish being taken from the fridge. As the body was wheeled over to the dark woman, the sheet was slowly pulled back, revealing the face of the young boy from the train: Caleb, Mr. X's nephew; the only child of his sister.

The deep cut around the boy's neck sent a clear shudder through her body. Behind her, her brother just looked on, studying the wound. It was deep, and executed with skill.

You have to remember: sooner or later, we all end up in a place like this, lying on a cold, metal tray, as our loved ones look down upon us.

Will they cry tears of happiness, that we died peacefully, or of sadness and sorrow, because we died so terribly?

By then, it is all too late to change: your soul has left your body and all that remains is to bury it in a box. No one can change what has happened; all one can do is ask the question - the same question we are always asked, by those we put on those metal trays, and in those boxes.

"Why?" she finally spoke.

It was unbelievable to her, that someone she had loved - had raised from infancy – had been alive just the day before being laid there like that, his flesh sliced open like poultry.

"Who was he connected with?" Mr. X asked. "Who were his so-called friends and associates?"

It was difficult for her to think about such things right now; at this moment she knew only of the huge hole in her heart.

"If you want answers, then I need answers, too – quickly, if I'm to act," he pressed her, gently.

She wiped her nose on a tissue, glancing his way. "And, do what?"

"What would you like me to do?"

She turned to face him fully, and slapped him hard across the face. "Don't you dare bring that in here!" she spat. "I'm still grieving; I don't want to hear that you intend to make this right. It won't bring him back. It won't bring my son back."

She turned back, to look down at Caleb's pale face. "It won't give him a fresh start. Or you."

Neither her outburst or the slight stinging on his face caused him to lose his composure. "He was my family, too; I need to know why he died the way he did," he insisted.

She eyed him, carefully now; "You think this was retaliation for *your* past sins; catching up with you, like it did for our father? The same as what it also cost our own mother and her sister?" She crossed herself. "He paid the price for his decisions, and now my son has paid, too. All that remains is you."

Mr. X didn't like the idea that his sister thought he was somehow involved. It had nothing to with him; his nephew had been deliberately sent to kill somebody.

And, it was clear that these boys had been given no idea who they were going up against.

She sobbed: "Whatever happened last night – and, whoever it was that sent him out there - have taken my child. There is nothing that is going to change that, or make it now alright. Now, just let me grieve."

He did want to leave this place, but he was determined to find the people responsible: "Tell me what I need to know, then I'll go, and leave you both in peace."

She finally spoke, naming a place he never again thought he would ever have to return to.

"Am I going to see you in here next?" she asked, no longer looking at him.

Placing a hand on the dead boy's forehead, he left her quietly, without another word, and returned to his car.

He wished he was able to see the lad off; to tell him to take care, wherever he was going. In truth, he really wasn't sure where the boy was even heade: Heaven? Hell? Perhaps nowhere.

It was the one question only the boy would know the answer to now – or perhaps wouldn't, if there were nothing beyond this world. In that case, eternal rest was indeed our final chance at peace!

In this job you can make too many enemies, and not enough friends; every time you kill somebody, you will forever make an enemy of their family.

For this reason, it is best to be very careful who you kill: one bad decision can turn you from predator to prey in an instant, and the benefit of any innate ability to understand the nature of other people like yourself dissolves, along with the blood and the bullets.

CHAPTER 16

So often, people mean to change their ways. But, the habits which come to rule our lives seem to take over our very will!

When you look into the face of the one you love, who wronged you, there is an honest sorrow. We wish death, rather than returning, once more, to the new master, who calls on a daily basis. Chained or bound, we cannot resist; we become a prisoner to our own weakness.

The biggest sin in the world is owing money.

The second biggest sin is owing money, but being unable to pay.

Laurie had been brought up as a good Christian girl, educated by her grandparents, always to show compassion for others in need.

People had always considered Martin, on the other hand, to be a low-life - just because he had done a little time in prison, for losing his temper and inflicting grievous bodily harm upon a drunken brawler.

His crime had been not near as horrid as those of his brother, Henry, who was nothing like Martin: no sense of right, no style and no future; just awaiting his release.

Laurie had taken pity on Martin, upon his arrival home. They had sort of known each other from school, though he never mixed much with other children. He had needed help and, as he had nobody else, she had taken him in – in spite of her father's disapproval - insisting it was a Christian duty to give someone in his position a second chance.

It had been her example which had helped to get him his first job: cleaning the town's church, at first under the supervision of the reverend, who guided him to see that it was the Lord who had brought him there, to start anew. He was surprised to find that there were people still willing to show him understanding and Christian love.

People can end up getting everything they ever wanted, but it still doesn't feel right; what they now possess may not feel as if it is theirs, because they didn't make it, or earn it.

To love is easy, but to earn eternal worship takes more than just physical affection. You can soon end up questioning whether it was what you really wanted; was it all for you, or was it for somebody else? It is easy to confuse what we want with the wishes of someone else.

We're free to make our lives what we want them to be, and our intentions may even be to act in the best interests of others, but does it satisfy enough, not to know whether they truly appreciate our efforts?

After Martin and Laurie got married, things slowly started to change.

Martin had once spoken of plans and ideas, but he somehow lost sight of them – and, in the process, her - speaking only to other people, despite her best efforts to support him. He would go to work, but when he came home, people would come calling, spending the evening there, or taking him out for hours on end, only to return after she had gone to bed. At breakfast, they would sit and talk only briefly. As time went on, their conversations grew shorter, until she began to look at him as if he were becoming a stranger.

Harry had invited both of them up to his house, for dinner and a business meeting, and was acting rather strangely around Laurie; Martin's jealous side was making him angry and suspicious, until Laurie had finally just come out and told him, when they were alone, that Harry was, in fact, her father; his job offer to Martin had been a personal favour. It was then that Martin realized he wasn't the only one with secrets. They had never mattered before, because the two of them had each other, and it was all they needed.

He thought about finding other work, in the city, but Laurie protested - she wanted him to remain close, as soon they would be a family.

The news of Laurie's pregnancy had shocked Martin; he just wasn't ready to become a father. He had lost his temper and said some horrible things, right in front of Harry and a prospective investor. This had caused Harry to become defensive towards Laurie, things had become heated and Martin had lost control of his temper, attacking Harry. Their struggle became a brawl, and the investor had taken a fist, right in the mouth.

From the moment Martin lost his job, things started to be tough on the both of them.

Soon, he grew distant, and the deep affection between them started to disappear. First had been the hot, then the cold, then they settled somewhere in between; after a while, things just became numb. The flame of their marriage, which had once burned in his heart, had been dampened; he just didn't seem willing to fight for the passion they had once held for each other. Martin still had something of a tortured soul, and I guess he believed his needs were always greater than hers.

The first night he went to the Big City Casino with friends, Martin won quite a lot of money. He couldn't believe how much his luck had turned, in such a short space of time. So, the following evening, he went back again.

The only happy person is a comfortable person, and money can make you very comfortable.

He hadn't exactly been flash with his money; he had just spread a little, here and there. Wasn't that the sort of thing one did in a big city casino? You wouldn't be there in the first place if you didn't have money to play with.

He found a spot open at a poker table, and what good was an empty chair? Martin played his cards and now found that each time he had been given a lousy hand. He should have quit, but he believed his luck was bound to change, sooner or later.

By the end of the third evening, he was down by a lot of money.

He tried to get ahead, but had instead fallen way behind - in this particular instance, from a great height.

That was when Laurie got a call from the emergency ward, regarding her husband. At first sight; she knew his injuries had not been the cause of an accident.

Finally, he confessed that he had gambled away not just their savings, but their children's future education; he owed the casino a lot of money. She couldn't believe that Martin would do something like this.

You can get to know someone, but you never really know what they're capable of. The things kept from you are probably what hurt the most; they always rise to the surface, in the end.

He promised he would get counselling and find more work. She had believed him, reassuring him that they would fight this problem together. They could have taken out a bigger mortgage, but that would only have made things worse for them. Martin was in way over his head; with the debts he owed, it would take years for him and Laurie to get out from underneath it all.

One week later, Laurie had come home to find the police, waiting on her doorstep. When she heard Martin had left town, she was, at first, shocked – even more so when she heard what he had done. By the time she went to visit the supermarket, the news had already spread; already, she was receiving the harshest stares from her once-friendly neighbours.

It was heartbreaking for her to acknowledge that someone she loved had brought her nothing but sorrow. Everyone had always known, and warned her, that he would bring trouble.

Still, she hoped he would come back, or contact her, full of regret for his mistake; promising he would make amends, and change. But, some men simply can't mend their ways, and are incapable of keeping their commitments.

Some men also can't maintain good eye contact, when awkwardness is present.

That was just as it was now, sitting across the breakfast table from Harry, as he buttered his toast.

"I hope the bed was comfortable; the spare room hasn't been used in a while," he spoke, pleasantly. "Should really keep it aired, but it's not often I receive guests." Harry was never really sure what to say when she was around. As she looked down at her untouched plate, her lack of appetite disturbed him a little.

"Is that what I am: your guest? Not a prisoner, then, considering you had one of your goons standing outside my door all night?" She eyed Victor, who stood at the door behind her, in a cheap suit.

Being ex-military, Victor had once single-handedly fought off thieves on one of Harry's construction sites – that was when Harry had decided to put his skills to more suitable use.

"He's there for your protection. I know you don't like being here, but it's only until Monday, then it'll all be over; you can go back home."

"And wait for Martin to come back?"

Harry remembered his lasts words to her, in his office, something he had regretted immediately. But, he simply couldn't understand why she would even consider taking Martin back, after what he had done to her and her unborn children.

"He betrayed you as much as he betrayed the rest of us," Harry stated, pushing his own plate away.

"And, how many times have you stabbed people in the back? Gone back on your word?" she countered.

It was true: the life Harry had led as a younger man was far from respectable and unsoiled. "What I do now is for the good of everyone, including you and my grand… your children."

Laurie folded her arms, resentfully, and sat back in her chair, addressing him, contemptuously: "And, who appointed you judge, jury and…" She paused at this, as an afterthought; "I forgot: you leave that part to others now. You're really no different, even if it's not you pulling the trigger anymore."

Harry could see the horrors of his past catching up with him again, but he felt it was all different now; he was a different man. As such, he chose not to live in the past. "Don't talk about things you don't understand, Laurie."

"I understand what my mother told me about you; why she tried to keep me away from you!"

She had him there; you can't isolate your young ones from the consequences of your decisions and actions forever.

"You can lie to yourself, every day," she continued, "but, we both know your hands will never be clean; you can't wash away your sins, no matter how much you try absolving yourself with good deeds."

She got up from the table and left him, once more sitting alone in his thoughts. Martin may have been out of her life now, but he was still causing Laurie a great deal of pain.

Returning to her room, she looked through a family photo album, at her wedding day pictures. It had all seemed so happy back then; a change she thought would never come in her life. Then, it had all crumpled away, as Martin had run away, leaving her alone, once again.

Those who betrayed him had got away clean, for now – but, hopefully, they would be caught soon enough. Right now, though, Martin was paying for all of them.

Violation of trust is an unforgiveable sin, if the perpetrator shows no remorse. As far as Harry was concerned, Martin's betrayal could not go unpunished: he would pay Harry what he owed, and something to all those he had stolen from - it was as simple as that. The money wouldn't make up for all the family heirlooms - lost sentimentality, for many of the town's people - but it was just, and it would give Laurie peace of mind.

Harry had discussed his concerns about Martin with Laurie, before the day of the wedding, but she was adamant that she loved him. Besides, her father had no right to say who she could and could not marry! It would have been simple to buy Martin out of Laurie's life, or warn him off, but Harry didn't want to rule her, so he had allowed the wedding to go forward. Anyway, Martin seemed to make her happy.

But now, from what I had told him, he knew that Martin no longer expressed any concern about his wife. Since our meeting, or even before the lottery win, he hadn't once asked after her. He had certainly made no promises to return to Laurie and make up for his behaviour.

If a husband no longer held feelings for the woman he had married, or the children she was carrying, was he any longer fit to remain in their lives? As far as Harry was concerned, the marriage was all over; Laurie deserved better than him, and a better life. He had already contacted his solicitor to enquire about Laurie's rights to a share of the money, and was assured that, once they were divorced, she would be legally entitled to half of what was his. The debts he owed would be cleared, and she would be free to get on with her life.

But, Laurie didn't seem to care about the money.

It is difficult for some people to decide what matters most to them. What was once held dear to their hearts can so easily slip away.

People live their lives so foolishly, then can perform one good deed a day, and pray that it will get them into Heaven.

Harry had put a lot of time and effort into the plans for the new shopping mall he was intending to build; he so badly wanted something worthy of redeeming his past sins. The company had changed: it was stronger and cleaner at the same time. But, his plans for future growth were not focused on the company, but the community as a whole.

Putting together a portfolio, he had already presented it before the council. By constructing the new mall, he was going to provide jobs, for the skilled and unskilled, both in the construction and beyond. He would require many labourers, most of which would be local youths, not only earning money, but also learning a trade. And, when finished, the retailers would hire local people as managers, sales staff, cleaners and security; it would no longer be necessary for them to travel to the city to find work. They may not have the skills to start but, through modern training programs, anybody could be taught and progress to, hopefully, make a good career for themselves.

When he had given this same speech at the community centre, the feedback from everyone had been positive; most questioned whether there would be jobs for the locals, as they were so often given to commuters from the city. Harry had alleviated their worries by insisting that the centre manager - who would run it all - would definitely be appointed from within the community; it would be important to have a liaison who understood local needs. Once this had put all fears to rest, the community was firmly behind the idea.

The project would also encourage outsiders to pass through the town, en route, which should be welcomed, because a small town could not thrive without prosperity. While most tried to avoid twentieth century progress, Ravenfall had chosen to embrace the modern era, accepting that times had to change, and that by standing in the way of progress, they would miss out on all of the benefits such future developments could offer current and later generations.

So, just as the local residence had supported Harry's proposal, they had been equally saddened to hear that he'd had to pull out, due to the investment being cut.

In a town such as this, the community looked to its own for support. But, for figures of this magnitude, it wasn't simply as if they could hold a raffle, or pass around a collection hat.

Harry was distraught. They had forgiven his past and were willing to give him a second chance; now, all he wanted to do was repay them all for their kindness.

Once he had the lottery money, he would be able to start afresh; perhaps redeem himself enough that when his time came to leave this world - no matter where he went from here - he would have something worthwhile written on his tombstone.

There are no coffin dodgers amongst those who choose to live their life by the sword.

What people say about us when we are alive contaminates our hearts, setting us on the path to self-destruction; it creates what cannot be erased so easily, from any human mind.

You can't hide your past sins; you have to wear them on your sleeve, like a scarlet letter. The deaths for which you are responsible can be seen clearly, through the windows to your soul.

But, if you look deeply enough, rhyme and reason can prevent society's entire withdrawal; whilst some things can't ever be forgotten, when replaced by good intentions, they can be forgiven.

You can't simply wipe blood from a stone, just as you can't get blood from it. But, the words engraved on the surface last forever; those who read them will remember not necessarily the man but, instead, his deeds. Both good and bad make up who we are. Nobody is born any different!

CHAPTER 17

It's funny how time can go so slowly at the worst of times, and so quickly at the best. Time can be short, the world passing by so fast that you miss out on the best things life has to offer. People can lead long, happy lives and be grateful, or they can lead short, miserable, pointless lives, resenting even their own existence.

They say that life is what you make of it, but there are times when even we cannot control the directions in which we travel. Nor choose how we get to a certain point in our lives.

I'd managed to get a little rest before our day began again, partaking of a good breakfast; I had settled up with the owner of the bed-and-breakfast, and Martin and I were out the door.

We had already stayed still for too long; the minute you stop moving is the moment you die! We had to be one step ahead of the opposition at all times. We had only two more days until we could claim the money.

Hopping in a cab, we arrived ten minutes before the train.

Why are we still travelling by train? I hear you ask. Well, the last town had no car rental and I wasn't prepared to wait to get one delivered.

Besides, faces can remain anonymous at public railway stations and on trains - amongst people meeting or leaving, packed in and ready to make their long journeys.

There would be no trouble in the middle of the day: it was unlikely they would make any overt attempt, with this many people around; far too risky to try anything on a crowded train, in broad daylight.

Mind you, no more dangerous than for those guys the night before!

Martin was still on edge, as he sat on the platform, glancing at anyone who came within five feet of where he was sitting. He was attracting too much attention, so I tried to apply some of my softer approaches. When the train did finally arrive I offered him one of my cigarettes, which he took and placed in his mouth, without a single gesture of appreciation.

Martin's eyes no longer looked upon me with the same interest as the night before; it was clear now that he could see nothing feminine about me, so why pretend to be a gentleman? Not that he qualified as being even close to that.

But then, who would class what I do as particularly "lady-like"?

Still, at least I knew how to be civil with people; at least, those who show me the same courtesy.

If you think we don't deserve courtesy, just because we take a life under orders of another person, consider all the people who do your *dirty work for you: those who sweep the roads, unblock your toilets... We're the people who take care of the garbage and get rid of your filth and shit: the dealers; the pimps; the bullies; the people who make our society a mess. We're no different to the road sweeper; the only real difference is that our garbage has a heart, which needs to be stopped.*

Picking up a newspaper, on one of the seats, I noticed a small mention of last night's disturbance on the train; the bodies had been discovered shortly after we got off. There was a C.C.T.V. shot of Martin, curled up on the floor of the carriage, while I was dispatching one of the machete thugs.

I thought about keeping it as a souvenir, but that would be pure ego.

"You've become a very important man, in a very short space of time." I showed Martin the front page. "Yet, I seem to be the only one who knows why."

Martin didn't answer; he just looked at his own image. Was he wondering if anyone he knew in Ravenfall was also looking at the front page, seeing him so cowardly? Perhaps his wife?

It had already occurred to me that he hadn't once asked after Laurie since we had met. "You know what really intrigues me? The fact that you didn't take your wife with you."

Martin turned a hard stare at me; "If she had come with me, you would have probably had to take care of her, too! Or, wouldn't Harry have the guts to kill his own daughter?"

I had already dismissed the question, knowing full well that Harry would never touch a hair on Laurie's head.

"Going back to our first meeting in the café, would you have traded your own life for hers?" I asked, not wanting to drop the subject. It seemed fitting, since he had tried to probe me so, the night before.

"Would you have killed her and our children?" He spat out a fingernail he had bitten, then answered himself: "I don't think so: not really your style, is it? Not really the sort of job you do?"

I noted the tone: it wasn't threatening, but it was impatient.

"You haven't talked much about her. In a situation like this, I would have thought a husband would at least have brought up his wife, just once," I pressed, trying to provoke some hint of emotion from him.

"Do you delight in tormenting me?" he asked.

I held up my hands, innocently, but I was laughing inside at his comment. I had one more card to play: "If you want to change the subject, by all means do so - a lot can happen in the next forty-seven hours." I leant over and whispered: "But, in case you don't make it, is there any message-?"

"Just shut the fuck up!" he barked, drawing attention to both of us. This time, I didn't care.

Clearly, the concept of family wasn't as important to some as it was to others, and it was obvious that his new predicament was having something of an ambivalent effect on his conscience, as though he were trying to wipe his mind clean of the past.

How fortunate that would be for all of us, were it possible.

But, then, not all of us win a hundred-million euros!

It was also clear that Martin was no longer thinking about escaping; his choices were now simple: spend a short amount of time in a very small room, or end up dead. It had very likely occurred to him that with his newfound fortune, he could hire the best lawyers and, providing he behaved, would receive an early parole.

He also knew now that something would be waiting to welcome him home, and clearly I don't mean the wife; at that moment Martin's mind wasn't on Laurie's well-being – only his own.

Ever since he became a wanted man, he'd had nothing - until his winning numbers came up.

As I watched him, holding the ticket, once again, between his fingers, I couldn't help but wonder what was going through Martin's mind at that moment. Certainly not the thought which had sprung into mine, and not for the first time; I knew it had never entered his for one moment: what if he were to get rid of the ticket; to destroy it? There would be no more need for all of this.

How much value did he place on that slip of paper, compared to his own life? It was funny how something so small and fragile could change a person's life so much. For the better, perhaps, but bringing so much trouble as the price.

Still a long way away from our destination, there was plenty of opportunity for more hoods to catch up with us and finish what their friends had started; just because we got further away, we couldn't feel that we had left our troubles behind us.

People always measure their own worth in this world. Yet, if they actually succeeded at putting it into figures, they would never be satisfied with the outcome. Having someone tell you your worth will most likely either flatter or insult you.

You can either accept or reject the value which is placed on your head, but your own value of yourself means nothing.

It certainly means nothing to the person collecting a bounty for you. Your life is meaningless, if it doesn't have a price tag.

So, how do you measure what a person is worth? Is it by their ambitions; their dreams; what they find the most precious; what they hold dear to their hearts? Even the smallest ambition, the shortest dream, can't be taken away. If someone tries, then you need to fight them; kill or be killed!

This was my new code; which I had been initiated into only the day before. I had been just a killer, then; now, I was as much a target as Martin. It made me appreciate my own life a lot more, even though I was not a rich woman.

Looking out of the window, the landscape was still urban and only a few trees and sparse greenery complemented the scenery of the towns and neighbourhoods we were passing through. I preferred the view of the fields and the distant hills and mountains, back in Ravenfall; city districts were like jungles, wild with lurking predators, hidden in the undergrowth, waiting to pounce on weaker species.

The human food chain really was no different to that of the animals, but as a species we just showed less respect for the world, polluting and destroying it, with progress and war.

I thought back to the dream I'd had briefly, relating to the stories my grandfather told me about life in the days of the second world war. Sometimes the best dreams are the ones which you so easily forget, whilst the most vivid from your childhood never seem to go away. If only we were able to go back and see the world as it really was, rather than just in our dreams.

There are, of course, the stories our parents tell us as children: of how their lives used to be, and how hard they had worked to make ends meat (pun intended, in tribute to my family trade). Life had been less independent during the war - it had to be, in order to get things done.

It is sometimes said that it is the little details - those we often forget - which are the most relevant, in shaping the future for the next generation. For the future to come, it is my generation's history of events, new ideas and inventions which will shape the destiny of the next generation. For the most part, a terrible world is necessary as, in most respects, the future can only be uncertain.

But, the destiny of a person may be something which many would claim to be pre-ordained. In the case of family, most will either follow in their parents' footsteps or break away and evolve, leaving behind hereditary principle. This is, of course, more acceptable in some cultures than others, seen by the latter as nothing short of a betrayal of one's legacy. After all, true wealth can not be found in a cash inheritance; it is the knowledge and wisdom which is passed on, which keeps a true family legacy thriving; reputations and respect of the family name. Thus, prosperity will always be assured; a person's individual destiny is never fully revealed until the end.

This thought made me feel, at that moment, like the richest person on that train.

Wealth cannot always be measured in paper or gold - you will not find these lining the walls of the human heart. It cannot be folded or melted down; some hearts are known to be as strong as oak, and glisten agelessly, captivatingly producing the most immeasurable love.

The most precious of riches can fit into your pocket. It can be simply found by opening a wallet: priceless treasure, forever captured in a photograph.

So often we say that we are not afraid to die, but we do hope to take something good with us when we go, leaving behind only the bad parts of our lives.

Continuously reliving the good - this is my idea of Heaven, if such a place truly exists.

Family is the always in the heart, both in this world and the next.

CHAPTER 18

There are some who are too trusting of those which say: "I'm looking after your best interests." Those who want to take you in hand; to show you the ropes, their way.

After a while, you may begin to look up to them; perhaps even idolize them, to the point where you'll do whatever they say. If they lie to you - tell you they see a lot in your future – you will go out of your way to impress them more.

And, when they give you a little taste of the business... well, before you know it, you're hooked.

Soon, you find yourself running with the pack, believing you're invincible.

That's when you start growing loud; self-publicizing, and before you know it, people are coming up to you, asking for small favours. You'll take the small money, because you're just starting out. Then, more come along.

Before you know it, everyone knows who and what you are.

Driving onto the council estate, it hurt Mr. X to see how his old home had been turned into a demilitarized zone.

To the locals, the place had certain charms; to Mr. X, it had only bad memories of his childhood.

Recalling the cramped flat in which his family had resided, it had not been suitable for a family of four; he had shared a sofa-bed with his sister, while his parents slept on an old mattress, in the other room.

Money had been tight in those days, and his father was only just starting out, but people were kinder to each other, in spite of the resemblance to more modern circumstance. These days, it was all hooded youths and gangs, trying to take over the neighbourhood; breaking into homes, vandalizing and stealing.

His father shot one person, a man who had come into their home to burgle - it caused the whole family to be evicted and saw his father awarded a suspended sentence.

Life was tough, punishing those who protected their own families, driving them to vigilante rampaging through the streets. It was as if there were no decency left in society.

The night his father never came home, Mr. X swore to seek vengeance. Taking his father's spare gun, he had found the people responsible, emptying the weapon of all of its rounds, until his finger finally rested and the fiery rage in his blood had cooled. This had been what started his career; following in his father's footsteps was something of which neither his mother or sister approved.

Now, parking his car next to one which was burnt out, and activating its alarm, Mr. X looked across the road, toward a group of youths sat on a nearby wall, eagerly looking his way. Double-checking the car's locks, he looked once more to the singed vehicle alongside it. Fucking kids nowadays weren't content with just stealing stuff; they had to destroy everything they left behind! Local police had reduced manpower on these estates, so these kids were free to do as they pleased.

He'd loved this part of town when he was younger; the parks were cleaner then. Parents didn't have to check the inside of the play-slide tunnels for glued-on broken glass.

On the grass, behind him, two little girls and a boy were playing with a ball, throwing it randomly to each other, with carefree attitudes. At least it wasn't a grenade! He caught the eye of one of the girls. She looked at him with no fear, before continuing her game. This made him sad: only in the eyes of innocence do we find hope for generations which will follow.

The day was getting on, and so was the task in hand.

As he approached the main entrance to one of the estate's tower blocks, he almost collided with another man – dark, with dreadlocks.

"Why don't you watch where you're going, *Fancy Man*?" the man spoke, exposing gold-plated teeth. "You're liable to get yourself in trouble, coming round here, dressed that way."

He looked Mr. X up and down eagerly, reaching slowly into his coat pocket. "You'd be lucky to leave with those fancy shoes you got on," he continued; "these streets are nothing but cold, you know."

Mr. X opened the left side of his blazer, exposing the handle of the automatic tucked under his arm. "Not as cold as the blood which runs in my veins," he said, moving past, slowly. "Be sure and tell your friends over by my car that I said hello."

Turning back, he made a childish gesture toward the man, with his fingers, as though pointing a gun, pulling the trigger and pulling it back, to blow on the tip of his index.

Taking the elevator to the fifteenth floor, he walked along the corridor, until he reached the door he sought, loud music being played on the other side of it. He knocked only twice, waiting patiently. Behind him, he heard the quiet creaking of a neighbour's door, before a figure slipped quietly past him and down the corridor. Finally, the door was opened by an average-sized man, his neck adorned with gold chains.

"I need to speak to your boss," Mr. X said, before being asked.

The man regarded him without interest, attempting to calmly close the door. Harshly, the door shoved him backward, as a web-hand strike to the throat sent him plummeting to his knees.

It is impossible to deny death when it comes knocking.

Walking into the den area, Mr. X saw a large man seated on the couch, with a semi-clad girl by his side; they were smoking from a bong.

"Who are you?" the large man asked.

Mr. X quickly took in his surroundings; there were only two other men present, sitting at a table in the corner, playing cards.

"I'm surprised you don't see the family resemblance. Did my nephew never talk about how much he took after me in looks? It's why he was so popular with the ladies." Mr. X beamed a smile in the girl's direction. Then, his expression grew more serious. "You boys had some business last night – business which involved my nephew, Caleb."

On the coffee-table sat a mountain of weed bags, along with a clutch of handguns - they were poor quality and not very well maintained.

"You're Caleb's uncle?" the leader said. "I see it now. Your nephew did mention you, briefly."

The worst people in this world are those you cannot easily read. Thankfully, this man was not such a person. Mr. X knew that those who gave orders were rarely at the top of the food chain.

"I hope it was all good." He looked again at the girl; "You really should give that stuff up; it'll kill you."

The man placed his arm around the girl's shoulders, as though marking his territory. "We sell it – we don't just smoke it. You want to buy some? It's very good quality."

Usually, people's eyes would light with greed when the topic of money was raised, but he could tell from this man and his associates that theirs were just swimming in a dope haze.

"Another nice little enterprise," Mr. X said, noting a slight scowl moving across the leader's face. "Helps when you can't get the work, I suppose."

"Everybody knows we run this patch. We sort out the problems here and we take care of our own." At these words, Mr. X noticed a show of camaraderie, from the rest of the pack.

"So, what are you doing about the person who killed my nephew?"

"We got other men looking for them," the leader said; "we're going to kill that bastard!"

Mr. X couldn't find the same optimism; even when the man's words were spoken with such conviction, there seemed very little emotion present, at the loss of their fallen comrades.

"Digging your blades out was a questionable move. So was sending three out for just one target; I've always believed in quality, not quantity."

He heard footsteps behind him; the man he had struck had recovered and was now standing in the doorway.

"Well, the guy wasn't alone, was he?" The large man reached out across the table and picked up a fresh rollie. "I thought they could handle it, while some of my better soldiers are away; I wasn't to know they were going up against a pro."

Promotion based purely on availability rarely made one the best person for the job. It had all just been a matter of convenience; the target had turned up in his area, at a time when he was short on talent.

"Well, that's what my point is: the quality of the information you've been given, or that you've asked for, should always guide how much arsenal you need to have to hand."

When the smell of blood is on the streets, someone is always making money from it, with no consideration to the methods, or the sacrifices.

The man continued: "We like to use blades. It's easy shooting somebody, but when people see you cutting-"

"Well, that's where we differ again. The whole idea is *not* to be seen, and not to be making some statement to viewers on the local news. The message is what you leave behind. It might be silent, but it's clear enough to read when it's written in red."

Looking at his body language, Mr. X could tell that the leader wasn't pleased with his choice of words. Respect for knowledge – in both the young and old - was lost on these guys, and it seemed that confidence had been replaced by simple arrogance.

"I didn't need your nephew, but since it was my gang he hung with most of the time, I took him on, and gave him a chance to prove himself."

Watching the king on his throne, Mr. X reached inside his blazer jacket, removing a pack of cigarettes; he noted that the soldiers had not stirred, even slightly, at his movement. "Do you initiate all your bangers in the same fashion?"

Lighting the tip, he inhaled deeply and blew out a long cloud of smoke, towards the leader. It appeared as though he were creating some kind of smokescreen, but there was really no need for trickery: even on the best of days, when not jacked up to the eyeballs, these boys were off their game

"Everyone needs somebody to look up to: a surrogate older brother, you might say." The leader lit his joint. "There are those who idolize, and those who *get* idolized."

"And, there are those who sit on their ass, while others die at the snap of their fingers." The air in the room was now starting to grow thick; it was not just from the smoke.

One could always respect family matters, but the leader would have no one show him up in front of his soldiers – soldiers who, at a snap, could take a blade to this man's insolent tongue. This wasn't a case of two boys from the same neighbourhood - not anymore; not with the fancy watch on Mr. X's wrist, and the smart clothes on his back.

"I'm starting to dislike your company. Maybe it's time you were making a move." He looked past Mr. X, to the man in the doorway. "Do you want me to make the funeral arrangements?"

To the seated man, none of this was about getting revenge for the deaths of his "soldiers"; it was still only about the money. This wasn't an army; they were just cockroaches, scurrying around, in the shit they loved most.

Mr. X, however, was not the type to be walked over or stepped on. And his was a simple matter of family. "He has his real family to attend to that. His mother is suffering right now, for the loss of her child. You just stay there, getting fucked up." Those who didn't get their hands dirty were those with no need to attend the confessional each Sunday.

The leader looked toward his associates. They had stopped playing their game, and were now watching the man they didn't know; his tone was obviously out of place here. One of them looked over to the coffee-table, where lay their tools. They had now clearly remembered the man they worked for; each was under his thumb, and none wished to get squashed like a grape.

Mr. X liked his grapes whole. And, the novelty of his current surroundings was fading fast; he had outstayed his welcome, and they had outlived their usefulness.

The leader gave a fake smile and continued: "I can't tell you how sorry I-"

"Usually it's the other way round," Mr. X interrupted him.

The leader looked questioningly at his men again, then back: "What is?"

Mr. X folded his arms across his chest, discreetly slipping his hand inside his blazer. "What were you about to say?"

The leader looked puzzled: "I… Sorry-?"

The first shot cut through his tongue and into the back of his throat, silencing the distasteful word.

The next two shots rang out; the two bodies had fallen from their chairs before even playing their last hand. Spinning, Mr. X dropped to his knee and shot the last man, in the doorway, before he had managed two paces forward.

The problem with this generation was that they thought themselves invincible; untouchable. No matter how powerful they think they are, even a king's best knights can be vanquished. No one lives forever; sooner or later, the throne always becomes empty.

Whether you called it "retribution", "karma" or "payback", it all added up to the same thing: these were not men; not people worthy of going about, in society, and all the horrible things they had done in their lives had led them to this point. Everyone wanted fame; to live fast and die young, as the saying goes. But, not his nephew, and certainly not under the orders of a drug-dealing degenerate.

Still alive, the girl was cowering, on the arm-rest. Her eyes were fearful, like those of an animal, but she was by no means a threat.

He holstered his gun and went to take a seat beside her, picking up a bottle from the table. He poured some into a glass.

"Look at you, all on your own now - it just doesn't seem right. How about you buy me a drink, and tell me all about yourself, and what all this is about?"

"I… I really don't know anything," she whimpered.

He didn't need to rely on psychic ability to spot a liar: it was easy to tell; there were countless signs which gave it away.

"That's a very pretty nose you have. Ever considered modelling?"

he asked her.

Human flesh was soft, but bone was hard, and could so easily break with the correct pressure. Taking hold of her nose between his index and middle finger, he lightly began to squeeze.

He didn't particularly like hurting women; it gave him no pleasure - as it had done killing her man – but, he wasn't going to stop until he got the answers he needed.

People will say – will do – anything, if you put a gun to their head; the things they say and do to save their life can never be taken at face value. It is therefore, sometimes, necessary to apply a little pressure, if only just to make sure.

They might plead, curse you, defy you... but, everyone gives in eventually.

When your questions are on a personal matter, you find that your patience lacks a little.

Just remember: if you are ever under questioning, the truth will buy you more time and less pain. Whether it will secure the rest of your life is dependent on how thorough you are with the details.

CHAPTER 19

When people look too hard in the mirror, they are sometimes frightened by the image staring back.

There are others who can spend a great deal of time in front of a mirror, without the slightest shiver; they are not so easily spooked by looking into the gateway to their soul. When a person knows oneself so well, inside and out, what is there to fear?

It is only when we try to fool ourselves that we feel the creeps climbing up our spine.

Mr. Braddock wasn't the sort to scare easily, particularly as the head of a fast-growing empire.

Looking admiringly at his own reflection, he straightened and turned sideways; he was still in good shape, for a man his age.

When you wear a suit, you look not only smart, but business-like, so that even the low-life punks come to respect you; it is intimidating to stand across from someone who looks sharp.

A good businessman takes the time to do his research; to get the right council employees on his side, and show how his upcoming project is in everyone's financial interest.

Unfortunately for Braddock, getting permission for his new casino was proving to be more difficult than he had originally anticipated. He had requested a variance in the safety code, regarding its structure, but, thanks to Timothy's report, certain representatives from the council had rejected it, saying it didn't meet with necessary statutory requirements. Thus, the law would not allow his application to be passed. Because it was going to be larger than the one in the city, and allow people to reside as guests, certain changes needed to be made, in order to make it safe, and thereby allow its approval. If they held out any longer, the delays would cost him greatly.

It was therefore time to make a personal visit to the council office; to see if he could work out an arrangement between himself and the Head of Planning and Development. At the end of the day, it was all conditional business, so Braddock had drawn up a waiver, to allow his construction project to continue. Since the funds had come into the bank account, he was quite willing to pay an exorbitant amount of money to ensure permission was given, without any further delays; he felt it was a simple matter of establishing the right people and placing untraceable funds into an account of their choosing - something of interest to most businessmen and women. Retirement packages were not what they used to be, after all. The problem with some men was they often had the urge to do what was not best for them.

In their defence, there were worse things imaginable; things so bad that they simply couldn't resist the temptation. Like Adam and Eve, when they had eaten the forbidden fruit.

They would start to hear the voices in their head, followed by an unrelenting craving. It was similar to love, only intensely more satisfying. Like being in a whole new world, and wanting others to join you.

Takers had been scarce in his younger life, despite the morals of loyalty and friendship. He had been part of a firm which had lost faith in the system - in the very government which was supposed to be protecting the people of this country.

Things had not always been better before then, but at least there was a certain order and respect. People counted their blessings, for at least having nice, clean streets, which kept unwanted vermin from plaguing their neighbourhood.

That was, until the outsiders from the Big City came, bringing their own filth with them: bullying, intimidating, making threats and taking what they pleased; targeting whoever they wanted, whenever they felt like it. Something had to be done. And the good people of this town all wanted to do their part in protecting their homes and their loved ones.

When one is starting out on a low budget vigilante enterprise, it is best to get a list of useful sources: informants, providing information on the movements of one's competition.

The firm began by targeting individuals: couriers, distributors and low-level enforcers. They didn't always know the real names of their targets, but they knew that all deserved what they got.

Going to war on a daily basis meant preparation, training and, most importantly, funding – and, what better way than to use the opposition's money? When Braddock had made this proposal, Harry - his best friend and partner at the time - had been reluctant to agree: they weren't thieves, and it wasn't about money. It only took a little persuasion to change his mind.

Braddock had managed to get in touch with an industry insider, who claimed that the city banks, which held the mortgages to most of the homes in Ravenfall, were overcharging against their rates. A lot of the Syndicate's earnings were also being laundered through these very banks. This was a violation, not only to the town, but to society at large.

Banks stayed in business because they kept taking money, whether clean or dirty.

So, the firm set to work, taking from the small banks, and they kept the bad business out of the town. Of course, it wasn't long before the authorities started to track them.

But, things could always be worked out; putting a bit of money in the back pocket of a few coppers ensured they stayed out of jail.

Turning a blind eye didn't always cut it, though, so of course they had to be brought in for questioning, when allegations were made. When they needed an alibi, it came, either from parents or other well-respected members of Ravenfall, only too happy to see someone taking the fight to the outsiders. The community was strong at heart, and had been ever since the war; it had fought for its liberation then, and it had broken free from tyranny. Nobody knew how many they were. Moreover, they now had youth on their side.

But that probably meant not boxing clever; they had, after all, started out inexperienced. Soon, they were becoming too ambitious and too reckless for their own good.

One day, the firm had raided a bank, where an associate, who was working there at the time, immediately recognized both Braddock and Harry, despite their face rags. In a flash, Braddock made the decision;

the gunfire scared even Harry, who immediately bolted from the bank with only half the takings, leaving Braddock behind.

A heroic bystander tried to tackle him, and was also shot.

You always remember your first kill: the terror in their eyes, as life is taken from them.

It was so powerful: Braddock had just got a taste for taking, then taking more besides. Not just life, but what others had; what he coveted; what he never had before.

After that day, the friendship between the two of them was rocky.

Braddock insisted that he had only made the decision to protect their identities, and those of the firm, but he had broken a rule: no unnecessary casualties.

But Braddock was not prepared to take all of the blame: the incident had been caused by bad surveillance, on all of their part. The dead associate – one of their informants - was not supposed to have been at the bank that particular day, which is why they chose it.

Anyway, their associate had not been innocent; he was on the take just as much as any of the rest of them. He should have just kept his dirty laundry to his own back yard.

Still, the taking of his life was not only wrong, but had been seen, from the point of view of the bystanders, as "no more than mechanical" – that was how it had read in the following day's newspapers. The firm was no longer considered heroic, even by the people of their own town, who feared they, too, would soon become victims. They had become no better than those they were fighting against.

Harry didn't want to be part of that world, but Braddock had already crossed the line. In fact, there was a lot going on behind Braddock's eyes, and Harry had started not to like what he saw. Before he knew it, everyone in the firm had also grown distant from Braddock, not allowing him to come along with them, due to distrust.

Braddock began to feel like Julius Caesar: everyone waiting to pull a blade, to stab him in every orifice, until there wasn't a part of his body left which wasn't in pain. He had started to become paranoid, that they were plotting to hand him to the law for his crime.

In the old days, rulers and emperors had one sure method of making sure they wouldn't be betrayed: killing everyone around them, or at least those of no great importance. Braddock decided it was time for Rome to fall, and for everyone to feel the walls crashing down on their heads.

So, it had been declared and, just like countries, families had gone to war.

But, no matter what the result of the conflict, it would bring about greater business opportunities. After wiping out the firm, Braddock took the opportunity to gain control over the free market and, soon, what started as a growing aspiration had built him his own little empire, while another fell.

He felt that his only mistake was not to finish what he had started.

Nowadays, Harry's own operation was of little consequence. As long as he didn't get the money from his son in law – a matter which Braddock hoped was being taken care of that very moment – he was no threat.

Going downstairs, he found his wife in the kitchen, accompanied by a bottle of wine and reading through the local paper. She didn't look up as he passed her, to fetch his car-keys from the counter.

Their relationship had been a show, since the day they said: "I do." Nobody admitted it, but it had been an arrangement between two families, merging in order to create a strong business and bring more economy to the town. It was obvious to everyone that they took no great deal of pleasure from being in each other's company. On and off, they both went looking elsewhere.

Over the years, Braddock built an image of smooth, successful man, created by the complement of an adventurous lifestyle. And, like a rollercoaster, it was more enjoyable at its highest point. This was his main attraction for the opposite sex: the appeal of slight danger was what the woman liked.

But, despite that, he remained a private person; he couldn't be bothered with open heartedness, and all that shit!

By nature, Braddock was the sort to just take and fuck without emotion, and he didn't feel the slightest bit sorry when the unexpected happened. He made a big mistake, getting involved with a professional woman, whom he paid for company and carnal favours. The girl started to think it was okay to call, or to show up, unannounced, on the doorstep, when his wife was out. Still, he didn't expect any issues.

Until the girl found that her period was late.

But, even something which you never plan, you can still make good. There are some women who like the old-school approach: being handed an envelope of money, and shown that a man cares just enough to give a little token for her trouble.

But, a woman without reason can be dangerous, especially when, for her, it isn't about money! Braddock had been placed in a tight corner, and started to pay out more, to keep her quiet. She accepted; sometimes survival means having to deal with second best: relying on those who promise to provide when needed, even if it is in exchange for certain information.

So, he became no longer her lover, but her pimp, using her to extract whatever – from whomever - he could profit from: little pieces of information, regarding important business acquaintances. Still, he did wonder what profit he could draw from a whore and a bastard child, in the years to come.

Braddock had ruled out children, especially at his age: there was no good in having a family which could destroy you. His own parents had taught him that, from a very young age. On the day his own father died, he had been found in bed, drugged and smothered. It was suspected that he had found himself in a situation similar to that which Braddock now faced, and had, at the time, demanded an abortion. The mystery mistress was never caught.

This made no difference to his mother: she still got her share of the estate, and he got his father's business.

Braddock had no intention of allowing the same fate to befall him, so when he failed to buy the woman off completely, he arranged a different kind of separation.

The same could be arranged for a spouse!

He watched his trophy wife, now at the kitchen table, looking through glossy magazines whilst indulging in another glass of his expensive wine, and pondered the possibility that sometime soon he may need to arrange another separation. With what he had planned, he could afford to have nobody turn against him, and watch his dream go up in smoke. He had never really trusted the opposite sex to do anything but one. Soon, they start looking into your work, then the stories start to spread; they just can't keep their mouths shut. So, eventually they have to disappear, or be silenced.

Right or wrong, what's done is done; you can now get back to fun, fun, fun!

The world is full of evil men. No matter how many laws man chooses to live by, he will always find his dark side, hiding in a shadowy corner of his soul.

There are demons in all of us, especially those who may believe in compassion and decency, but have no choice but to also believe in the pain and suffering of others. Perhaps no different to a priest, who believes in God, but also accepts the existence of the devil; you cannot worship one, without believing in the other.

But, which of the two is stronger? Which is more seductive?

If mankind isn't generically evil, how do we account for all of the horrors he has committed, throughout history? Even my great grandfather came to consider the concepts of "fairness" and "justice" no more than another simple human invention, neither created by God or the devil. What we humans create for ourselves is only accountable to our own nature. Who bestows that nature upon us, I'll leave you to decide.

CHAPTER 20

There is no question of being on the right or wrong side of the law; the line is not drawn, in our profession. In this work, it's easy to get used to pulling the trigger for another person.

But, that doesn't make the client any less responsible. When they choose get their hands dirty, there is always soap to hand; we're just a device: a tool to fix a problem, when needed.

The trick is to not feel dead inside; you need to be thankful for being alive, every day - it is the most precious gift bestowed, and not something to be taken likely.

Life certainly could dish out unusual circumstances, for which we weren't always prepared.

Lying on the living room floor, Laurie went through her daily exercises, and being in Harry's house was indeed something of a new perspective. She had never visited there before, even when her mother was alive.

Growing up, Laurie would often ask after her father - a man she never knew, but who still provided for them so well - but her mother had always shied away from the subject. Finally, when she was around the age of fifteen, Helena got around to telling her that Harry was her father, and they had not married because both of their parents had disapproved. They had been young at the time and Harry was just starting to work for his father's company, but he had not shirked his responsibilities; he was an honourable man, despite his reputation as a gangster, part of the criminal fraternity. He was a good provider, and she only spent the money he contributed wisely.

Helena had been a good and sensible woman, unlike her childhood, when she had first fallen in with Harry's group, finding him to be charming and flamboyantly generous with his money. On Harry's eighteenth birthday, he had invited her for a night on the town, arriving at her house in a limousine, dressed in a stylish tuxedo with flowers in his hand - even Helena's mother had been impressed. They'd gone into the Big City - as did all the youths - and hit all the best nightspots; the other girls looked on her with clear envy. After a few glasses of Champagne and a few puffs of a joint, they couldn't keep their eyes - or hands - off of each other.

It wasn't the nicest way to learn you had been conceived - in the back of a limousine, whilst partially drunk and stoned out of their heads – but that night, he had made her mother happy. Until the harsh thrashing she received a month later, when she tested positive at the local family clinic. The doctor, attempting to pull her father off of her, had received a backhand across his jaw.

Helena had gone to Harry and asked to stay with him, fearing for the child's life. His first reaction had been shock, and this cast doubt and shame over Helena's face, for which he was immediately repentant, chasing after her and vowing that he would do right, by both of them.

Unfortunately, their unity lasted only for a short while: some men can not change their natures, and Helena would not give up her family. When her parents came to visit and asked her to return home, at the end of the day, family was family. But she wanted to keep the child, and they had no choice other than to respect her decision.

Harry still kept in touch, though whether it was out of love or guilt, Laurie's mother had never been truly sure.

Both Helena's parents became very supportive and, on the day of her birth, baby Laurie had been an immediately beloved sight, driving any feelings of shame or disgrace from their hearts. When word finally got around - which wasn't surprising, in a small town - they no longer cared.

Even Harry was permitted to visit, and just as easily fell in love with their daughter. They both agreed on the name "Laurie". When, in the end, the truth all became public, Harry started to visit more, with her parents' blessing. They hoped he would live up to their expectation, asking for her hand but, for some reason, he never did.

As Laurie got older, the visits started to grow shorter and farther-between. When he was around, Harry would try to make polite conversation, but he never seemed able to get close. At Helena's funeral, he offered that Laurie come and stay with him, but she had declined, telling him that she needed to be around familiar surroundings, to help her grieve.

Then, of course, Martin had come back into her life, with all of his predicament: arriving back in town, with no one to turn to and nobody caring, since his own mother had deserted him.

Laurie helped to try and track her down, but they found that she had recently died. That same day, she took Martin into her bed. It was, at first, out of pity, but lying in his arms she had seen a softer side, buried beneath the hard exterior he had built, during his time away.

Maybe they had rushed into things a little too quickly, she now thought, for the first time. She was supposed to be his wife, but he hadn't confided in her, or even spoken of his plan. Laurie had assumed that Martin would send word to her, to somehow come and find him, but as the days passed, it was becoming increasingly clear that she was not going to hear from him.

It was also painstakingly obvious that Martin could never hide from someone like Harry: the people he knew could find anybody, no matter where they ran.

She heard the phone ring, bringing her out of her thoughts, and listened: footsteps could be heard in the hallway, then the sound of Harry's voice, talking very quietly. She went to the phone in the living room, lifting the receiver to her ear.

She listened in to his conversation with a mysterious woman - someone around her own age, she guessed. The woman told Harry that they had arrived safely at their destination, where they were going to hold up for a couple of days, and keep their heads down, in case the opposition turned up unexpectedly. There was talk of a courier, with documents, who was not far away; he would meet them at a location which would be disclosed nearer the time. Until then, Martin was safe and well protected. As long as they all stuck to the plan, nothing else should go wrong.

Laurie waited until Harry had hung up, before replacing the receiver.

The sound of Harry's voice, so enthusiastic, replayed in her head. He had finally got what he wanted: Martin out of her life - permanently, if he had his way, just as soon as he had the money.

Laurie had thought about leaving Martin for what he did, but she wouldn't, and she knew it truthfully wasn't about the money; there were never guarantees that money could make you happy. A person could so easily find oneself a victim of their own greed; just looking in the mirror each day could make a person hate their own image. Because, when a person's financial motives weren't fuelled by greed, that left only one: hate. As she had quickly learned, hate could keep you warm at night.

Entering the living room, Harry saw Laurie standing by the phone, making no effort to hide the fact that she had been listening in on his conversation.

"I would usually consider that a liberty, under my own roof," he said. "You don't have to listen in: anything you want to know about this business, you can just come straight out and ask me."

She went over to the coffee-table and lifted the morning newspaper, displaying the front page; "I've already learnt quite a lot, already."

If looks could kill, Martin would be half dead from hers. Like a volcano, she seemed ready to erupt, and somebody was about to get burnt, badly; the vengeful fire broke through her eyes and bore straight into his. "To you, this is all business, but Martin is still my family; he's the father of these children!"

Harry could see that she was angry, but it really wasn't his fault that

Braddock had found out about his lottery win and Martin had become a target. At least Martin had escaped with his life, and was being protected.

"This is not about revenge," he told her: "just getting the money. People are depending heavily on what I've got planned for this town." He came over and took her shoulders in his hands, softly. "Everything I do, every step I've taken, is in the community's best interests... and yours."

Laurie broke away and turned sideways to him, her eyes downcast. "Every step forward you take, you take another two back. You're trying to be someone else, but every time I look at you, you're still the same person. You can't change what's underneath, because I think you're afraid you won't like the new you. People feared you in the past, yet now you want to be their saviour - you'll be a walking contradiction for your whole life."

Harry couldn't deny the things she was saying, but every man had the right, at least, to try mending his ways, even if, along the way, he had to resort to questionable methods. "I am me, and I am all the bad things that I did. But, the one good thing that came out of my life was you."

He touched her hair, lightly; "I was always grateful you never turned out like me; you are your mother's daughter, and for that, at least, I have to be thankful."

She looked at him sombrely, now, as she caught the sadness in his eyes.

"Martin didn't just fritter away your money, Laurie," Harry continued, cupping her cheek; "he took away your future together, just like I did with your mother. He tried to take it all for himself, and I believe he will try and do it again, because I know men like him. It was a man like him who took your mother away from the both of us."

Laurie became empathic, as he turned to walk away, still talking: "When I took over my father's company, and started to make something good of myself, I wanted your mother to be proud; I wanted *you* to be proud."

Giving him her full attention, curious of where this was all leading, Laurie kept quiet. It took a strong man to own his mistakes; this was a side she had never before seen of him, in her whole life. Her mother had always insisted that even the darkest of souls had a slight glimmer of light, and this glimmer was a lighthouse, occasionally guiding men away from their own destruction.

When she realized he had finished, Laurie spoke: "My mother said there were moments when she saw another you. I was always away at school, so I guess I never got to see it. I always wondered what that man looked like."

He turned back in the doorway, to look at her, briefly, the new man still presently before her eyes.

"Maybe one day I could come to know him better," she concluded, "if he ever chooses to stay a little longer."

He left her alone and returned to his office, where he impulsively began flipping through an old photo album; sometimes, he could feel a touch nostalgic.

In his life, he had been given a lot to thank God for, which he did, in church every Sunday. At first, this had been the simple pleasures: going out with friends; drinking; partying; being with girls, and coming home to a father who never once cautioned his choice of lifestyle: each man and woman walked their own path - for how long didn't matter; it was the end which counted.

Laurie's mother had been a beautiful girl and, in his eyes, had never changed. He had loved her very much, and he always believed that she was too good for him; not deserving of a life being married to a gangster. That life could only lead to one end.

And, it had. His cautious nature had failed him that night – the result would be restless sleep and haunting images in the darkness, replaying over and over again: images of the both of them, lying side-on-side on the ground, riddled with holes and he suffering in pain. At least she had been spared that part of the ordeal.

All he could do was hope that the pain wouldn't last for too long, before he, too, was taken from this world. But, his destination was probably not the same as hers.

In this business, there are few who can expect to see old age. Few who will die comfortably in their beds, surrounded by family.

A person can say their prayers, over and over, before going to bed. But, how can we really be sure that anyone is listening? So many people put their faith in a force they have never seen or heard; how do we know that God even exists?

Harry had never questioned his own faith; he had always believed that everything happens for a reason.

Never once had he raised a harsh word against the Almighty, although he had spent most of life defying His wishes - particularly one:

"thou shalt not kill".

In fairness, and maybe in hindsight, Martin's decision to turn against the community and run had forced his hand. But then, of course, some unexpected luck had granted him clemency.

What was he supposed to do have done? Just let Martin leave, because now they were better off? Leave it all to the authorities? They'd had had their chance to make him see the error of his ways; to try and reform him; to save his soul.

And now, Harry's family were again back where they had started.

He had spared Martin's life in the hope of washing away the debt, which now loomed over Laurie. With two children on the way, she was now alone, and an outcast.

Laurie had desperately wanted her independence, for years, and she had married Martin believing that they would go away; leave Ravenfall forever. Not that Harry could blame her for wanting something better than this town could give. But, where could she go now? What had she now, in life, to make her future seem anything but bleak?

The money. It would give her the freedom she had always wanted. If she chose, she could leave Ravenfall and start afresh; Harry would not stand in her way - not if it meant she could finally be happy. That sacrifice - of maybe never seeing her again - could finally give him peace over Helena, at whose graveside he had vowed to always watch out for their daughter.

As for Braddock, Harry knew it was best to take his need for revenge to the grave.

Some things we know; others we hope will never come to light.

There are things in this world that matter, the most precious of which we choose to allow access inside of us; the most horrific, we try to drive from our memories.

You can't kill everything or everyone that reminds you of your past; it's more worthwhile to just put a gun to your own head and pull the fucking trigger.

Or, better still, sacrifice your own needs, for those more deserving and more worthy.

Atonement comes at a heavy price, either way - only the strong are truly willing to pay it.

CHAPTER 21

The most common question you might - no, more than likely will - *ask, since humans are such inquisitive beings, is: how many people have I killed?*

Well, first, I don't keep count, and second, my family doesn't keep those sorts of records; it is probably kind of incriminating to have something like that in your possession. All documentation connected to any job is immediately destroyed upon completion. When the job is over, it is best to forget and move on.

Unless, of course, it is personal.

A flower rosary hung in the shop-front window, just above an empty display coffin. Mr. X looked at it, as he passed through the shop's entrance.

He was greeted there by an elderly lady, who welcomed him reverently; she was dressed, as you might expect, from head to foot in black. She immediately offered her services, willing to answer any questions and show him whatever he needed to know, in regard to his visit that day.

Dealing with the dead was just as important a business as any of those which dealt mostly with the living. In the old western movies, empty coffins usually meant that the undertaker's business was slow; his life was only good – his business only frequent - when people like Mr. X did their jobs well. Even the gunfighters, back in old days, had this profession - it was even legal, to some extent.

Of course, most of them would not have the opportunity to bask in their glory for long; there was always no shortage of enemies on their way, to challenge another mortal combat; sooner or later, someone else would always come calling.

Which meant more business for the undertaker; no matter which side won or lost, his boxes would always be filled by the end of the movie.

What's it like to kill somebody?

When personal, it can be a relief: that one problem you've wanted out of the way is finally dealt with.

When it's all just business, after a while you start to feel numb.

It's best not to be religious about it, crossing yourself after each kill, as is customary with some cultures - you'll find it becomes a branding; a scar which will never heal.

The woman opened the lid of one of the display caskets, before its soft inner padding was removed, to reveal an assortment of some of the best handguns, ranging from revolvers to semi-automatic pistols.

Of course, the carrying of firearms was restricted in certain countries, and illegal in others - this made their supply a limited market.

Reaching inside, Mr. X took his time to examine a Glock .22 and a Jennings small-calibre pistol. It was not advisable to carry a hand-cannon, like some big action hero in the movies; the weapon only needed to be a suitable size for that which you wished to kill, and unless you were going on safari, your target was not an elephant.

The smallest guns were the easiest to conceal and would always get the job done - man or woman, all people have vital organs to damage.

Guns are the one thing that every professional knows about.

Throughout history, to some, they have been as important as oxygen; as a merchant of death, you wouldn't live one day without having one by your side.

To the layman, guns always hold a unique fascination, with a mixture of fear.

When you hold it gently in your fingers, it seems at first so innocent - until you fire your first round, and you feel the power surge up your arm, making your whole body shake. Your breathing ceases for a moment.

Then, you look inward.

You may want to stop, but you feel the need to fire again, then again. By the time you've spent your last round, you find that your breath has returned; the shaking has stopped and you're, once again, in control.

What you now see, before your eyes, is the damage you created, with just a squeeze of a trigger!

The prices charged at the shop were always reasonable and, if regular, customers could usually expect a discount on any ammunition purchased with a weapon. They even provided a recycling service, where one could safely dispose of used firearms, without any fear of it being traced to any of the business which may have conducted. It was a good operation, and the merchandise was always good quality.

But, when it comes to getting up close and personal, a good knife should always be at the ready. It had certainly done the job on that train – as well as what he guessed was probably a wire; the hand wielding such weapons was surely that of a skilled and anatomically-educated person: a trained killer, like himself.

Descending the stairs to the basement area, he found himself positioned before a compact firing range, where he could test his new purchases. A target had already been put in place, so he took aim and fired off a couple of rounds.

What was Caleb thinking, going around like that: all tooled up?

Only amateurs used heavy implements. Sure, it looked scary, but the last thing we need in this profession is thugs, running around and trying to make names for themselves, in that way.

The truth is, he never really knew his nephew that well. Family wasn't like it used to be: kids grew distant to their kin so quickly these days. But, it was nature; chicks had to leave the nest, sometime. That didn't mean they wouldn't return, now and then, to pay a visit.

The last time Mr. X had seen Caleb was at his sister's birthday celebration, where the boy had given her a very nice, gold chain necklace - how he had got the money, nobody asked.

His mother had never told him what his uncle did for a living, but Caleb had been smart enough to figure it out for himself and, soon, he grew curious, and started to ask questions. On his nephew's fifteenth birthday, Mr. X had taken the boy for his first shooting lesson; they managed to find a small dirt quarry, which was secluded and far away from others.

These days, all people knew about guns is what they saw in the movies. The way he handled the weapon - like some punk gangster, holding it sideways and slightly bent at the wrist - made his first attempts look like the actions of a clumsy child. Even after being instructing in the proper curriculum, Caleb still couldn't hit the target.

But, he hadn't been a disappointment: it is never easy the first time, especially if you let the excitement get to you; this will always throw your aim off.

Clearly, the boy hadn't been much good with sharp steel, either.

All in all, it had been a bungled hit, generally lacking the necessary professionalism; Caleb had entered a world he knew very little about, outside of the movies. His world consisted of a bunch of undisciplined punks, drunks and junkies, who thought they could just pull a trigger and dig a few holes; could run around slicing people up, as though it were the Congo!

It is vitally important never to underestimate one's target, especially when they know the game like the back of their hand, and are always ready to play the game they like the best. Targets who won't run and hide in fear, like a mouse; the only time these targets ever get eaten is when they are not quick enough.

The person who had dispatched Caleb's group had been a pro, but only known professional outsiders were ever given a free pass, when doing business on other territories. This fact had put the Skulls' gang onto them - now leaderless, though no doubt still looking. They had, by now, learnt of the attack at their base, and would soon be looking for vengeance. That would not be easy.

Nobody knew anything about Mr. X, and nobody knew anything about me, which made the two of us amongst the most dangerous quarry they could go after.

Mr. X, on the other hand, was no fool: he knew when he was coming across the path of someone just as lethal; someone who could kill in an instant, if he dropped his guard. It is always necessary to get the first shot off; not to talk, or to brag, nor to wait for them to make the first draw, like some old-fashioned gunslinger - by the time you even reach your weapon, they'll already be bottling your last breath!

He knew we were currently hiding out somewhere, but he was confident he would find us; nobody is untraceable, if you have the means and the manpower. The Skulls were still in play, but it was doubtful they would ever be able to find their target – us - any time soon. Mr. X knew that I was good at my job, and taking all necessary precautions to make us difficult to find, even for him. So, he decided to conserve energy and do the next best thing: wait for my next kill.

When the bodies started to show up again – which they surely would – he'd find us soon enough.

We didn't have numbers on our side, but we had, at least, the resourcefulness to turn a disadvantage into an advantage - all we needed was the right place to hold up and work out a plan of action. Like some invisible army, we didn't need to go looking for trouble: we would just wait for it to come to us.

When you go onto the opposition's playing field, they aren't often where you'd expect or want them to be; you've often already lost, before the war has even started. Mr. X wasn't the type who liked to lose, so, for now, he would leave that to the Skulls. When their bodies started to turn up, that's when he would be onto us.

But, first, he had another matter to attend to.

Returning to his car, he started the engine and made his way out of the city, towards Ravenfall, somewhere he hadn't been in a long while. Still, he knew it well.

He felt bad for his little sister; mourning the loss of a son must be something you can never get over - this is why he currently opted against having a family. He was in a relationship, on and off, but a family was different: it required a lot of commitment and trust.

It wasn't every day that you told someone you were a contract killer. How would they respond? If they took it badly, how would you deal with it?

He had learnt these lessons from past mistakes and, at the time, he had been lucky not to pay with his life. It was just a shame his nephew had not been so lucky.

Often, amateurs make too many mistakes, mostly resulting from their own ego. As a specialist, you need only to limit your exposure; only do what you are paid, unless caught in a contract which requires last minute adjustments - as you see from this story, this can and will happen, if not often.

Some people are born into this kind of life; others have a choice to turn away from it. But, we all have to live and die by our decisions; in the end, we have no one else to blame but ourselves.

CHAPTER 22

"Do unto others as you would have them do unto you!" (Luke 6:31) – a memorable quote from my childhood.

When you specialize in a career involving the deaths of other people, you don't always take the opportunity to pause and think of how, one day, your own end may result. Maybe the quote should read: "What you do unto others will be done unto you."

It is equally easy to say: "Do unto others as they would do unto you." People have enemies, and are, themselves, enemies of others; if you don't do unto them first, they will, most certainly, do unto you.

So, what is the result of our actions? How will their sum shape our future? Nobody is karma-proof; we all need balance. We all justify our actions in this life, to serve us when we move on to the next.

There are always those who remain trapped in the realm between the two worlds (Limbo); only those who cleanse their souls of all the wrong they have done can expect to find eternal peace.

Martin was feeling far from cleansed: he hadn't washed or changed his clothes for three days, now. The lights were off, to make the room appear unoccupied to the outside world.

The harsh feeling of Purgatory was beginning to crawl over his skin, like an army of ants, irritating him to madness. Additionally, there was no television in the room in which we currently resided, to keep him entertained, or distracted from his ever-growing fear that perhaps he was not going to live to the end of this. My nearby presence – as I stretched on my bed, quietly reading - was like sharing a room with the Grim Reaper, mocking his misery; simply waiting to collect another soul.

For the past hour, Martin had been sitting on his bed, looking through magazines, and occasionally glancing at the walls, every now and then. His paranoid imagination was starting to affect him in a bad way, I thought. I wondered if he was starting to see images, appearing before his eyes, like movies on a screen.

Suddenly, he launched himself onto his feet, as though evading a sudden spray of bullets which came right out of the walls - walls which, themselves, were starting to feel like too much; it must have felt like being in jail already.

Moving over to the window, he opened it and looked out, into the dusk. The feel of fresh air on his face did some good, but it wasn't enough: he needed to get out; he needed to be in a public place and feel normal. Even though he knew it was dangerous, he couldn't wait for his sanity to finally slip. He started pacing up and down, scratching his head and perspiring like a junkie doing cold turkey; he held himself and began to shake.

The combination of sweat and fear breeds a horrible odour; he was putting me off my reading.

Martin knew he was still carrying a price tag on his head, and was clearly starting to worry that perhaps even I wasn't enough to protect him from it; if those people succeeded in catching up with us, the last anyone would see of him would be in the obituary columns.

He couldn't bear the thought of it anymore; he had to get away from it all. The money didn't matter now - he just wanted out!

Moving quickly, he tried the door, but it was locked - I had taken the precaution. Still, I followed immediately after him, catching him by the shoulder.

He hammered his fists against the door, in frustration: "I have to go out!"

"We're staying in tonight. Just two more days; by Monday-"

He snatched up my phone, from atop the chest of drawers, and threw it against the wall, hard; it broke. I'd had enough, and decided to administer the necessary disciplinary action: a right hook across the jaw seemed suitable.

The impact sent him flailing against the door, hard, but he was only partially stunned. He made a grab for my gun, which had been next to my phone on the drawers; the look on his face was one of vengeance.

We all have different images of ourselves, whether compatible or incompatible with how others may or may not see us. My own view of Martin was that of a coward and a weakling; an amateur. But, he had some spunk, at least, and was suddenly pointing my own gun at me.

I was curious as to whether or not he actually had the balls to shoot.

Click!

He pulled the trigger. The gun didn't fire.

Click, click, click... He continued, reflexively, as though trying to empty the gun into me.

Like I said before, the idea of killing changes a person. He was looking down at me like I was just an animal.

Maybe, but I was not a dumb animal; smart enough not to keep my gun loaded when it wasn't close by. Removing the ammunition clip from my jacket pocket, I held it up, in amusement. His eyes lowered to the floor, as I slowly took the gun from his hands.

"I need to get out of this room, either alive or dead!" he whispered, finally.

Karma is universal, so it is impossible to run away from it - wherever you go, it will find you. It will haunt you; beat at your body, wherever you are. It will drive you to madness; to tearing out your own eyes, just so you don't have to look at your own reflection, and see karma standing right behind you, peering over your shoulder!

There is, of course, other means by which people dull the pain inflicted by karma.

I, myself, had forgotten what it was like to sit in a local pub and be around other people, talking about the normal shit they had to deal with in their own lives. But, at least they chose not to hide out at home, where nobody could see them; they were not invisible to the world, and neither were their troubles. A problem shared is a problem halved, and when drinking it down with good ale, it doesn't taste so bitter.

Unless, of course, you're the only one buying the drinks.

I have never drunk alcohol when working: it dulls the reflexes. Martin, however, did not follow the same logic: his first taste of alcohol was especially welcome, having spent the past two days dry. He decided, that night, that he was going to relax a little, asking me to keep a tab, which he reassured he would settle at a later date.

I watched over him, like his guardian angel, again. In this place, we were not invisible, like in our room, but as long as we kept things friendly - without allowing tempers to flare up, again - we would be considered socially acceptable by the locals, who had, by now, recognized that we were strangers.

"Why don't you sit across from me?" Martin asked, placing his already half-finished pint on the table. "This kind of looks like we're on a date."

We were side-by-side. In a closed environment, with a lot of people about, it is always best to position oneself so that you are able to see everything and everyone. "Good: then we won't stand out so much," I answered.

Mostly, we sat and talked about what he would initially do with the money – his anticipation was growing more and more, now; much stronger than when he had first seen his numbers drawn. He had never really known what it felt like to have real money; no more than just a few notes had ever passed through his fingers at one time. Now, he could practically fill a swimming pool with them; he could dive in and wade through the cash, feeling it immersing him - there was nothing in the world that could feel that good! He would allow the ecstasy to build, until he let out the loudest cry of joy!

I think it had finally hit him, now, as it did with most: the endless possibilities now open to him. He was now ready to walk through those doors and claim the prize - the treasure that was going to change his life

It would be nothing like it was before. Sure, he was looking at doing a bit of time, but, with good behaviour, he'd be out soon enough. And, now, he had something to come out to: namely, a fucking fortune! How many ex-cons had something as good as that to look forward to, on their day of release?

One-hundred-million euros. Money he would never have to pay tax on. He would never have to worry about paying any bills. Nor eating lousy food, or watered-down beverages.

I tried to bring up the subject of his wife, again: would he be looking to restart his life with her, away from Ravenfall?

He shied from the question: "I'd much prefer to talk about you."

I took a sip from my glass of Coke and lit a cigarette. "I don't get to know people when I'm working… particularly…"

"Guys you've been sent to kill," he teased, putting some nibbles into his mouth. "I'd thought maybe you were starting to warm to me."

His hand appeared, pulling a loose hair from my collar, in a clearly affectionate - if not seductive - manner.

He could not manipulate me, nor was this a flirtatious scene; his touch was neither warm or inviting, which I made very clear, by pulling away from him, disapprovingly: "You're not my type, Martin."

If we were not in public, I would have given him another slap. But, it is not professional to draw attention to one's actions.

Martin drew away, clearly disappointed. "I suppose you're the type who likes to get drunk, get laid, then wake up alone."

That comment actually hit a raw nerve, but I managed not to let it show. Instead, I looked at the group of girls at the bar, who had caught Martin's eye the moment we walked in. He was not going to get lucky that night, nor as long as he was in my charge!

"You don't know me," I said. "This isn't all that I am; this is just *what* I am - what I need to be - at this moment. I have no interest in you because you're still a target, and not just because I'm not the one looking to put a bullet in you."

The words hit hard, filling him, once again, with gloom. His upbeat attitude and playful banter had left him exposed, and he once again felt the touch of death on his shoulder. Well, he had started it, with his unwanted personal judgements of me.

"I'll bet *nice* isn't your type," he continued; "you're probably into some freaky shit!"

Stereotyping is a common mistake applied to all contract killers. "Just because I kill people like you, doesn't mean I can't have deep relationships," I countered, now not wanting to back down. He was baiting me, but I wasn't the type to be reeled into the net so easily, so I let him.

"I'll bet they never hang around long," he dug deeper. "You're just a mercenary; a filthy killer for hire - what do you know of love?"

If this was how he wanted it, so be it. It might make things a little easier, for later, should it be necessary.

"I know enough to recognize that love is not made stronger by a man who runs away from his responsibilities," I countered; "if he truly cares for the ones he loves, he'll face whatever problems come along, and still remain true to the vows he made on their wedding day."

Martin's eyes now became sorrowful, and the air between us was growing stale. This wasn't productive; I needed a change of scenery.

Getting up from the table, without excusing myself, I dropped my unfinished cigarette in his pint glass. A visit to the ladies' was in order – unfortunately, it wasn't just a large turd that I needed to flush!

I had to remain focused to the business in hand: Martin was still on edge, and perhaps even looking to get away from me, at the first opportunity. But, for the moment, he had to be patient - just until the time was right; he needed me to protect him, until he got the money. Then, when I wasn't looking, he would either take care of me, or do a disappearing act. Subsequently, if I, or anyone else, came looking again, he would hire other people to protect him - people just as well trained as myself, or maybe just any other paid thug.

When it came down to it, his money could buy anything, and - almost – anyone. But, not me.

Now, I was the one who was a target; I needed to watch my own back.

In this job, sometimes, you really do wonder whether the money is worth it all.

Money. What can I tell you about it that you don't already know? There is no particular combination of words I can use which will surprise you.

If you don't count war, money is the most unattractive of all of human creations. All over the world, currencies are printed in red - I wonder if you even knew that fact. Open your own wallets and purses right now and look closely: somewhere, between the lines, you'll see that little shade hiding.

You probably won't believe me when I tell you that every penny of it is blood money. From one hand to the next, you are all passing money which has been paid at the expense of someone else's life.

In ancient times, it would be gold - you could wipe the stains away easily.

Washing my face in cold water, I felt a sudden presence, behind me.

Spinning around, I caught the person by the throat, pushing hard, up against the wall. Staring back at me was a pair of terrified eyes, belonging to a middle-aged woman with red hair.

"Who are you?" I demanded.

She held up her hand, something shiny and familiar between her fingers. Releasing the pressure, I allowed her to speak: "You dropped this, outside."

I looked at the object now, realizing immediately that it was one of my earrings. I released her neck and coolly stepped away, if a little embarrassed.

She dropped the earring to the floor and quickly ran out of the ladies' toilets, leaving me alone, once again.

Some people believe that nature selects people to be cold-blooded killers, and that it's something you can't change about yourself.

No matter how bleak that may sound, I, too, believe it to be true.

And, if there is no hope of change, there is only acceptance.

Unless there is someone out there who can prove it wrong. I won't spend my life waiting for that someone to appear.

What I do is a job, and it's best not to like it too much. Because, yes, you do get to like it! You need to find a way to maintain some form of balance, or else you may find that you lose yourself. Your own shadow becomes darker and more disfigured, with each passing day.

CHAPTER 23

Does anything scare me? Do I think I'm invincible; untouchable?

I feel fear, like anyone else. I bleed like any human. And, like any woman, I enjoy the feel of a man's hands over my body.

I've already said that my relationships are not fleeting, nor bought with money. It can, however, be difficult getting close to other people, without allowing them to step into my world. I'm protective, by nature and by profession, not just for myself, but for my family, too.

When do the lies begin and end? You might as well ask: when does love start and when does it stop?

It's not like I don't have any feelings. But, when you get too close to someone, you find the pressures and the hassle of having to lie can affect your abilities, becoming a huge burden. That's when you have to choose whether to keep lying, or end the relationship. I have to ensure that my personal life doesn't interfere with the job, and vice versa. Who I am at home and who I am right now are two different personas.

It is sometimes difficult not to let the mind get sidetracked by thoughts of love. One can always train the mind, but the heart is so easily neglected; there are days when it can just come over you – it is unavoidable. You just deal with it the best you can.

There is a guy I see, on and off - nothing too serious, which, surprisingly, we're both cool with. There is no mutual element of "Based on my observations, I'd say that you're more than you appear."

Coming out of the ladies', I found our table vacant.

It seemed that Martin had done pretty well for himself, and was now mixing with the group of ladies at the bar; laughing and fooling around, clearly oblivious - once again - to our previous conversation.

At least seeing him in a good mood was better than seeing him in a bad one.

We were enjoying the local hospitality, up to this point. Unfortunately, he then decided to place his lips on one of the unwilling girls, receiving a harsh slap in return - stronger than my own, earlier. Clearly, this wasn't Martin's day.

Nor mine: he had now drawn everybody's attention.

Somewhat like our own little tavern, back in Ravenfall, it was immediately clear that the locals didn't take kindly to strangers coming in with their filthy ways and disrespecting the women.

I immediately made for the bar, intending to grab Martin, but some folks had already enclosed him at the bar, blocking my path. A large, bald-headed man, in a brown jacket, approached Martin.

"You keep your lips to yourself," the man growled.

Martin's male pride would not allow him to be made to look weak and, foolishly, he squared up to the man, smiling: "You're just jealous I didn't ask you first."

One single jab to the mouth sent Martin flat on his back, a trickle of fresh blood seeping from the corner of his mouth. He tried to kick out at the man's shin, and received an empty glass over the top of his head. The cracking sound of the glass breaking to pieces shocked many at the bar.

But, though I hate to admit it, I actually enjoyed watching Martin take the subsequent beating, which he'd had coming since leaving Ravenfall. Part of me also wanted to get even, for our earlier conversation. So, I hung back and let the blows fall.

You couldn't honestly blame me: for a long time now Martin's comeuppance had been drawing nearer; karma had a funny way of appearing, out of nowhere - it was one thing you couldn't outrun or hide from. In the end, it was still less than he deserved.

But, nevertheless, I couldn't just stand by and watch him beaten to death in that pub; even if the guy was a worthless piece of shit, I was still responsible for his safety.

Fighting my way through the crowd, I grabbed the bald man's arm and pulled him around to face me. "I think he's had enough."

The large man's face was red, and he was now panting from the exertion; he wasn't in the best shape for this type of activity. For some reason, he looked upon me with the same repulsion – why, I don't know; perhaps he didn't like a woman contradicting his judgement.

"He took a liberty with a friend of mine. He came looking for trouble, and I gave it to him!" he growled, following up with a kick to Martin's groin, which caused him to cry out and grimace in pain.

"And, you did it very well," I complimented him, with complete sincerity, "but, we will be going now, and leave you in peace, to lick your wounds." At this, I looked at Baldie's raw knuckles: they weren't in very good condition; being big had done nothing to make the flesh hard. The bartender, standing behind the girls, looked on with increasing concern.

There was no shame retreating from conflict, on any side. We were supposed to be keeping a low profile.

But, my main concern was for Martin, who was already nursing a bleeding head. His shirt was torn beyond repair. He seemed relieved to see me now bending over him, as I reached down to pick him up off the floor.

The bald man took me by the arm: "I'm not finished with him yet!"

"I think you are. Let us be on our way." I put a slight edge into my voice: "Let's not make this any worse than it has to be; you won't like it if we stay."

Now, other men joined us, clearly with Baldie. There was nothing worse, to an alpha male, than being disrespected in front of his pack. "What you going to do to stop us?" Baldie challenged.

It was clear they were not yet done with Martin, which put me in an awkward position.

The fear is always with you - you can never be free of it, for as long as you value your own life.

But, sometimes you just have to fight, no matter how bleak your chances might seem. By focusing on your main survival instinct, you can unleash an unstoppable rage.

It was in my nature to do what I was good at - accepting your own nature can make you more than you ever thought yourself capable of being; the only thing that can hold you back is compassion – and, it had no place there and then. As a killer, the concept of love for humanity has to be blurred at times. When it is all gone, the only thing left inside you is a dark creature; a starving predator, hungry for prey.

It was unfortunate that it had to come to this, but I'd been left with no choice. They were bigger than me, and perhaps stronger. These people were not assassins, but it made them no less dangerous a threat to Martin's life. Or my own.

It was a useful tool to play the part of the pacifist: hiding one's true intentions left the opponent vulnerable; wide open to a surprise attack. My sideways thrusting stamp onto Baldie's knee was enough to surprise anyone.

His sudden loss of balance dislodged his grip on me, and the force of gravity propelled him onto the table behind him. I delivered a severe hammer-fist strike into his groin. It wasn't very sporting, but I couldn't well use my gun in there.

My body was a well-conditioned fighting machine, trained to take on more than one opponent. The group had been ready for anything… except me.

Once the fear is behind you, the strength inside begins to grow.

Forget any illusions about code of conduct: there are no rules in this arena; you do what you have to do to win a fight. When you feel the adrenalin cut you loose, it is then that you attack, like a rabid dog.

Taking up my *pensador* guard, I lashed out with my fists and elbows, pulverizing the men to their knees, in merciless, efficient fashion.

Then, of course, the girls started in on me, grasping a handful of my hair. I twisted around, almost breaking the wrist of the first, throwing her onto the floor to join Baldie. More came at me, but the look in their eyes now indicated hesitance; they were not fully committed. The last thing you need, going up against somebody of my skill, is hesitation in your actions, or any sudden cloud in your judgement.

They had all picked up bottles from the bar, which were now raised aloft. This was turning into something other than a typical cat-fight and, as such, I was entitled to change tactics.

It is commonly a good idea to employ all resources in the environment, in order to gain the advantage: cue balls, glass bottles and ashtrays are excellent choices for improvised weapons, when fighting in bars. My particular style of combat had taught me to use such weapons, accompanied by multiple strikes from my hands and limbs, in order to overpower any number of adversaries.

For example, a broken pool cue makes a good impact weapon, whilst also being useful for locking and grappling.

The maximum damage you can inflict on an opponent - whether a trained combatant or not - depends on their willingness to back down; mercy can only be awarded once they have conceded.

Not that that means they would do the same for you!

By the time it was all over, there wasn't much of the bar furniture left intact.

Martin hadn't been hurt too badly: just a flesh wound, above the eye. But Baldie was going to need some rest – and, the rest of his friends, a little dental work - by morning; the girls could live with just a manicure and some fresh eye make-up. Generally, it hadn't ended too badly.

As usual, Martin didn't have much to say for himself on the walk back to the bed-and-breakfast. It wasn't until we were in the bathroom that he started to address me directly, again: "It seems that whenever you're around I get drawn into blood and violence!"

I found the statement inaccurate, to say the least.

"The whole world is full of blood and violence," I retorted; "you see it on the news, every day: wars; crazed killings; we're only a small part of it."

Martin winced, as I padded his head with cotton wool. He had been lucky: the wound wasn't that deep - at some point, it would require no more than a few stitches; I'd seen a lot worse in my time. The guys at the bar had received far worse from me!

"I tried to persuade them to do things civilly," I said, sincerely, "but there are some men who won't listen to reason, or control their temper."

Martin regarded me, questioningly; "Know a lot about men with tempers, do you?"

I could see where the question was leading. It was insulting of Martin to suggest that a woman like me would ever allow a man to treat her in the manner he was implying. "The only man who ever raised a hand to me was my father, when I did something bad. But, there was always genuine love – that's the part which kept me straight."

Martin chuckled: "You call your job 'straight'?"

I looked him hard in the eyes; "I never kill the innocent."

I pressed a little harder on the clean dressing, in an attempt to steer away from the conversation, but Martin wasn't hurt badly enough to be put off. "You're kind of attractive when you're threatening and beating people up."

Then, he straightened himself up, in a macho posture; "Course, I had everything under control." I found myself smiling at his comment, again seeing Baldie booting him between the legs.

I finished the dressing: "I don't think there'll be much of a scar, and this should stop it from getting infected. Though, plastic surgery might be worth considering – you can add it to your medical expenses, when you become a millionaire."

Martin frowned at the lump, in the mirror, wondering if it really was that bad; seemingly, he missed that my plastic surgery comment hadn't been referring to his injuries.

"As for your clothes, we'll have to see to them in the morning," I continued, moving into the bedroom, to slip onto the mattress. Though I was still energized, my fists and arms were aching after the brawl.

Martin came in after me and started to undress, right in front of me. He stripped down to his boxers. There were no bruises on his body, probably because it wasn't in a particularly fit condition: he was saggy and round at the midsection, undoubtedly due to his choice of diet and lifestyle.

"I don't suppose you'd consider giving me a rub-down?" he asked. "It might help me get to sleep easier."

So would another knock on the head, I thought, looking away. "Not a chance, but feel free to rub one out yourself, if you feel lonely during the night," I replied, rolling onto my side to face the wall, if only to hide my childish grin.

It was just typical of men: go home hammered and expected to get laid! Well, he wasn't going to be lucky tonight. At least, not in the love sense, anyway.

If you're having any doubts about whether I am going to deliver on this contract, just keep reading: you might be pleasantly surprised. Or, perhaps you may not. This is not your typical story of redemption - not for him, or for me; that, at least, we have in common.

No matter what happens along the road of life, we will both have no regrets, because the journey we took, we both chose of free will; what is there to regret?

Martin would never change who he was; would never apologize for the way he has lived his life.

Throughout this account, I have spoken mostly of death, and little of my life. It's not because I think I'll die young; it's just that my life has - in more ways than one - always revolved around death.

I'm not asking for sympathy; just understanding, and perhaps even a little compassion. I think that, by now, you'll agree that I deserve it more than Martin.

CHAPTER 24

How can you live with what you do? This question isn't just aimed at me; it's one used commonly in society.

Up until now, you've probably put me down as being unusual. Well, granted, it's not the life or career a normal person could ever imagine; you can't spend your whole life going around killing people - it would seriously fuck you up in the head.

But, these days, is it possible to define any person as "normal"? Individualism thrives on people having unique desires and passions.

It isn't my desire to spend my whole life taking others, just as it is not the desire of others to spend theirs in misery.

There are always certain vices to help, of course. Everyone has their passion – and it is often their biggest weakness.

The most commonly welcome blessing was the one which came straight from a bottle.

Braddock's wife had spent her whole life trying to find alternatives, but unfortunately it was never the love of marriage that had filled her heart – just as at that very moment.

Pouring the liquor from the neck of the bottle, she thanked God to have found at least one pleasure she could indulge fully, on a daily basis. Filling the glass to the top, she necked half of its contents in one go; her head was starting to swim, along with the rest of her body.

When her husband was away, she would often go out to the pool, and soak away the years of depravity and disappointment, if only for a short moment. He had never really been the athletic type, unless you counted him running for a getaway car, as a youth, with a bag of money in his hand. He wasn't particularly energetic between the sheets, either.

So heavily invested was he in his vision, he had barely looked at her over the past few days; clearly, she was no longer considered a solid investment, nor their marriage. He was currently moving into a new area of power.

She wasn't exactly thrilled by his activities of late; clever and honest don't often apply to those who choose to work outside of the law.

Power and pure tyranny gives some men the ability to control everything around them. Women often think of this as a means of safety and strength.

Some, such as Braddock's wife, come to see it all for what it really is: there are some men who just cannot control the darkness in their hearts, even allowing others to use it, from time to time, to carry out their own retribution. This will be given at the cost of anything and anyone.

Braddock had lived a foolish adolescence, but had managed to survive, due to a life of serious business and serious money. Along the way, he had seriously fucked up his marriage.

Not that he had been totally to blame: some strong support for the failure had been contributed on her part, too.

Nothing is ever what it appears to be in the public eye; this is one of the most valuable of lessons in life. Some considered her husband to be a moderate kind of gangster – that was, until they met him face to face, up close. He called himself a businessman, but really he was just another criminal of the old term - he liked the image so much, he wore it on his sleeves, literally: the diamonds he'd had made into his cufflinks had come from a jeweller whom he had personally robbed!

The sound of the rear door opening brought her attention back to the present; the sudden appearance of her husband, clothed in his best robe, seemed to make the water turn tepid.

"How has your day been, dear?" he asked, chewing on an unlit cigar.

It was strange for him to bother asking anything with regards to her life, ever; nice, intimate chats were practically a distant memory.

Even more shocking was seeing him stripping off, placing his cigar in the ashtray and coming to join her, in the water. Noting her sudden change in mood, he asked: "Were you expecting anyone else?"

She considered the question anything but an insult.

There were many nights that she would sleep in her own bedroom, which suited him, since he often slept away from home - it made breaking their vows an easy sin for her to live with. Their relationship wasn't even close enough for them to hold each other in bed at night, so it felt strange having him join her like this, for a moonlight swim.

Wading out to the centre of the pool, now behind her, he held her frame, moving his hands up to softly massage her shoulders. Was this some weird foreplay? It wasn't at all like him to be so affectionate, and in the most upbeat mood she had seen him for a long time.

"Are you playing games with me?" she queried.

He seemed uncharacteristically hurt by her distance from him. His business at the council had gone well, and he had chosen to enjoy this news with her, but maybe now he was reconsidering.

This was fine by her: just because he had finally got clearance to build his grand casino, didn't give him conjugal rights to her body, whenever he felt like it. He may have had big dreams - the sort one would only whisper into a loved one's ear - but they were nothing to her, compared to knocking back all of the alcohol in the house. There was a time when she would have listened to anything he had to tell her, but now, as he moved his mouth to her ear, his words were nothing more than irritable static.

Their marriage had been a big disappointment, slowly taking away her strength and respectability; a legacy built on the bones of others, whom she was no doubt soon to join.

It seemed the right time to tell him that she'd had enough and was going to bring an end to the charade which was their marriage.

This certainly got his attention. "Are you asking for a divorce?" he asked.

She laughed, childishly, at the question. "I would be crazy to remain with you, especially when there are other men willing to provide for me - not just financially, but who'll take the time to give me true physical pleasure, an act of which you seem incapable or unwilling; services a husband would gladly bestow upon his wife, on a nightly basis."

The man with whom she was currently having an affair was just a simple shop-owner, but he was a true lover, who showed interest in her uniquely dark and passionate desires. It felt wonderful to be loved again. He dealt mainly in antiques, and business was very good in the international market; there was more on offer from him than she would ever receive from her husband. Within a week, she would be leaving Braddock for good.

She knew he no longer needed her anyway - not now that he'd had his dream casino approved, and his luxury mansion, where he would take all of his whores. She would not be one of them, waiting - maybe - for her turn at his attention.

She would be glad to be getting out of this town, and spending her evenings in the city again; dining in the finest restaurants, rather than having staying at home with grilled cheese sandwiches and a bottle of beer, or some other watered-down beverage. The ice in her glass was melting fast, and so too was her loyalty towards her husband.

Braddock was not invulnerable to what she was telling him. But, nor was he the sort to overreact; he was well aware that their marriage was formed of family desperation and obligation, rather than love.

So, surprisingly, he respected her wishes; if she was going to leave him in the morning, and file for divorce, he wasn't going to stand in her way. He was, after all, soon to be a very wealthy man soon; a king needed the right queen by his side.

Unfortunately, for a mere princess like her, only fairytale stories had a happy ending. Some power couldn't be shared; it could only be held by one pair of hands.

It was this pair of hands – those which had caressed her shoulders, as she took her nightly dip – that were now holding her head underneath the water's surface.

He held her there until the struggling stopped.

She had come to know too much about the way he operated, and was now a danger - a useful tool for the authorities; she could be used to fix him proper, if he did ever end up in court.

Killing one whore usually made all the others fall into line, and perhaps show a little more respect.

Lying back on the lounger, he now looked at the tarpaulin, just toward the edge of the pool; he would arrange its removal first thing in the morning. It would make a good addition to his mansion's foundations.

Lighting a fresh cigar, he listened to the evening's silence.

He suddenly realized that he was not alone; a dark man in a white blazer was observing him, thoughtfully, from the back gate.

Braddock had a manner which never reacted to anyone or anything out of the ordinary; he was very good at reading a character, and always allowed this part of him to do its work before any reaction: the visitor carried himself with confidence and control, he noted. Unshaken by the man's presence, Braddock asked: "Can I help you?"

The man didn't break his stride, as he made his way over to the pool. "I believe it was you who required *my* services."

Mr. X sat down on the lounger opposite Braddock, who immediately recognized the meaning to the retort.

"I didn't expect a visit," Braddock said, now interested in the stranger: "I understood you turned down the contract. How did you find me?"

"Through a mutual associate. I know about you and the Skull gang: you use them, from time to time, to carry out certain business transactions," Mr. X replied.

Slight unease crossed Braddock's face now. Like any businessman, he liked his own to run smoothly, and didn't take kindly to people interfering in his affairs. Even hired assassins. "Can't buy the same discretion you used to be able to, I suppose."

He continued to smoke and drink from his glass, showing the man that his manner did not intimidate in any way.

"The price of life being what it is these days," Mr. X said, cryptically, "what I offered, he couldn't turn down. Nor could that nice little piece of tail you see, from time to time."

Of course, Braddock knew that he was referring to the Skull leader's mistress, a girl whose name was inconsequential; only her favourite parlour tricks mattered, when the lord and master came to visit her. "I suppose he sent you here," Braddock enquired, slightly amused. "I'm surprised he didn't make it a personal call."

"He won't be making any of those again. As for the girl, I'm sure she's already attached herself to the new, self-appointed leader by now."

He eyed the fresh corpse, now beneath the tarpaulin: "Rotten way to die: too slow; very painful."

Braddock turned back to face him, clearly disapproving of the remark. "May I ask what concern this is of yours?" he asked, impatiently.

"What you do with members of your own household is your

business," Mr. X said, eager to return to the previous topic. "Just think of me as an interested party, who would like to know why a certain young boy was killed on a train, a couple of nights ago."

Braddock took a moment to remember the article, then guessed that this man was a relative of one of the young boys, slain by the other contractor Harry had set after Martin. He spoke cautiously: "They took the job; I was paying well. It wasn't my decision to send those boys; it was their gang's leader - if you want specific answers why-"

"I asked," Mr. X interrupted, "but I didn't get very satisfactory answers. It seems that you weren't very clear regarding the full situation - a situation they were neither prepared or capable to handle."

Braddock shrugged off the statement; it was hard to find good help these days. "They knew what it was all about; they could have said no and walked away, at any time."

Dissatisfied by the statement, Mr. X reached across and removed the cigar from Braddock's mouth. "Just tell me what exactly this is all about. The girl said it was about money - which is usually the case - but I didn't see a bag being carried by the target, in the newspaper, so it wasn't on him."

Braddock was not accustomed to demands being thrown at him in his own home. Nor was it usual for men of this stranger's profession to ask questions. The attitude was not going to persuade him to give up information. Family matter or not, disrespect could not be tolerated. "I suggest that you refrain from any further involvement. Whilst it is unfortunate, regarding whomever you are- *were*, related to, business of this kind has its dangers!"

Mr. X recognized the statement to be a clear warning – he had no slight concern. There is a very simple philosophy in this business: we recognize the right of all people to exist, until somebody pays to have that right taken away.

"I've met many people like you… many times: successful business-types, who make their money out of the pain, suffering and blood of others."

"So do you. We're no different; I've been where you've been, and I've done some questionable things." Braddock took back his cigar, casually. "Don't underestimate me: people who get too close find my scent quite harmful."

Some people, no matter how nicely asked, are reluctant to accommodate sound advice of their own free will. Mr. X could have just let it go, but this was what he did. Besides, it was still a matter of family. Some clearly had no idea how important family was. That was clearly the case with regards to this man, judging by the figure wrapped up in the tarpaulin.

"*I'm* a killer with a smell of death. People like you always come up smelling of roses, because you risk nothing," Mr. X corrected. He knew people like this man well, ever since the school playground: those who relied on fear had no real power; it was no more than a mask, which could be put on and taken off – it concealed what was really beneath. Behind this man's false tough image was genuine fear; it reeked from his pores, like a bad stench.

"I don't think you even know the meaning of harm, or pain, or suffering," Mr. X rose and reached, slowly, into his pocket. "But, we can remedy that very easily."

In one fluid motion he had delivered a brass-knuckle punch, straight to Braddock's face, knocking him out cold with one strike.

Sometimes it is necessary to teach people by example; the use of initiative, when it came to difficult students, was his specialty.

Luckily, he kept smelling salts to hand – otherwise, it was all just a waste of time.

Awakening suddenly, with a throbbing in his cheek, Braddock found himself bound to the lounger. Mr. X was standing over him, smoking his cigar.

"I'm going to ask you again. I suggest you think hard about the answer this time, before speaking." He moved forward, placing the cigar's hot tip near to Braddock's face. "Why did my nephew die?"

Braddock spat blood, in defiance. "I'm going to have you and your whole family butchered!" he grinned, through a dripping, red stain. "You'll know what it feels like to have your limbs cut off, before you die!"

Mr. X realized that he must be a little off his game – but then, a death in the family could do that to a professional.

"The thing about a threat is that it's only effective is the person who made it is still alive!" Mr. X took the bottle of alcohol from the pool's edge and started to pour the contents over Braddock's body. He then proceeded to retake his seat on the empty lounger again, continuing to smoke the cigar, with enjoyment - it wasn't a bad brand.

"This really is a fine cigar – it would go well with that particular beverage." He noticed it was starting to go out, so he lit a match, bringing the tip of its flame close to Braddock's body.

No matter how tough a person appears on the outside, we all have phobias - there is none more common than dying in excruciating pain!

Not to mention, in Braddock's case, such a humiliating fashion.

Still, when faced with impending death, there is very little left to prove; it is better to swallow one's pride, than to have it burnt from you.

"The target's name is Martin. He stole from the townspeople of Ravenfall, and he lost everything. But then the lucky fuck won a hundred-million euros on the lottery." Braddock added, hastily: "The man I'm competing with wants the money, to pay back the people."

Mr. X's mood lifted, the information having been imparted so easily now - there is nothing like a good bit of honesty to ease a person's suffering.

"Is that all?" he asked, bringing the flame closer still to Braddock's face - Braddock tried to pull away.

"He also wants to build his own project: a mall, to provide jobs. He believes, probably misguidedly, that this will absolve all of his sins."

The last statement was of little importance, but had some small relevance. Pulling back, Mr. X shook the flame out, placing the cigar back into his mouth again. "You don't think it's possible for a man to be absolved?"

Braddock allowed his head to sag forward, in resentment. "For the things he and I did in the past, it's going to take more than a fucking shopping mall to wash the blood from his hands." He spat, again. "I always thought it would be him that would come for me."

Mr. X wasn't concerned with this other man's vendetta towards Braddock, though at times even he was willing to forgive. It was when he couldn't forget that you got to see his real bad side.

"Well, thank you for all your help, Mr. Braddock. I will be taking my leave now." Mr. X rose, looking at the body wrapped in plastic once more; "It's a shame you married folks can't settle your disputes in a more civilized manner."

Braddock raised his eyes in a look of disgust: "Who are you to talk: you were about to burn me alive!?"

There is a great difference between a clean kill and untamed slaughter; Mr. X would never have truly killed a man by fire, just as he would never use water. As a professional, it was always best to make it quick and simple.

"I just sold that well," he replied, turning to look down toward the pool. "Just like I could have just dunked you right here. But, like I said: too slow and painful."

Braddock hated nothing more than being treated like a fool. "This isn't over!" he screamed. "You and your whole family will know what it is to be roasted in your beds - after I've peeled the flesh off your bodies and ripped out your insolent tongues!"

People never seem to learn that you should always ensure that you mean threats made at a person's back; if you've truly got something to say, you should always do so to their face.

Looking a person in the eye as you kill them doesn't appeal to everyone. Few throughout history had ever received that privilege.

One clean shot to the forehead silenced Braddock forever.

Mr. X was never really fond of killing people when they were sitting down, or tied up and vulnerable. In this instance, though, he could happily make an exception.

Replacing the cigar in his mouth, Mr. X made his way back to the gate, looking up to admire the moon as he did; it really was a beautiful evening.

With a last goodbye Mr. X turned and walked away, leaving another king on his throne.

The simplest of deaths are the ones in which you simply let go, immediately.

There isn't always time for that one last speech, before the heart stops - the body doesn't even have will enough to make the effort, but you should try to be content with that final thought, which goes through your mind, as you feel yourself die and leave your body - and the pain - behind. They say that your whole life flashes before your eyes; that memories come back in an instant.

The harshest of deaths is when you are not completely gone from existence. As you start crossing over, into the next life - as though walking over a bridge – and, looking down, you find Hell beneath you. When you don't make it the whole way across, as you think about all the bad things you've done in your life.

It's best you just keep walking, with a closed mind; to focus on good memories, of good deeds, so the ground doesn't disappear beneath your feet.

CHAPTER 25

There are three types of person in this world: the shepherd, the sheep and the wolf. If you don't know which category you fit into, you're automatically labelled a "sheep".

At that moment, I was unsure which I considered myself to be. Now I was amongst the sheep, hiding in plain sight: whether a shepherd, a wolf, or even a sheep, I could not decide.

Most of the time I was a wolf, snatching up sheep every now and then, behind the shepherd's back.

The wolf, by its nature, is a carnivorous animal - always looking for its opportunity. If it chooses to hide amongst the sheep, sooner or later, it is bound to strike.

Walking around the department stores, I could no longer feel that same hunger; instead, huddled amongst all the other people, oblivious to who I was and what I did, it was the fear I felt. For some reason, I felt as vulnerable as everybody else around me.

I hadn't shopped for a man since I bought my father his birthday present, some months earlier. My own choice of clothing was somewhat masculine, but in these modern times a woman was entitled to wear whatever she wanted.

Selecting the appropriate attire, which I had chosen for Martin, I made my way to the checkouts. There was a mirror behind the counter, and I hesitated for a moment, looking at my own reflection, as I had done earlier that morning, before leaving the bed-and-breakfast. Now, something seemed off.

Perhaps it was my jacket; it felt a little unsuitable for the following day's appointment at Lotto Centre; I couldn't possibly walk in there with Martin, looking the way I did. I wasn't sure if they would even question my presence, but saying that I was his girlfriend or wife was out of the question, and I couldn't let Martin out of my sight.

Selecting a dark blazer for myself, I paid for everything, smiling pleasantly at the girl behind the counter who served me. I looked down at the bump of her belly.

It made me think, again, of Laurie, back home, now under the protection of her father. Though, this girl wasn't at all like Laurie; she was completely comfortable with her situation.

Harry had made the right decision: taking Laurie in until all this was over, despite her objections. He should have done it years ago, but Laurie had been too proud, and too stubborn; despite her current predicament, the girl still had a lot of strength and conviction. It wouldn't be long now before all her troubles were behind her.

And I, too, could go back home and return to my life.

You probably think that life would be easier not doing what I do; maybe I could retire; settle down to be a mother myself; just work in the butcher's shop.

So far, you have been asking a lot of questions!

Let me ask you one: have you ever killed anyone - in war, self-defence or murder?

Your first kill always stays with you, no matter where you go or how old you grow. Some people will do anything for the right price, but there have to be limits, especially when it's business and not personal. When you kill for emotion, it goes beyond your code of conduct.

And, believe it or not, we're not all sick psychopaths.

The instinct to kill can come as easily as second nature. When you are given the qualities and conditioning required to be a professional killer, it makes you wonder what you really are, underneath.

After my first year of basic training, it wasn't long before my father started taking me along on jobs. Of course, I was only there to watch and learn, but it made me want to do it more. I had no idea what we were going into, so I just kept quiet and let my dad do the work.

I recall one assignment, in which I was acting as lookout.

My father had gone to scope out the target's house, and it wasn't long after he left that things had gone wrong. Loud gunshots rang out, through the walls and into the street, making me jump.

I swiftly made my way round the side of the house, to the rear, drawing my knife. Before I knew it, the side-gate swung open, and I was met by a pair of eyes, open wide, in shock and surprise.

The gun fell from the man's hand, to my feet, as I slowly retracted my blade from his chest. For my first attempt on reflex; it had been executed perfectly!

The target was in his early forties; a dope-dealer and known sex offender. He slumped against the gate, sliding down it, to sit on the floor. I had instinctively thrust deep; it wouldn't take long for him to bleed out. Father's bullet finished him sooner, to the side of his head.

"Are you trying to steal my contract?" he mused, as we were walking back to the car.

"We could go halves," I playfully retorted, before we drove out of the neighbourhood.

Although none of the neighbours had seen anything, my father was a little upset that I'd left my post; on the drive home, he lectured me: "Never assume your target is the only one; things can change at the last moment: one target can easily become two, if they are under protection, or a loved one is present."

I hadn't thought about that; I'd been more worried that my father had been shot, and was coming to his aid. But I, too, could have been killed.

"Also, if you start something, you should always finish it," he added, as we were pulling into the driveway.

"I would have done, but it was your contract," I said, getting out of the car.

Going inside, we found that Mother had already laid the table for dinner.

He could have chewed me out more, but we were now home; he let it slide. Besides, it had paid off, that time.

All-in-all, I had made my father proud: my contribution had ensured that the target never got away, which would have been sloppy.

We are a great breed of killers; we have been through the decades, yet known only to a few. The price of our success is that the world can never know of us. To carry on our family legacy means everything to me; there is nothing more important in my life.

It had been so easy that first time. In fact, I couldn't help but question whether it had been too easy; was taking a life that simple? A person had died by my own hand and I felt nothing; it had been as easy as sticking a pin in a cushion. My father put it all down to training; he always seems to shy away from the suggestion of ease.

Though he does continually criticize my use of a firearm: I'm better with a knife than I am with a gun, for which my dad always teases; he says I have a sharp personality! A knife is a good close-quarter weapon, deadly in the hands of a trained - or untrained – combatant.

To be truly effective, you must never hesitate, or overreach beyond your own safety zone. Sticking a knife into another person's body is not about being cold and ruthless: it's about precision and technique, ensuring incapacitation just before death, so your opponent can't fight back; it all comes down to possession of a very particular skill set, lots of training and practice.

Of course, you also need to be of the necessary mindset.

It isn't easy using such a tool to take a life, in a stand-off. If you are meeting your match; if you underestimate your target; or, if you overestimate your own ability, that's when your ego will always defeat you, faster than any blade.

There is nothing like a clean shave and new clothes to make you feel like a new man.

Standing by the sink, draped only in a towel, Martin's fresh wounds were still raw, but the pain didn't seem to bother him, as he towelled himself off after his shower.

Brushing the razor carefully over his face, he looked for a moment as though he had changed, and then again, with each scrape of the blade. It was as if he were peeling off another layer of false front, until, staring hard in the mirror, he could see no more of his old self anymore. Looking through that window into himself, he was finally seeing the soul beneath; he was truly seeing himself for the first time.

His whole life was playing, over and over, but it was not happiness he took from those images – instead, he felt his body grow cold, at the realization of just how weak a person he had become, the façade having been stripped away by his own hand.

All his life he had believed himself to be strong, his will making him tough and impenetrable. But, after the last two days, he was seeing how weak and needy he was.

As he gazed into the mirror, an image of Laurie appeared beside him, combing her hair, whilst listening to the radio. It was part of their usual morning ritual, which he had taken for granted, for so many years. In recent months she would look downward in the mirror, paying no attention to her hair, as she caressed her baby-bump and felt the maternal pride of every woman in her condition.

Suddenly, the barrel of a gun appeared behind her head, there was an explosion, and Laurie's reflection disappeared, in a thick mist of red.

A knock at the door brought Martin out of his daydream.

Wiping the shaving-foam from his face, he came over to the door, outside of which I was patiently waiting.

I immediately noticed his somewhat pale complexion, and ignored it. "I need you to get dressed quickly; we need to leave here now."

"Where are we going?"

"Change of address."

He took the new clothes from my hands and glanced at my own, in approval. "Do we really need to?"

"It's best. We only have one more day to go, so it's best that we keep on the move - stay ahead of anyone who might still be after us."

I left him and returned to the bedroom, making a final sweep and wiping down anything we might have touched since being there.

It's best not to stay anywhere for too long: twelve hours max.; not a moment more. When you're on the run, never stand still and never run in a straight line.

Planning and organization are key elements to staying ahead, and to staying alive. Not to mention out of the reach of the law.

The police had no doubt heard about last night's brawl and were already making their enquiries.

Martin came in, looking very flash in his new attire, though he seemed to wear it with disdain, which was not very gratifying, considering I had paid for it - as I had done for everything else. I needed to make a stop at the A.T.M. machine.

The bank account I used had been set up by Harry. It was in a false name and used only for business expenses; transactions were carried out when the job was completed.

The cost of the expenses on this job was becoming considerable: accommodation, food and now clothing. This work was expensive; it wasn't just all about the cost of a gun and a bullet. It was a lucky thing that Harry was going to be receiving a lot of money from this; compensation for my trouble was certainly assured.

In the movies, you often see people in this profession living a fine life. But, the highly paid jobs - ones with considerable risk - don't come around every day; the target is usually somebody very important: a political assassination, for example. Those targets are well protected, normally with an entourage of bodyguards.

Later, taking a brief rest at a local café, I began to imagine myself in the shoes of a close protection officer - the role I was currently undertaking. It felt strange, no longer considering myself to be playing the part of the assassin; it all felt so different to be on the other side.

Martin was playing the typical role of V.I.P. Sipping his coffee, he looked at all the people passing us by, seemingly without a care in the world. Dressed in his new blazer, he looked fully as though he believed himself to be something of a newborn banker sort.

But, right then he was no more than a worm on a hook, a fact of which I reminded him; no matter how hard he wriggled, he couldn't get off this line.

Being bait was no fun, and the resentment which re-emerged - of my comment and my presence, in such constant close proximity - could not be hidden behind the dark glasses he now wore. Martin wasn't warming to the idea of being saved all the time; it made him feel insecure that he needed me to keep him alive and safe.

I had never seen anybody so tense; Martin was not coping well, the psychological fatigue showing on his face.

Whereas, my own training kept me cool under pressure; my sixth sense will always warn me when there are eyes looking at the back of my head. The trouble with that is that one begins to see every third person as a potential enemy, because seeing the same faces repeatedly often means that you are under surveillance. I had to keep my eyes peeled and my reflexes sharp.

The psychology of fear is something everyone experiences, from time to time. Some people never get used to it, whilst others do - it all depends on the person. Paranoia can be distracting, or it can keep you sharp.

There were a few pinheads across the street, messing around on roller blades, trying to impress a group of girls, who couldn't help but laugh at their monkey act. One, however, managed to perform a spectacular feat. He immediately moved over toward the redhead of the group, to receive a generous kiss for his efforts.

The corners of Martin's mouth turned up, ever-so-slightly, at the scene - it was as though he had never before seen two people kiss so passionately.

I could feel Martin's eyes moving over me, from behind the dark rims and, at that moment, I was damn certain that he was not thinking about his wife. Now my attire was less butch, he was clearly starting to like what he saw.

"Is your wife a good kisser?" I enquired, in a poor attempt to take his mind off of its current course.

He shifted in his chair, immediately uncomfortably at the subject being brought up. "She *was* very good; there was a time when all I needed was to feel her touch on me."

I was surprised by his words, and started to recognize that something seemed to have stirred, deep inside him – perhaps that very morning, before we left.

"All you need is the love of a good woman," I paraphrased. "I was starting to wonder what's going to happen to you after all this, when I'm not around to protect your ass."

He took a moment, then leant across to whisper: "Maybe I could hire you full-time. The pay would be good, and a career change might suit you."

I found his change of direction desperate, and I wasn't going to be steered so easily off-course. "As precisely what, might I ask? Your protector, or maybe a nanny?"

The thought of his children, back at Ravenfall, brought a dark cloud across his face. He sat back and said nothing more, clearly no longer in a conversational mood.

This was probably just as well: I was supposed to be looking out for our wellbeing; if our safety was to be maintained, we couldn't drop our guard for a moment.

Slipping back into my previous role, I found that the question of whether or not I was actually willing to take a bullet for Martin was starting to nag at me. I had been told to keep him alive, but I wasn't prepared to give my life for this man, whom I had been originally sent to kill.

If I did my job well, hopefully I wouldn't be forced into making that decision.

There was a payphone nearby, so I made a quick call to Harry.

He had welcoming news, which filled my heart with hope, for the first time that day. "We're on our way."

I hung up and turned to Martin; "The courier is going to meet us with the documents, in about an hour."

We had to get moving: time was wasting and, unlike those kids across the street, there wasn't a moment to spare, for any more of these fun and games.

That doesn't mean to say I don't like a little fun, now and again.

Riding the subway, I eyed a young man - around my age, with the same well-toned physique as my current "bit of rough".

We all have our weaknesses; even for trained professionals, it's hard to ignore the appeal of the opposite sex. It's not like I don't have a will of my own: like any young woman, I have feelings and desires. From time to time, there is a voice in my head, telling me to be adventurous. We cannot always resist temptation. Like Adam, I long to taste forbidden fruit.

I used to think there was no room for love, but it really can't be that way: if you want a life beyond the world of killing, you have to find something or someone to love, or you are just as dead, inside, as those you were sent to kill. Sometimes, despite your worries, you have to take a risk.

Love is the biggest risk, but it is also the most precious possession. When there is no longer any doubt, and you release control of your emotions, you finally see more than just a cold-blooded killer staring back at you in the mirror.

Love is a trap which ensnares you, and keeps you a willing prisoner; the more complicated it is, the more you want it.

My heart is for love, not just a target for a bullet.

CHAPTER 26

I'm a ghost by trade; I appear and disappear at will, like some apparition. Most witnesses are not even sure if I was ever there in the first place.

I work in the shadows; what you see is but a glimpse.

What I know, I keep to myself - those who know me do the same; any talking is done directly through my employer.

The only time you'll see me is the last day you'll ever see anything!

I was being called out, in this circumstance; meeting the courier in a supermarket – a public place - wasn't my preferred choice. But, Harry had arranged everything. I just wanted to make it as brief as possible; being a Sunday, it wasn't long before closing.

People were going about what seemed a resemblance of normal life: shopping and working – but, one could never be sure who amongst them were what they appeared.

We found ourselves browsing the pest control aisle, looking idly at the various traps and poisons. I had never used drugs or poison to carry out a contract: they are complicated and most - unless very sophisticated - will show up on an autopsy. Besides, if you wanted to kill someone with poison, why would there be any need to hire someone like myself?

Unless, of course, it's a task that you've been putting off, for some time.

We all have chores we put off until the last moment.

When it comes to dealing with infestations, we tend to treat vermin with tolerance and humanity for too long. But, sooner or later, the inevitable becomes harder and harder to face.

And, the problem only gets bigger, if you fail to do the job right the first time around. You tried to solve it yourself, but you didn't use the right sort of repellent, or you took the cheap route and bought an inexpensive brand. So, now you need to call in an exterminator.

If you want the job done right, the first time around, pay up front for quality!

I felt a presence approaching my right-hand side, and the well-built figure of a young man in a motorcycle jacket lingered, seemingly browsing for rat poison.

"You wouldn't, by chance, know the number of a good exterminator?" he asked, casually.

"Depends on the size and scale of the problem you want removed."

The recognition codes had been given, but he wasn't what I had expected.

"Are you sure you weren't followed?" I asked, still keeping watch around us.

"How could they? Nobody knew where I was," he said, in a self-assured manner; "I got rid of my phone, like Harry told me, so no one could track me." He had an edge of cockiness to his tone.

"Did you bring them?" I asked, wanting to leave straight away.

"No, I decided on a different course of action: I put them in a coach-station locker, just in case something went wrong." He looked over at Martin, briefly. "I stashed the key on a statue, not far from here."

I looked at him, now with curiosity. That had not been the arrangement.

"I didn't know if you were going to turn up," he continued, "and, I wasn't about to walk into an ambush, and be caught with them."

The guy was cautious and smart; Harry had clearly chosen well.

I was just about to ask which statue, when he rose a questioning eyebrow; "I know you; you're from Ravenfall. You... your family runs a butcher's shop."

From beside me, Martin looked around with keen interest, at this news.

"Your sister was one year below me, at the local high school," the courier continued.

I immediately took back my previous opinion of the lad's aptitude; these very words had sealed his fate, and also Martin's!

Why had Harry sent this boy?

He knew things about my family, he knew my sister, and now he knew all about me! I had to protect all of them, as well as my own anonymity; I had no choice but to take steps, to ensure that this information went no further.

I won't ask if you would do the same as me - the answer resides only in your own heart; it is your judgement and yours alone.

To survive, you'll do anything for the ones you love.

I decided we would leave together, and that I would make it quick and painless - at least I owed the young man that much for his efforts.

My attention was drawn to a passer-by, in a red coat, with dark dreadlocks. Stopping not too far away, in a neighbouring aisle, a dark-skinned woman suddenly appeared to be browsing, with little actual interest in the items on the shelves.

As I looked around, I saw two dark-skinned males, keeping their heads down and, again, not truly focused on what was before them.

On the opposite side of us, two heavily-built men seemed to be interested in nothing but the three of us.

It was obvious now that the opposition had found us again, and this time with heavier numbers. How they could have located us, I wasn't sure. Had the courier led them here? Was it a double-cross? I looked over Laurence's face, but he seemed just as concerned as I was. No, he had nothing to do with this - that much was clear. True, he knew who I was, but he was still Harry's man.

He had to leave, before this turned ugly: I didn't want any innocent lives unnecessarily lost.

"Where did you stash the key?" I demanded.

"It's in the local park, on a statue of a royal guard on horseback," he replied, quietly.

"They're here for us, not you; go straight out of that exit there," I said, looking to an open door, nearby. "You've done your job. Now go back home, where it's safe."

I could see the hesitation in his eyes, but by the time I cleared my jacket and revealed my holstered gun, he had already made his way out of the area. The gang let him leave.

They started to band together now, approaching with great caution.

The largest man, wearing a bandanna, stepped forward, and was now no more than fifteen feet away. He addressed me, through gold-plated teeth: "My best guess is that somebody is going to die tonight - who that will be is up to you. We came for him; you would just be a bonus."

Beside me, Martin looked pale, feeling the touch of death once more - now approaching from all angles. They had spread out, to box us in, each man blocking an aisle.

"So, how did you find us?" I asked, keeping cool in the moment.

If you show any sign of fear, there will always be one person who calls your bluff. Like in a game of cards, though you may not always be holding the winning hand, the day you win is the day the other guy folds. That, or he takes everything from you. I never show weakness.

There's an old saying: "It's only the coward who dies a thousand deaths!"

Well, if I am to die, I only want it to be the once!

"We heard about your brawl in the pub, on the news last night; we thought you'd be in the area. So, I had my boys here keep lookout at the local hotels and B-and-Bs: one of them saw you two leave your last place; he recognized our friend there." He looked eagerly at Martin and told him: "There's a large bounty on your head!"

Often, assassins never asked and were never told the reasons behind the bounty. At this moment, that could be a blessing in disguise.

"Do you actually know why the hit was ordered in the first place?" I asked, reaching slowly inside my jacket. I brought out the lottery ticket: "This ticket is worth over a hundred-million euros. It belongs to our friend here, and someone doesn't want to see it cashed. Maybe you guys have other ideas?"

The leader considered the tempting thought for a moment – which was all I needed, to step in front of Martin and position myself by the end of the aisle, partially obscuring one side of my body. By my thigh, I held my gun; I pulled back the hammer with my thumb.

"You can walk away now," I warned them, "or this is going to get messy."

Amused, the leader now grinned, with a wide flash of bullion from his teeth; "I beg to differ: I've got a lot of help. These guys want to warm you up first, then maybe you and I can have our own little party?"

It was clear I would have to kill them all; it was all of them or both of us

When it went down, it went down hard.

I grabbed Martin and ducked for cover, as the whole store erupted into a live-fire zone. Bullets tore through packaged goods on shelves, spraying dried foods and condiments everywhere, as patrons screamed and fled for their lives.

Returning fire, I immediately took out one, with a round in the chest. He fell back against a second dreadlocked women, who unhesitantly made a run for the main exit. That was typical: at the first sign of death, most people showed their true colours.

Gangs such as this were only strong in numbers, and the sudden decrease in theirs now put them at a disadvantage.

Not to mention their lack of skill with firearms: they were hitting everything in range… except us.

Sometimes it felt good to pull a trigger; to hear the sound of the gun, feel the hot steel in your hand, and smell the cordite as it fired. Like some unstoppable drug lust, it made me want to do it again and again.

Keeping down, as well as I could, I again returned fire, now more controlled and much more accurate. A lucky shot caught the second man in the throat, causing blood to spurt from his mouth - I dropped him, with another shot to the temple.

That left only two: the leader in the bandanna and another man, whom I had lost since the shooting began. Unbeknownst to me, the latter had managed to manoeuvre himself behind us, taking me by surprise, until Martin decided to take up arms, and tackle the man with a kitchen knife.

The guy might have had guts, but he was not very efficient when it came to hand-to-hand combat; the other man was well built, and clearly stronger than Martin.

From my cover position, I couldn't intervene personally. I chose, instead, to give Martin the upper hand, by putting a bullet in his opponent's leg, sending them both tumbling to the floor.

Spinning back around, I suddenly found myself peering into the barrel of the leader's gun. Behind it, a wide smile beamed on the face which looked down on me. I waited, but a bullet did not immediately come my way.

"Why don't you suck on my barrel, seeing as it's-?"

A large, heavy fist came down onto the back of his neck, followed by two more blows to the kidneys. It took me a moment to realize that Laurence, the young courier, had crept up behind Bandanna, and was using his own form of boxing style to pound the leader to the floor.

I quickly looked around, to see Martin on top of the fourth man, fighting to plunge the blade into his chest, as the larger arm of the dark man managed to hold him at bay.

I took aim again, and delivered another shot into the man's bicep, immediately collapsing his obstructive arm. Martin's blade penetrated deep, and the man ceased struggling altogether.

Spinning again, I delivered one final round into the middle of the leader's face. As he dropped, Laurence stood in shock, breathing heavily.

Behind me, I could hear Martin grunting and the repeated sound of the blade plunging into the thug's defenceless body.

The thing about using a blade is that it's difficult to stop yourself, even when you're sure that the other guy is dead!

Sometimes, all you see is red, and you can only wait until the fire burns downs, and your head clears.

Those who say they aren't afraid of dying always show their true colours when death comes close to removing them from the world. It is only when a person is faced with death, and can feel it touching their soul, that they will find an appreciation for life; they will then either flee, or stand up and fight, to keep it. They will fight by any means necessary, so that they can go on to live a life to its fullest.

It's amazing how much pain a man can cause – and how much he can take - when he has a fortune waiting for him.

Some will try their very hardest to prevent the very soul being ripped from them.

It is the most emotional of sensations you will ever see, in a person's eyes, as they realize that they will live no more - no more days; no more hours; not one more minute of enjoyment!

A dying man's last thought is truly precious; it is the hardest thing: to say goodbye.

We had made a mess of half the store.

Walking slowly towards the front entrance, I noticed a middle-aged lady slowly pop up her head, from beneath the counter; she looked my way.

I looked at her and made a decision: it was always best to be careful, when it came to situations like this; a conscience could drop you, right where you stood, faster than a bullet. Besides, for all I knew, she was concealing a weapon behind that counter; people often did foolish things in stressful situations.

A cold-blooded kill can happen anywhere, at any time, with anyone watching - that is where most amateurs fuck up.

The only time you leave witnesses is when you're sure they can't identify you. Witnesses result in complications, no matter who they are or how old? If I have to, I'll kill a witness, should I believe them to be an immediate threat.

In some cases, I might instead just write them a letter: remind them that they are in my thoughts. What I choose to remember, and what they choose to forget, can make all the difference, to them.

Walking outside, the three of us made our way, hastily, from the store - it wouldn't be long before the law turned up.

Laurence had felt bad about letting Harry down, the way he had before leaving home; he had genuinely thought he could trust Debbie to keep their conversation to herself.

But, what was done was done; nothing could undo the mistake now. In his mind, though, as he was leaving the store, he decided that when you fuck up, you put it right. And, it just did not feel right, somehow, walking away the way that he had: he owed Harry much more, considering what Harry had done, in years past, for his mother and father.

Harry had briefly mentioned the situation to me once, and it suddenly struck me who Laurence was: Ravenfall's very own hometown boxing champion – at least, at the local high school. With his choice of clothing - hoodie and cap – I hadn't recognized him sooner. Harry should have told me, but I guess he counted on me making the right connection.

"I'll make sure Harry knows what you did," I said, with sincere gratitude. "You're fast with your fists; your reputation is well-deserved, Champ!"

With Martin dawdling behind us, we walked briskly across the pavement, trying to make some distance between us and the now decimated store.

"You ever have been to one of my fights?"

"No, but my sister is something of a fan." I looked behind, to make sure Martin was still in sight. "She thinks you have a shot at going pro, so I should look after those hands if I were you: they'll see you right, in the future."

When Laurence finally left us, to return to his aunt's home, I found myself relieved that he was still alive: killing him would have been regrettable.

I had left the cashier behind the counter alive, even though she had seen us both. By now, she would have called the police, giving our descriptions.

And, Martin was now starting crack, badly.

Things were starting to get out of hand!

Now at that time of day, public places were beginning to close. The only option now open to us was sanctuary.

When you do this for too long, your fascination with death – and, seeing the desperation of another, to cling to life - becomes a hunger, which can never be satisfied.

Sometimes, we are capable of doing things we never thought we could. But, often, when faced with our own impending death, we can also end up doing things of which we never thought we were capable! So many people never truly come to understand their own nature.

Most of us never look into our own hearts, or understand the darkness for what it is: when evil is untamed, along with our free will, human nature lies in indulgence. Understanding free will is to understand that the choices we make only have an impact on ourselves. If we remove the consequences, which restrain us from continuous indulging, we break free,

We can choose to judge ourselves, punish ourselves or accept that it is human nature.

Some might consider this a cold way of looking at it, but remember this: when any single life is taken – whether justly or unjustly - the rest of world carries on!

CHAPTER 27

The first time you see death up close, you are scared. Then, if it is by your own hand, you are excited.

You have never felt more alive than when you take your first life - at least, that's how it was for me.

The worst thing you can do in those moments is dwell on the lives of those you kill: wives; kids; girlfriends... whose were the the last faces they envisioned, at the moment they died? Questions like this will get under your skin, and there your sins don't just wash away. You can try asking for forgiveness, but some things cannot be redeemed.

In the end, you just need to find a way to live with the horrors, of which you would never have thought yourself capable, even as a novice.

Martin had been young when he had seen his father murdered, by his brother, Henry.

It had taken him a long time to admit that the action had been wrong, despite all the abuse they suffered from his father. But, pretending that it didn't happen changed nothing so, in the end, he had to face the fact: killing was wrong. And when he stood before the jury, his own testimony had sent his brother to prison, for ten years. He might have wanted his father to die, but he hadn't been responsible for his brother's actions.

Maybe a small part of him didn't care; he just wanted it all to stop.

But then, that drunken man had spoken so badly of his brother, and of his mother, for allowing it to happen, Martin had lashed out.

Now, he had done so again, this time, resulting in a death.

Sitting now, in the centre pew, he held his hands together tightly, and looked upward, to the figure of Jesus crucified - it looked very similar to the one in our own church.

Approaching from behind, I asked: "Not interrupting anything between the two of you, am I?" He didn't respond, so I slipped in to sit beside him. We were the only ones there.

Right now he was no better than a cockroach, hiding from exterminators; it felt like the whole world was looking for him at that moment. This was the safest place to remain at the moment.

But Martin couldn't stop himself from dwelling on the past, on all the wrongs he had done in his life.

"When was your last confession?" he finally spoke.

Sometimes, a church was enough to prompt anyone to spill their guts.

"I never confess in the house of God: He is all-seeing and all-knowing, so why confess in the first place?" I said, simply.

He looked down at his palm, still slightly stained with blood. "What about repentance?"

It was a question one would think should be on my mind all the time, but there was no conflict - not at this stage of my life, anyway. "That's God's decision: whether or not He will choose to forgive." I looked up toward the statue. "It doesn't matter what we ask Him; it all comes down to what kind of mood He's in when it comes to our day of judgement."

Martin held his tongue, then brought his hands up to his mouth, trembling slightly.

"I would refrain from vomiting; I'm not going to rub your back like Mummy," I said, indifferently. "It's just delayed shock. Difficult, I know, but it will pass."

"Is it always so easy for you?"

I wasn't really in the mood for a heart-to-heart, but where we were really didn't seem the sort of place to hide secrets. "It takes a certain personality to kill without hesitation or remorse," I said, honestly. "It was either him or you; a fair trade, in my book - in God's, too." Even now, the Church reiterated the condoning of killing in self-defence. But in today's society, taking a life to save a life was a tough argument.

"If you want me to say something which will help you sleep better, I've got nothing to give," I continued. "Just remember: they were going to kill you! You chose to live; you made that choice. Now, you have to make up your own mind-"

"I need to confess something," he interrupted, placing both palms together, as if to pray.

"Well, I'm not a priest!" Looking downward, I joked: "I'm not even a guardian angel! Nobody's hands are totally clean in this world. If they were, I wouldn't have a job."

He looked at the statue again, and I noticed tears appearing in his eyes; "I've done a lot of bad things in my life… but…"

"You want to weigh up the consequences of your actions? Well, you're in the right place, but you're talking to the wrong person." Refusing to allow any emotion to get to me, I said: "The blood you spilt tonight probably won't matter when you're living in your big house, sending your kids off to a fancy school, and fucking your wife stupid every night… all paid for with someone else's blood…"

"Someone else's lottery ticket…" he added, in a whisper.

I wasn't sure I had heard him correctly.

Before I knew it, he was proceeding to explain that he had come across the dead body of a man, in the town where I found him, cleaned out the guy's pockets and took his wallet - the ticket had been amongst the meagre cash inside it; enough to buy him one meal.

"You stole it from a dead body?" I said, now outraged. "I don't believe this; it wasn't even yours! You actually won a hundred-million euros with someone else's lottery ticket!"

He remained silent, lost in his prayers for forgiveness.

"Who was the dead man?" I asked, refusing to let the subject drop. "What was his name?"

"I don't know. I was looking for cash; I didn't look at his identity card."

Slumping back in the pew, I was now beginning to feel a little off-colour myself. "I was wrong: you're not lucky, you're still just a screw up!" I could feel the anger starting to build now; "You just left him there, didn't you? I bet you didn't report it. Did you take anything else? That fine looking watch – is that really yours?"

He merely shook his head, bowing his head in shame.

"I've got a good mind to shoot you on general principle!" I declared, reaching for my gun. But he surprised me, turning to look at me, for the first time.

"Who are you to judge? You're a killer!"

His judgement made me even angrier, and my trigger-finger started to itch, irritably. "I don't steal from the people I kill – it's not good business; it's immoral!"

He giggled mockingly, then, out of reverence, brought his hands up to cover his face.

After all this time, he finally understood guilt.

The harm we do - the decisions we make - can haunt us, until our dying day. Before we know it, we start to regret all the things we took for granted: the missed opportunities, handed to us by life, but which we chose not to take.

"You've got a wife, and kids on the way, but that just wasn't enough, was it?" I queried, now holding nothing back. "Will that money really make up for all that you've done?"

I knew he wasn't sure anymore; all he wanted to do was start his life over.

"That ticket is not yours," I continued, "any more than that watch. That man might have a family."

Suddenly, as he withdrew his hands, I could see a flash of light appear in his eyes; "You're right! When all this is done, I'll send it back to them; I'll send them… some money…" He again looked up at the effigy, with hope, as though quizzing whether his notion was worthy of his absolution.

"How?" I asked. "You don't even know his name."

He thought about this for a moment, and I could see that touch of salvation quickly drawing away from him.

"I could check the papers… the obituaries; I'm bound to find him," he said, as reassuringly as he could manage. "I still remember his face; I remember where we were when I found him… If he's got family, I'll make it up to them, I promise!"

The last two words weren't for my benefit, I knew: he was still holding out for some kind of forgiveness, from a power higher than my own.

"What do you care, anyway?"

His question hit me in the gut, hard; considering all we had been through, I'd thought it was plainly obvious: "You're here because that man's death was your last piece of bad luck – now it's all finally coming to catch up with you. And, it's not over yet." I took a breath, calming myself; "Not for me, either, for that matter."

I knew there could still be people coming – people who, like me, would not care for reason, because, like me, they were highly trained and very dangerous.

"Well, for whatever reason, some good luck has finally popped up, out of nowhere!" He pressed his palms together and placed the tips of his fingers to his lower lips. "I'm going to take this second chance; I'm going to make things right. I have the means to do it now."

When was this man ever going to learn that money can never solve everything?

"There are still people out there who will not stop until you're dead," I said, matter-of-fact. "I'm here because of you: first I'm meant to kill you, then I'm protecting you, and now I'm right back to thinking about shooting you again!"

He turned to look at me, noticing my hand beneath my jacket; "Seriously?"

"Give me a reason why not," I challenged, although even I had to admit that the idea of killing in a church was sacrilegious.

"I have a pretty good one," a voice spoke, from behind us.

Turning quickly, I looked up to see the woman with the dreadlocks, who had run from the store shootout - she was again aiming a gun at me.

When it comes to near-death experiences, we might ask ourselves why we didn't die: was it not our time, or were we just lucky?

Perhaps a guardian angel was watching out for us.

Well, that sounds great, but if guardian angels do exist, why do people die at all? Because if they didn't, I guess there would be no Heaven or Hell at all. But, how is it that those who live good lives seem to die sooner than those who live sinfully; some seem to go on forever.

Still, sooner or later, death comes for all of us.

Both God and the devil have the ability to control life and death, with just the touch of a finger.

Some say Death comes as a phantom of darkness, draped in a black robe; others say it comes in the form of a boatman, taking you across the sea, into the land of the dead, and that if you don't have the money to pay him, you remain between the two worlds.

So, I guess it's always best to be prepared, and carry a little change in your pocket, just in case.

The woman was good: I hadn't seen her coming, because I'd been yarning with Martin.

"Now, the both of you up and move out, where I can see you," she ordered, keeping the gun aimed at my chest. She reached out and took my own gun from its holster, tossing it away.

When it comes to death, you're either always afraid, or you're never afraid - some days, you're not sure which. Either way, my chosen vocation depended on my staying calm in difficult situations.

Though my gun was now out of reach, I still had my backup, as a last resort.

The fact that we weren't already dead suggested that this girl was after more than just the contract bounty; she knew about the ticket – she had overheard me talking to Bandanna about it, back at the store.

"Where is it?" she demanded.

"Well, we have it… It is the ticket you're asking about, I assume?" I asked, looking her over, carefully. "But, what good is it to you?"

She wasn't much older than me, and not necessarily as skilled or disciplined with a gun. She held it with enough confidence, but in her mind, I suspected it to be a prop, rather than a life-taker.

"Simple: first I'm going to kill you, then your man and I are going to go to the office, instead. There he is going to arrange for the money to be placed into an account - not one of his own, of course."

Indeed, I should really have seen her play coming.

"So, what's your cut?" I said, keen to keep on the topic of money.

"Cut?!" she sounded amused by the suggestion.

Since I'd taken care of her associates, it was apparent that she now looked to keep the lion's share. It was no longer the client's money with which she was now concerned: it was the big payoff.

"So, you go in together, get the money...? Then what? You both walk out and you let him go?" I asked, indicating toward Martin. He looked at me, questioningly, clearly not liking what I was implying.

"That doesn't concern you," the dark woman spoke. "Where is the ticket?"

"I think it concerns Martin. You see, without him, the documents and the ticket, nobody gets that money," I said, grabbing Martin by the collar, and pulling him in front of me, like a human shield. "I'd say we have a Mexican standoff."

She stood poised, but did not fire. "I will shoot; I'll kill him and you!"

"Do it. You kill him and all you get is the bounty," I said, backing towards the altar, as I looked around for an exit. "Me - I was *sent* to kill him, and the money is just a bonus for my employer; personally, I don't give a shit about it!"

Martin was starting to tremble against me, no doubt believing every word I was saying. The woman, however, looked doubtful: "If you wanted to kill him, you would have done it already."

"Maybe, but you're the one who wants the money. You can't get it without him, so I know you're not going to take that shot." I backed away from the pews, into the centre of the crossing. "So, why don't we talk a little business?"

She looked at me, hard, but kept her aim level. "What do you propose?"

"Let me and Martin live, and you can get a slice," I tempted.

She was at least considering it; even a cut of the money meant much more than the small bounty Braddock had been offering. Martin was now in no real danger.

And, as long as I kept him between myself and the bullets, neither was I.

"Alright," she said, finally, "we can call a truce." There were some propositions one couldn't refuse.

However, backing down didn't make her any less of a threat. "First, you need to get rid of your gun, to show good faith," I said, keeping myself covered.

She slowly lowered the gun, throwing it in the same direction as my own. Watching her moves carefully, I released Martin, pushing him aside.

Moving out to join me in the open, the woman said: "I think maybe we should discuss my share. Assuming I choose to keep my word."

Martin looked on, his concern resuming, as we squared up to each other.

In business, certain parties always had other agendas. I knew that I was only a fifth wheel, and not an equal partner – but that was no different to how I looked upon her, in that moment.

"I was actually thinking the same thing," I replied; "I don't imagine you're the type that likes to share. Yet here we are, on equal ground; just like me, you have no gun now."

She looked me over and sized up my physique; "I don't need a gun. Killing you will be entertainment."

"Winner takes all, then," I conceded.

She took up a defensive position, raising her arms in a fighting stance. Lowering myself, I positioned my arms into my preferred defensive cover.

Immediately, I took the first hit: a roundhouse kick to the head, which had little effect.

Delivering my own flurry of punches and low kicks, I was able to deliver effective strikes to her soft target areas. Still, she was tougher than she first appeared, and she took every blow I delivered, with little more than a slight grimace.

Executing a spinning back-kick to my abdomen, she sent me falling backward against the altar, slightly winded. She quickly withdrew a knife from behind her back. Pulling my own, we circled each other.

She was on the attack first, cutting and slashing at my jacket, whilst nicking the surface of my flesh; she was proficient with a blade, just as I was.

Thrusting outward with my foot, I stamped hard on her knee, hearing a pop. From then, she was limping, giving me the edge I needed: moving fast, I made a front jab to her face, as a distraction, following up with a diagonal slash, cutting the side of her neck. She withdrew, clutching the wound; though it wasn't deep, it was enough to shake her.

Staying on the defensive, I waited, patiently, for her to make another mistake.

Unfortunately, my ego was getting the better of me, and my reluctance to maintain discipline caused me to slip up: knocking the blade from her hand, I was about to deliver the killing blow, when she swung a round kick to my knee, following it with a jarring knee to my jaw.

Collapsing to my knees, I looked up to find that she was straightening up, apparently not as badly hurt as she had been feigning. With a flick of her wrist, something shiny appeared from her sleeve – a gunshot echoed through the church, as the bullet struck my arm.

It was commonly the most fatal of weaknesses: I had underestimated my opponent.

Still, she had, too: hers really should have been a kill-shot. But, with one eye as badly swollen as hers was, it hadn't been such an easy shot, and she could be forgiven.

You may take away one of my eyes, but with my one good eye, I'll watch you die!

What are my chosen last words? How about I tell you where I want your bullet to go? I won't try to give any heart-melting speeches; I certainly won't beg for my life: it's not a life worth begging for.

There are no regrets in this business; this is how it is.

Personally, I had never executed someone on their knees: it was too undignified.

At the end, you can kill yourself with one last effort, and retain some honour, or you can have your opponent put you down like some sick, wounded dog. I can't think of anything worse than leaving this world like a dog.

"You're good, honey," she taunted, mercilessly, "but this match is mine, I think."

Taunting was not professional, and it could cost a person dearly.

Our match was merely in check; it was not over, by a long shot.

Besides, I was never much for chess, anyway.

I preferred card games; never fully showing your hand. And, always having that one card hidden, which could get you out of trouble; an ace up your sleeve.

You can only survive situations like this if you have the mind of a machine - a killing machine.

My arm was troubling me, but I kept my attention focused, overlooking the pain just enough to retrieve a tiny throwing spike, concealed in the cuff of my jacket. With a last effort, I delivered a reverse side throw, sending it through the air, straight into the woman's throat.

Her eyes opened wide and her hand grabbed for the deadly item – it was deeply embedded. She fired another shot, but her vision had already become blurred; she missed me by some ways. Collapsing to her knees, she toppled sideways, onto the stone floor. Her eyes stayed open, even after she had stopped breathing.

Rising back onto my feet I saw Martin, still where I had last seen him, his face sombre. I retrieved my gun and we made for the exit.

Stopping by the fountain, Martin washed his hands, cleaning them of the blood stains; he then crossed himself, at the door.

When it comes to believing in God, an average person's faith lasts but the few seconds required.

I remember every kill; every face.

That's all they are: "faces", like so many walking around out there.

The question they're all too afraid to ask is: "When is it my turn?" Well, if you're lucky, you won't see it coming.

Maybe it will be so quick that you don't feel any pain. But, honestly, in my opinion, at the very end, feeling one, last sensation is better than feeling nothing at all - it's the one last great gift.

How do I do what I do?

How will I atone for my sins?

I'll just leave a small donation in the box, on my way out the door. Then, we're square again.

CHAPTER 28

Have you ever had one of those days when everything is going wrong and everyone wants to kill you?

Well, perhaps the first part, but you can't even begin to comprehend how it feels when your life-force is draining from your body, making you clumsy and weak.

When you have a bullet in your body, it's not like you can even reach out to ask for help. Particularly when you are being sought by the local police. Being hunted, like an animal, does somewhat remove you from the rest of society.

That's when you come to hate everything and everyone that crosses your path.

As we walked the streets, every step behind us sounded like Death knocking on my door.

At one point, I turned, to see an old man, smoking a pipe, as he strode behind us with his walking stick. A glowing, cheerful expression was on his face, as though he were enjoying the best evening of his life.

Allowing him to pass us by, we continued on. I couldn't help but consider how lucky some people were, not to be victims of the world. For a moment, I hoped that he would fall or get hit by a passing car, just so that Martin and I were not the only two people who had experienced so much misfortune in these past few days.

Even my own hand had been repeatedly forced to take lives - all for the sake of a little scrap of paper.

Entering our room, I was immediately thankful that it came with its own sink. Stripping down to my bra, I inspected the hole in my upper arm.

The problem with a gunshot wound was that we couldn't go to a hospital: there would be too many questions. Eventually, the events of this evening would come out, and would be connected to us. Thankfully, it was only a flesh wound, and could be tended to by myself.

Using a sharp knife, I dug into the wound and turned it, until it opened further. It was something of a trick to extract the bullet, with tweezers, without pushing it deeper. Gripping hold tightly, it took only three tugs to remove it fully. I cursed so loudly that I must have disturbed the neighbours - as if all the swearing in the world would stop any of the pain from this wound. Placing a clean dressing over the wound, to stop the bleeding, I took a moment to clear my mind. The sensation had been excruciating, but my father had taught me to endure pain.

Dying usually hurts, so by overcoming the pain, one can overcome death; denying pain is proof that your spirit is not yet ready to leave your body. You simply have to believe in the two different parts of yourself: the first is the mind; the second, the body.

We are born with both, but most people are taught to balance them unequally, so one can become greater than the other, as needed. The mind will decide whichever goal needs to be achieved, and the body executes the action required to do so. In order to achieve balance, each has to fully trust in the other, if they are to work together efficiently, as one; as a team.

I wished the same could be said of my relationship with Martin.

Ever since I'd met him, my life had turned to shit. Even though he supported me, and helped us get back to the bed-and-breakfast, I knew he was still only acting for his own benefit.

Martin was afraid for his own life, yet he knew nothing about death, save for one kill, in itself an act of self-preservation.

Now, he was just a man full of drama, as he lay on his bed, facing away from me, and cried himself to sleep, whilst I stayed awake to keep watch.

Perhaps he was changing; looking to start a new life. Well, that decision was in my hands, not his.

And the night wasn't over yet: we were still in hostile territory.

I clearly wasn't going to get to sleep so, again, I took to the streets, still seeing everyone as a potential enemy. If anybody else came at me that night, they would find one pissed-off killer!

It's not always easy justifying to myself what I do. The number of people I have killed, in such a short space of time, you wouldn't have thought possible!

True, on this occasion, I've mostly been defending myself. But, still, I had taken all of those lives, and for what? To protect a petty thief and a small scrap of paper, worth more money than anyone could ever spend in a lifetime. Now, I had more death on my hands than I had ever intended - it bore a great weight upon my shoulders, for which I hated Martin even more.

It's not like I'm psychotic; it wasn't a killing rampage. All of those deaths were unnecessary... for Martin, a man who himself deserved a bullet - just as do others who betray their loved ones. I was trying to keep alive someone who had no right to be walking the Earth.

My instincts told me to just end it all and walk away: one last death, and this madness would all be over.

I needed something to warm me up, but there was nowhere open to buy a drink. After all this mess was over, I would be looking to take a long rest.

I kept trying to tell myself that everything was going to be alright. This wasn't something I usually did, and I would not be looking to do so again, any time soon.

I aimlessly walked up a flight of steps, onto a footbridge adjacent to a broad river, and looked across, to the lights on the other side of the water. Tomorrow morning, all we needed to do was cross the river, and we would be at the end.

Looking down onto the water's surface, it looked opaque, not at all like the one near my house in Ravenfall, which always looked fresh and clean. There, the streams flowed clear, like bottled mineral water, and the meadows were beautiful, green patches, soft and pleasurable to the eye.

It made me nostalgic to think of home, allowing everything else to become a blur - even taking the cold pain away from my arm, for just a short time. I was missing the open country; I was never the kind who was into the Big City scene, where everything was louder and more dirty – and, not just the streets.

As I looked down onto a nearby street corner, I saw a group of girls, standing around as though on display – hookers, more than likely, given their choice of evening attire. Desperation could lead some women into the most desperate of acts. Men, too. Surely there were better ways to make money. But, then again, who was I to judge?

What I was doing, getting caught up in all this shit, I didn't know any more. I had very little invested in all this; I had just been sent along to kill someone. Harry was expecting me to deliver on my obligation, but it would be delusional to say that I hadn't thought again about going back to the bed-and-breakfast, right at that moment, and putting Martin out of *my* misery. So far, all he had done was cause a lot of problems - all because of his own selfish necessity to escape his problems. Only just today had he faced up to the things he had done; all the people he had hurt.

Everything he took from Ravenfall was gone, and his money couldn't provide solace for it all.

But, there were still people – hard-up people - depending on me to finish this.

I felt another presence drawing close, and I couldn't help but stroke the butt of my pistol, as a little old lady, from the bridge's far side, passed me by.

I felt nothing now but fear, creeping up my spine.

Fearing for the loss of my own life was something I had been taught never to dwell upon. But I was now the prey, and I didn't like it. The whole situation was starting to make me paranoid - perhaps even crazy.

When it becomes difficult to tell the sharks from the guppies, in times of crisis, the only people we can safely turn to are our own family - there is camaraderie to be found in most. Even those with whom we don't always get along: our siblings, at the worst of times; or our parents, when being too over-protective, and disapproving of our decisions. We may not even feel the same connections that we did when we were younger, and over time we may even worry that the strength we had as a family is gone. But, we're always bonded by blood; any of life's other conflicts seems futile, compared to the possibility that we'll never get the chance to straighten things out with them.

But, even though they're not present, it gives us strength to feel they have our back, even if that just means the sound of their voice, from a long way away.

I'd already been to the statue and recovered the key, locating the locker and the documents, but the job still wasn't done. All I wanted to do was end it; as far as I was concerned, it was time to go home.

Harry was usually the only direct contact when I worked. But, in this instance, with his being the actual client, it was difficult to report the current situation.

Reaching out to my family - to my father, in particular - was a difficult decision for me to make. It wasn't a particularly proud moment in our family history, as I stood alone in a phone booth, talking with him.

He was at home, sitting next to my mother on the couch, while my little sister was in her bedroom, finishing her homework.

I was ashamed to realize, for the first time, that I was beginning to doubt my own abilities to fully see through this contract.

"Harry phoned me and said that you've been through quite an ordeal," my father's voice came across somewhat concerned. "Did you meet up with the courier?"

I immediately started to feel bad again, recalling how I had even considered killing the boy Harry had sent up with the documents; I was beginning to lose grip on my own sense of objectivity. "The courier's on his way back home, but we're still on the run." I took a deep breath, before continuing: "But there's more, Dad: today I killed three others in a supermarket, and a woman in a church." Many lives were being lost - it wasn't professional to kill so many outside of the contract.

"I hate that this is happening! I never want to kill so many people in such a short time!" I felt the pain in my arm start to irritate again. "They're not even contracted targets. Now I don't even consider myself to be anything more than just a target, alongside Martin."

Evidently, we were both in serious danger, but I hadn't wanted any concern to come across in my voice, allowing my father's doubt to make him think that I couldn't do this on my own.

"I just want it to be over - to just kill this guy and come home. There's been too much unnecessary death; there was only supposed to be one target. This isn't what we do; it isn't our concern, the money; it isn't what we're about!"

My father had seen the article in the local newspaper, regarding the incident on the train, and had accepted that there were times when the unexpected would happen. At least I had been prepared, and I had kept my head down well, so as not to be identified.

"I can only guide you; only you can make your own decisions," he said, affectionately. "When I was your age, all I ever wanted to do was protect our family's honour. I'm actually relieved that you are taking this as you are, although I don't mean that to sound cruel. It's not as if you enjoy the killing any more than the rest of us, who came before."

At times, it was a tough thing, to live up to the family name, especially amongst those who were at one time considered to be heroes; those who did what they did to ensure liberty for our countrymen.

"We all chose this path, but it's our free will that keeps us human," he said, with a proud tone. "Why else did you let that courier go? I knew that you wouldn't disappoint on that account."

"It was a test?" I couldn't hide my shock.

"I asked Harry to send an unknown courier, when he phoned me. We worked out a way to put you in a situation in which you, alone, can decide whether or not you have the power - the right - to take the life of a person, just because they happened to be in the wrong place at the wrong time."

It was true: most of the time people ended up dead, just for being in the wrong place.

"How did you feel when you found out who he was?" Father asked.

"I was afraid for all of us. I was prepared to do it, but he wasn't the target," I said, justifiably. "He actually saved my life, so I owed him one. He won't tell anyone - I believe that much to be true."

My father knew that I was smart and had good judgement, but I was still young, and open to self-doubt. That was only natural in this profession; it kept one sharp and alert. Asking questions makes one pay attention to details, which may arise out of nowhere.

"I never wanted to disappoint the family, or to let Harry down."

"You would never have killed Laurence: I taught you better than that," Dad assured. "If you finish this, the faith will be restored. You're still young - Harry understands that, and he's just as proud as your mother and I. I admit, even I had doubts about sending you out like this - solo – on your first time. But now I'm sorry that I was so harsh when you suggested it."

I remembered our conversation in his office; his objections to me going it alone. But it had been these very doubts which had made me even more determined to prove myself.

"I had to do it, Dad, despite your reservations; I had to see if I was good enough," I said, feeling as though I had perhaps made the wrong decision.

"This is a lifelong commitment - I told you that before you started," he said, now in a more serious tone. "Finish what you started, then you can come home to us. When you do come back, we will never need to talk about this again."

I had got so used to his preaching, it made me lose track of time. It was getting late, and I knew I wouldn't be safe, out in the open, for much longer. I said what needed to be got off my chest: "There is only one way I'll be free of this burden: if that man doesn't make it to that office, I'll have failed - I can't allow that to happen. If he is to die, it needs to be by my hand."

At this, I finished the call and hung up, making my way back to the bed-and-breakfast.

So, now you know the truth: this is my first solo contract; all the other times have been under the watchful eye of my father.

Since you now know that, you might as well know the rest: my first name is Bethany, I'm nineteen years old, and I've been doing this work for the past twelve months. I come from three generations of killers, assassins, mercenaries, or whatever you wish to call us; we kill people for money. But we don't just kill anybody - that much you should have already gathered.

There will always be times when even the best of us stumble and fall, but if you land right, you won't injure yourself; you can pick yourself up and walk on, without any shame.

False confidence is a person's worst enemy, but it doesn't apply to me. I'm everything my father made me - everything he taught me - as taught to him. I know what I know because, without my skills, I would be dead right now. Faith in your own strengths and abilities is enough to get you by, at times.

I walk in the shadows, but they merely cloak my light, because that is what the darkest predators come to feed on. They hunger for the light, because they have none; there is nothing more than darkness in their hearts. What remains of the world is only kept lit by the actions of a few.

It has been my family that have fought the darkness with our own light. As the predators try to extinguish the flame which burns in the heart of our society, we counter by wiping the darkness clear, so the flame burns on, illuminating the world; mankind need no longer fear the darkness. Nobody else was brave enough to make the kind of decisions that needed to be made, so we took it upon ourselves to see that such people die, by the same light that we are trying to protect. It is a terrible burden to bear, but it is the only sure way for our society to survive.

Even my own mother, who was once a victim, came to see this.

Don't be mad at God: He did not create the darkness; He made the light, for all things to live. He gave us the free will to ensure that His creation never ends. We are not pawns on a chess-board; we are His knights and, when called, we vanquish the evil. We are the soldiers - the warriors who win the wars, in His good name; we carry this burden and fight our own wars until, finally, all the evil is removed.

One day, hopefully, we shall be able to lay down our swords, open our hearts and receive the love He has blessed us with. We will come home, to His kingdom, and we shall finally know peace. And there we will look upon His face, and He will place a kiss upon our brow.

With that kiss, all our sins will be washed away and our hearts will know forgiveness.

CHAPTER 29

Is it possible for people to change?

Well, externally, yes, very easily; people change their appearance all the time. It sometimes helps them, psychologically, to change who they once were. Or, who they want to become.

Unfortunately, what is on the inside takes a little more work.

You never lose or forget what you are, or have been, because you've spent most of your life making it part of your soul, and a human soul cannot be so easily changed.

Not as far as the devil is concerned, anyway.

If you stare into the light for too long, hoping to catch a glimpse of Heaven, it can blind you. However, you can spend your whole life walking in the darkness, and never feel the warmth on your face.

Harry used to love watching the sun rise over the hills, each morning, after dawn. It gave him small comfort to see the darkness dissolve before his eyes.

But, it didn't always bring a change in circumstance.

The most he could be certain of was strong black coffee and a nice, warm breakfast, as a way to start the day, no matter what it held in store. As his father used to say, the best thinking is always done on a full stomach.

The worst way to start a day was with the police paying him a call, in the early hours, as he conversed with his daughter, at the breakfast table.

Upon first seeing the local police sergeant and his young officer coming through the door in an official capacity, Laurie feared they had come about Martin: had somebody at last caught up with him; was it all over?

They had, in fact, come about a completely different matter, and had heard nothing regarding her husband, which really came as no surprise to them at all: Harry had already told them he was looking into the matter, which usually meant that the only time they would hear anything would be from the coroner's office.

In fact, the police had received a call from Braddock's housekeeper, who had found two bodies, out by the swimming pool: the wife appeared to have been drowned and Mr. Braddock shot.

Surprisingly, the news came as a shock to Harry. As he sat at the breakfast table, with Laurie seated opposite him, he was quiet. Rising from his chair, after a while, he asked the sergeant to come into his study.

Everyone knew that Harry hated Braddock, but they had also been friends - almost brothers - as younger men, and he was now faced with the dilemma of a feeling of grievous ambivalence. The man had been a nuisance for a good number of years, but hearing of his actual departure from this life now left a hole in Harry's heart. The anger he had kept there was suddenly relinquished, as though ripped out of him; he was now left with an empty space, without so much as a cork to plug it.

He had never been sure which would be the first of them to go, and whilst he was glad it was Braddock, he was a little regretful not to have been the one to have personally ordered it.

Now there was, of course, the question of his whereabouts last evening - strictly procedure. Harry had been at home, which his daughter would be able to verify; they had been reminiscing in the lounge, for most of the evening.

Harry enquired if Braddock's murder had yet been announced to the press, but not so far; few, if any, in the town, had yet heard the news. There weren't many who would shed a tear, despite Braddock's past deeds for the town, when he and Harry had acted in its interests.

The sergeant - who had first started out as a copper when Harry's crew begun their little enterprise - chose to believe Harry's statement; for the moment, he decided to leave the line of enquiry there. Making for the door, followed by the other officer, they both left, as quietly as they had arrived. As always before, Harry could count on their discretion, when it came to matters as sensitive as this.

The town needed to start its day normally, just as it always did. Word of Braddock's demise would get around soon enough and, no doubt, he would be suspected. But, would they blame him, if he had pulled the trigger? Harry, at least, retained some dignity, always putting the community first, as with his mall project - this afforded him clemency for his past mistakes.

Those times were nothing but weak shadows now, being slowly dissolved by the day's new light rising over the town, burning away the darkness and bringing a new beginning. He could finally let go of the past; justice had come for Braddock, and it had not dirtied his own hands.

His family had always seemed to have this strange immunity surrounding them, generation after generation. Questions had been asked and sometimes charges had been, fleetingly, filed, but never once had Braddock, or any of those around him, ever been sent to jail.

Nothing can be proved if you can prove nothing.

Yet, sooner or later, guilt will come around to pay out.

Payback can come around fast, and so can death.

The trail of bodies you leave in your wake will eventually lead back to you. Even should you choose to hang up your killing ways, your time will come, sooner or later; the road you have taken has led only to this - you can have no complaints. In your own eyes, you may not be guilty, but in those of society, nor are you innocent.

But, when it comes around, you'll never have imagined it would come so soon.

Like it or not, when the decision has been made, your life is taken away from you, just as you took it from others.

And, now, is it Hell or Heaven waiting? That is only for the dead to know.

Laurie waited until the cops had left, before joining Harry in the study.

She didn't share his confidence that everything was going to be alright. The man with whom Harry and been at war, for many years, had now turned up dead, and no matter what a person had done in the past, in

Laurie's eyes, it still wasn't right.

"I know you think you're the king of Ravenfall, and I know how you used to deal with competitors and liabilities," she said, perhaps harshly, "but you said that you'd given that part of your life up. Was that just another lie?"

Harry had lied about many things, but never about his oath to go straight. "I assure you, I had nothing to do with it. But, let's just say it was long overdue!"

Laurie did little to hide her distaste for his comment.

Harry had tried so often, earlier in life, to pretend to be something he wasn't, and where had it got him? Heartache, and perhaps even now the permanent loss of his child.

"Why aren't you defending yourself, like you always do?" She pressed harder: "Why can't you be the man my mother wanted you to be? The man I know that you truly want to become, but in the end, you haven't the strength to fight against your own dark nature? Why can't you free yourself?"

It isn't always easy living a life you are not proud of, whilst others find it difficult to find any form of pride in anything they ever did. In this case, Harry couldn't just say: "It's time to start over."

"Because I don't want to; this is my burden to bear," he said, taking a sip of whisky. "To me, it's either living life under someone else's ideals, or choosing to live your life free. Either way, there's a price to pay."

He had, at one time, considered himself to be the last of a race of giants - even giants had to start out small.

"Your whole life you profited from the illegal actions of others. You use people to do your will - to dirty their hands - so you no longer have to stain your own." She knew only too well how many lives his word had taken, in the past; his hands were just as stained with their blood.

"I'm not sure if there ever was a good man in you, but you were always good to your word, both good and bad." She challenged: "You pretend you do a lot of good work for this town, but it will never make up for the bad you did - the harm - even to your own people!"

It was true: there were evil deeds which he could never fully wash from his hands, no matter how much he tried to scrub away the blood; it was even under his fingernails.

A life of witnessing brutal – even inhuman - acts either broke a person or made them strong. When the time was right, he had hoped to tell her all about it. That time had now come.

"You know I'm not a God-fearing man, but they do say that the first step towards redemption is confession." He took something from his desk drawer and came over to stand before her. "Well, I choose to confess here, to you, not God."

She remained quiet now and just listened - to what she hoped would be the truth.

"We can choose to pick our sins; we can choose to ignore the ones we make against God, but not the ones against those we love," he said, with clear sincerity. "I've always chosen to believe what guides us is fate - I don't fear it like others, who are happy to deafen their ears and turn away; I could never walk away from the both of you."

Laurie wanted to believe his words, but she still needed to hear more: there had always been something he had been keeping back, and it was time she heard the truth.

"You may have stood by my mother all these years, but you never took her as your wife," she said, bitterly; "she died never knowing if you would ever come knocking to ask her."

Harry nodded, feeling the deep regret resurface, once again. "People want things so much, and hate to be told they can't have them. So, we try our hardest to make those things happen; to prove to ourselves that it's not in our interests to listen to others. But, it is so easy to build or destroy something; not so easy to know whether it will make you feel full or empty inside, once you actually achieve it.

"I was no good for your mother, or for you, so I chose not to make her a part of my world - not until I decided to change my ways. I bought her a ring, and was going to propose that very night; she didn't know yet, but that was why we were out celebrating."

Laurie could see pools forming in his eyes.

"I've never been able to stop thinking about your mother, as she passed away, by my side - killed by bullets that were meant for me." He allowed the tears to flow. "I never told you, but she was the first to see the danger coming, and she stepped in front of the gunshots… to protect me!"

He stopped, trying to compose himself. But, he would make himself fight through it: she deserved to hear everything, at last.

"Despite irrefutable evidence, Braddock was acquitted. I did think about taking his life once - went to his house with my gun and waited in my car, until he came home - but I never went after him. I knew that your mother and you deserved justice, but if I'd killed him, you would have thought even less of me."

Some people carry a hell of a grudge with them - like cancer, it eats away, until little human decency remains. A man's dignity is something he must hold on to, or he will become little more than a monster - most won't even realize it is happening, as they become worse than the person they originally despised.

"After I came home, I went to my old coat and got the ring." It had appeared in his hand; he held it out to show Laurie. "I thought about returning it, but for all these years keeping it helped me hold on to my love for your mother; this kept the anger at bay."

Foes can take away your possessions, but when you allow them to steal your humanity, your empathy and your compassion, all you see, from then on, becomes distorted, and you risk losing sight of what really matters.

"I came to realize that the reason your mother did what she did is because she believed that she could give me the chance to redeem my life, through you," he said, taking her hand, gently. "But I am not as decent, or as strong-willed, as you, and it is not so easy for me to turn from the dark forces driving me."

She continued to look at the ring. It was very beautiful; just what her mother had dreamt of receiving, all those years ago. He placed it in her palm and folded her fingers closed.

"I don't deserve this anymore… or you. I've done what needed to be done: this prize money coming your way is now your best opportunity… our best opportunity; it will wipe the slate clean for the both of us." He turned from her and shuffled back to his desk, picking up his glass, once more. "Tomorrow, you will have everything you need; you can go anywhere you want, and never have to see me or Martin again."

Looking down, into her hand, she knew, for the first time, that he had held intentions toward her mother, and believed every word he was saying. But it wasn't simple for her, after all these years, to just accept this moment as a new start.

"We all have darkness," she said, moving nearer to Harry, again: "I chose to stay with Martin, even though I knew he was becoming distant and no good for me; I was a coward not to admit that to myself."

Harry couldn't allow her to think of herself in this way; she had to remain positive. She and those precious children had a bright future coming to them, for the first time in their lives. But, he knew that to Laurie it wasn't - had never been - about the money.

Starting over wasn't simple, of course, no matter how much money you had, or where you went; the bad memories would always follow you, and sometimes haunt you to your dying day. She couldn't just run away, pretending that none of this had ever happened, any more than the neighbourhood could: it was her own husband who had caused all of this, and in their eyes, she would have to accept some responsibility for that - even Harry couldn't shield her from this. If Martin were to come back, she would be tarred as guilty as him - whether she were in the defendant dock or the witness stand - just as he had been, in the case of his brother.

But, no matter what he had done, she could not betray her own husband. If someone had to answer and go to jail, they would do so together. Regardless of him, she would keep her vows, to stand by her husband, and rehabilitation would be the new cause their family would fight for. Only then would they be absolved, in the eyes of God and their neighbours, and their children would be able to stay in Ravenfall.

She didn't want to move away; her mother had raised her here. Now she was being given the opportunity to do something her father never could: to make a difference, using means other than violence and bloodshed.

Harry was surprised, but not at all saddened, to hear the words coming from her mouth - she was truly her mother's daughter, and not at all like him; Laurie had chosen a different path, and he couldn't have been any prouder.

In his own eyes, perhaps he had been justified in wanting to kill her husband, but Laurie was a forgiving soul, who chose not to run from her demons - she had the strength to face up to them, and she knew how to fight for her life, and the life of her family. If only he had been that strong at her age, then maybe things would have turned out differently.

He no longer wanted to remain in the past; instead, he wanted to look towards the future. If she wanted to stay, all the better for him: perhaps he could get to know his daughter more. Helena would have wanted that. For the very first time, he really did, too.

Holding Laurie close to him now, he couldn't contain his happiness.

Whereas, she couldn't contain the water which had just broken in her uterus!

Should he call for an ambulance!? No, that would take too long!

He called for his car to be brought around the front; he would take her to the hospital himself.

Death can bring sadness, just as new life brings happiness. Either can bring immense relief: no more worries; no more cares.

When you are young, it is best not to feel too much, too soon; you have the rest of your life to be open to new sensations – to perhaps relive past experiences, long gone, but never forgotten.

Choices are made, mistakes are regrettable, and life owes you nothing.

There are days when you can make up for them; you cannot repair the past, but you can build a future. If you love your life, it's never too late to start it over. All you need is strong foundations, constructed from new life. Rather than bodies, long since buried.

CHAPTER 30

Bad dreams - we all get them, from time to time.

There are those who believe they are meaningful, and others who believe they are meaningless - a side-effect from bad food, or perhaps something on our minds, which just won't settle.

Dreams can be so bad that a person will endure insomnia, just to avoid them altogether.

Nobody can control their dreams; like opening a strange door, or the lid of a box, you never know what you're going to find.

In some cultures, the daydreams you have, whilst awake, are believed to be visions, indistinguishable from conscious imagination or your projected destiny. Your past and your fate can come together, as if setting your life along one main road. One can change how they travel on this road of life - deciding which turn to take, and which not to – whereas some people are just inclined to make every decision offered to them wrongly. The actual destination of your road is permanently undecided, because you never know when you're close to the end. Until you've arrived, and the journey stops.

What comes next is not for us to know, in this world.

It was a terrible dream which had kept Martin awake, for most of the night: he was once again back in the pub, only now he was standing in an open space, with his wife Laurie, father-in-law Harry, his parents and the man he had killed, all circling him - eyeing him, judgementally. As guns appeared in their hands, they all took aim and smiled, as though all were finally happy. Before the triggers were pulled, he had awoken with a start.

After that, he couldn't sleep. He tried to take his mind off of everything: browsing a free community magazine, he read about local charities, and how they had helped so many in need; the smiles on the grateful faces had moved him, somewhat.

Martin was beginning to understand that in his past, behind him, all the wrongs - the betrayals and the deaths - had perhaps been a curse. And now a gift was being presented before him: to start over. There was much that he could do for others, and not just financial aid.

Up to this point, the whole of his life had been a story, which needed to be told. He had been rescued from darkness, saved at the last moment, and made to witness and endure the worst of horrors.

But, he had learnt now that evil could be fought, if with another kind. Even though he recognized me to be an instrument of death, I had delivered him from damnation, and he walked, now, with both eyes fully open. It had been a long walk, but we were still taking it, together.

Thankfully, it was only a ten minute walk to Lotto Centre.

It was a little cold that morning, which irritated my wound. Thankfully, the injury wasn't too bad, so I still had good mobility and was able to function well enough.

As we strolled along the street, Martin seemed lost in his thoughts. I knew that he was starting to feel things he hadn't felt in a long time:

genuine regret, for what he had done to his wife, and to the people of Ravenfall. He had even been talking about finding a way to make it up to everyone: perhaps using the money to build a better school, or maybe a new community centre.

There were a lot of professional-class people walking by us – well-dressed and off to their jobs, in some office. We were now on the respectable side of civilization. But, as we made straight for Lotto Centre, situated in the heart of the city, my full attention was on the main entrance to the building.

It was wide open and uncovered; perfect for a sniper to pick us off, on approach. I had to check the situation fully: we couldn't go ahead until I was certain nobody was waiting outside, or hiding nearby, to make one last attempt on Martin's life.

The area was clear, for now. But that, in itself, was suspicious, despite the early morning hour. There was only one person in the vicinity: a road sweeper, going about his daily routine.

Leaving Martin in a nearby alcove, I approached slowly, hearing music from the sweeper's earphones - it was loud enough that the guy couldn't even hear me pass him. Totally focused on his work, he was no phoney.

I retrieved Martin and we walked across the approach to the automatic glass doors, stepping inside without any trouble. We crossed the foyer, into the reception area, which was also clear.

Once identified and greeted, we were offered a drink and asked to wait in a very plush office.

Then, the most unusual questions had been asked of Martin: was he on medication; did he suffer from high blood pressure, or diabetes…? He asked them if he was there to claim or for a health check! I guessed that some winners, under the circumstances, may need reminding to take their medication; in a high-stress situation like this, it was easy to see how some might forget.

You would think that the arrival of a massive jackpot winner would spark some excitement amongst the staff, but we were met with perfect professional calm and efficient etiquette. These people were trained, and very well so, to deal with people walking in off the street to claim millions. Of course, it is not like a large wad of cash is placed in your hand; usually, the transaction is made by cheque or electronically, depending on the amount, so it was all very administrative.

The calm was also necessary not to attract attention, in order to protect the winner's identity; the company operated very discreetly. Usually, these days, the process was carried out in the winner's home, but we had already concocted a reason for being in town on other business, making this visit more convenient.

As the official representative came in to greet and introduce himself, I immediately caught his eye – only winners and family members were welcome.

"She is my personal security," Martin told the man, with a hint of authority in his tone.

The official looked over Martin with clear interest: it was surprising how calm a person could be, despite winning such a fortune; most people were desperate to claim!

"I am to remain with my client for the duration of the transaction;

he's been placed in my care," I added, also in an official manner.

I wasn't prepared to wait outside, in the hallway - Harry had been clear not to let Martin out of my sight for a moment – so I took up a defensive position, in the corner of the room. Martin sat at the desk, across from a "Winner Counsellor", whose name was Khan.

The process was going to take from forty-five minutes to an hour, which was fine, considering there was no rush. We had made it inside and nothing more could prevent our success. This made me smile, internally, thinking how proud it would make my family.

Martin first had to present the winning ticket, to have it verified, officially. For the most part, by this stage, few claims weren't genuine, though often made from claimant confusion: looking at the wrong weekly draw; confusing numbers, etc. In this case, it was no false alarm.

I couldn't help but wonder how many fraudulent claims were made each week. It wasn't unheard of for people to copy and paste numbers together, creating forged tickets, which looked so genuine one really couldn't tell the difference. I wondered what would happen if they realized that the ticket wasn't even Martin's.

I guessed, in this case, possession was nine points of the law. Sure, he hadn't bought it, but he had found it, and signed it with his own signature. Was that actually illegal? He wasn't claiming under another name, so could they rightly claim fraudulent activity?

Martin then had to complete the prize claim form and present his identity documents.

It was usual for people who had won a considerable amount to open a private bank account at the meeting. This was made possible by attendance of a representative from a private bank, who was waiting in another room. Now he came in, carrying a laptop. Banking online, with a secure connection, the account could be set up immediately, along with the transfer of the prize - a cash advance could even be arranged.

I knew about the advance, and assured Harry that he would be the first to receive compensation. At this point, I quickly stepped in and handed Martin a piece of paper. "You have other business to attend to first, Sir," I reminded him, politely.

On the paper was the numbers of Harry's bank account - I had written them down at the train station, when Harry and I discussed Martin's documents.

Of course, in these circumstances, there had to be security checks made; there came the question of who the money was going to. Whilst it was usual for people to give money to friends and family, there were certain legal implications when it came to large gifts, such as this one; undoubtedly, a large tax bill awaited your beneficiary.

Thinking fast, Martin explained that the advance would need to go into another account, regarding a certain venture investment, back home; a construction project which would benefit the community. This wasn't a lie.

So, with no further questions, the process began. I was asked to witness the somewhat modest transaction of half a million euros - the most which could be gifted at such short notice. For the moment, it would be considered no more than a small down-payment.

There came a clear shiver of excitement from Martin, as his own, somewhat larger balance appeared on the monitor.

Then, came those words: "Transaction completed."

I think he wanted to erupt in a victory scream, but he managed to keep his composure, as a press representative took his photograph, for tomorrow's news article. It no longer bothered either of us who saw it or knew about the win because, as of that moment, nothing would ever be the same again. There then followed a short interview with Martin.

"So, we finally have what we need, and I feel a great relief has come over me," Martin said, as we walked back outside, into the open. "It's a shame I won't be able to spend it any time soon."

It was appearing that the endowment of so much money was already prodding the temptation in his mind to plan a giant spending spree. After he got out of jail, he would go on holiday and buy a new house – where, he wasn't exactly sure, but he would be leaving Ravenfall for good, keeping his earlier promise. "I can't say I'll be sorry to be out of that place; it never held anything for me but bad memories."

We walked up the steps, looking at the view from the footbridge: over the river, now busy with working vessels. The water was calm and seemed much clearer that morning, than the night before.

He spoke with clear sincerity: "I think it was wrong for me to ever have returned; I should have just stayed away - made a fresh start, when I had the chance. Then, maybe, all of this would never have happened."

"But, then you wouldn't be standing here right now, with a hundred-million euros in your bank account," I said flatly, then added, wryly: "and, I also wouldn't have met you, and all those people wouldn't have had to die because of it."

Martin turned to look into my eyes, deeply, for the first time. "You really don't care about money, do you? I mean, about being rich? To you, it's just about the job, and doing what you're good at… when you're not at home, being a butcher's daughter, that is."

This led to more personal questions from him, as he recalled the moment Laurence had recognized me, back in the supermarket: "Just how long do you think it will be before people start to realize what your family really is - how you finance your little shop?" He spoke now with a serious edge: "Sooner or later, everything comes to light; you can't hide in the shadows forever, any more than I could."

I didn't take his statement to be a threat; he was just talking openly. It was as though he felt we had developed enough of a trusted bond to do so.

"I don't live my life in darkness: it just appears every now and then, and, like a thick fog, I have to work my way through it. I always find some light to guide me."

He nodded his concurrence: a guiding light had certainly aided our little adventure. And, along the way, he had found his own - it had helped him to see life more clearly.

Perhaps he would do some more travelling; have a few more exciting experiences, in the future. He even went as far as to offer me a postcard and a small gift, from some exotic location, where he would be recuperating, following his release from jail.

He thought it sad to be temporarily going back to Ravenfall again, simply to answer for his crimes; perhaps it would be simpler if he just surrendered himself at the local police station.

“Why can’t you stand the thought of facing the town’s people?” I asked, disappointedly

“I feel that if I’m going to pay, then it should be under my terms. After what I’ve been through, you could at least grant me that dignity?”

I wasn’t sure if there was any reason, or any price, that bought him such grace.

He looked out at the boats again, with sorrow in his eyes. “I’ve had a lot of time to reflect, from the beginning of all this: I will try to forgive myself eventually, and I’ll make it up to those who I’ve hurt, like I promised.”

This time, I didn’t bother to ask if that included Laurie. The answer to that was already obvious: he had once again chosen not to bring her up, just as had been the case from the very first day. Perhaps he was a new man, in some ways, but the change had still not come about in his heart, only the thought of a new life, and of escaping his past life and past mistakes. In many ways he was still running, and always would be; he would never outrun his demons. All he really cared about was the money.

Unfortunately, he wasn’t going to live long enough to appreciate it. He would not be sending any gifts from where I was sending him.

Descending the bridge on the other side now, I stayed close by his side. Suddenly, I quickly swept my left heel backward, catching his footing - gravity sent him hurtling, head-first, down the steep steps. Only the impacts of his body tumbling could be heard; not the slightest sound came from his mouth, as his life bounced and spiralled out of him.

Finally, his body remained still and twisted at the bottom, his eyes open, but unmoving; a dark stain started to cover the pavement around the back of his head.

I quickly looked around: the streets nearby were deserted, and there were no vehicles or pedestrians in sight, to have witnessed the horrific accident which had just occurred.

Like I said: there's no such thing as free money. There is always a price, and this one has just been paid.

If Martin really was interested in trying to pay penance for his sins, his only intention was to gain enough of a pass to allow him entry into the kingdom of Heaven.

I did tell you it might not end as you expected. Orders are orders!

Harry got some of his money, and would soon receive the rest, and the town's people would undoubtedly receive compensation from Laurie; she was, at least, an honourable woman.

There was enough money to go around.

It did give me some comfort to know that even after she had paid off what she owed, Laurie was still was going to be a very rich woman. Hopefully, she would use the money for the good of the community.

Unfastening the watch from his wrist, I pocketed it and moved swiftly out of the area. I couldn't stop thinking about the old guy, whom Martin had found dead. I decided that straight after I had gotten something to eat, I would look into that matter.

I'm a killer; in your eyes, perhaps, a cold blooded assassin. But, I do have ethics.

There is no sense in trying to change what's in my nature, just as there was no sense in believing that the money would really have changed Martin.

Still, there is always a little light in everybody, which can cause a tinge of grief when you have to extinguish it forever, like blowing out a tiny candle flame. In Martin's case, it felt more like smothering an inferno, which had been burning out of control.

When you spend so much time around death, you start to understand it more; when you do a job well, and properly, you start to see nothing wrong with sending someone on their way.

One minute you're here, and the next you're not: you're elsewhere, making a new journey - maybe experiencing a new sensation.

In this world, the very need to breathe only leads to pain, fear and panic. In the other, maybe it means pure freedom.

Death is just another stage, no different from being born. It doesn't require any thought; nothing, really, to think that hard about.

Truthfully, I had been scared of it once. But, after I had faced it, I was ready to accept that there is freedom in death; it brought liberty, from life's horrors and burdens.

We all had to go - the only real question was how.

In reality, most could choose this, or elect to have that choice made for them.

I had been lucky that nobody was around to see me deliver Martin to the next world, so it had been quick.

And, now I was on my way home, reflecting on how lucky the day was turning out for me.

Of course, sooner or later, luck has a tendency to run out.

I'd been in too much of a hurry to ensure that no one had followed me from the bridge, where I left Martin's body.

So, as I swiftly turned a corner, the feel of a blade being pressed against my throat, and a cold pair of eyes right before my own, came as quiet a surprise to me.

I realized it was the first man I had shot in the supermarket; I had hit him in the chest, or so I thought. A dark smear of red on his shoulder indicated that I had not been as accurate as first thought. I should have been more wary, but I hadn't had the time to confirm the kills - he must have been playing possum.

Still, if this guy's intention was to fulfil the contract, he was too late; it had expired, following Martin's sudden demise.

"It's over," I said, calmly: "the money's already been claimed. My client has received his compensation and the target has been terminated."

"And, what about my crew?" he growled, pressing the blade a little deeper into my skin.

Loyalty is very touching, but it is not really what I expect from this sort. Even his associate, back at the church, had tried to take all the money for herself; there had been no mention of revenge.

"It was just orders - nothing personal on my part," I said, slowly reaching for the handle of my pistol. As soon as I saw an opportunity to redirect the blade, I would deliver one quick gunshot to his heart.

This time, I would be sure not to miss.

"Well, you killed my crew, so for me this is about as personal as it gets," he snarled, his eyes growing redder by the second.

Despite my wound, my reflexes were still of an excellent standard; deflecting the blade and redirecting it would have been easy, were it not for the unforeseen force which suddenly struck my assailant from behind, just like it had in the supermarket.

This time, though, it had not been a fist which struck him, but two bullets, dead-centre, to the heart. The blade slowly fell away from my throat and clattered to the floor, along with the now lifeless body lying at my feet.

"Afternoon, beautiful," a familiar voice called to me. "Was that young man bothering you?"

In a rough neighbourhood, it is always wise to have some form of backup; you never know when you, yourself, are being shadowed.

It had occurred to me that there would be a few surprising turns of event, doing this kind of work. But there is nothing more surprising than seeing your own boyfriend looking at you down the barrel of a gun, which he is pointing in your direction.

Eyes hidden behind dark sunglasses, he was dressed in a white blazer and dark pants. His face was, at first, set like stone. Then, with a tiny smile curling up at the sides of his mouth, it softened. He slowly lowered the gun to his side.

My hand remained in check by my own gun, still not knowing the full intentions of Mr. X.

CHAPTER 31

Death aside, there is no such thing as a natural conclusion.

Some people are just beyond saving, and with every death comes new life.

By now, Laurie was giving birth to her children. At least Harry was there to support her.

Hearing that a loved one has died can be quite a shock; perhaps more than you could ever imagine.

But, whilst it wouldn't make you feel immediately better, it was always best to have somebody there to talk to. Harry wasn't exactly the shoulder Laurie would have preferred to cry on, but there would be many tears to come. At least the worst part of her life was now over.

Sometimes, harsh methods had to be used, to allow happiness and progress.

It was now a time for happiness. She had been blessed with two children, and with the money they had coming to them, they all would be exceptionally well provided for.

Harry didn't expect a warm invitation into their lives any time soon, but at least she was taken care of, just as he had promised her mother she would be. At this thought, another good feeling returned, replacing the haunted images of the past. Now, he could rest more easily at night.

He would not answer to the laws of man. As for God, he would need to wait until his day of judgement.

Waiting in the corridor, he was anxious to talk to the doctor, and to see his daughter and his new grandchildren. He grew a little nostalgic, thinking about the birth of Laurie, all those years earlier. This time, he had planned everything near-perfectly.

Unfortunately, there was one thing that he could have never foreseen, nor had any power to control.

When the doctor asked him into his office, Harry knew; before a word had been said, he felt a force stronger than the impact of a bullet, tearing through his heart.

Maternal death was uncommon these days, unlike a hundred years ago, but even modern medicine couldn't prevent some fatal complications of delivery. Laurie had battled hard, but the muscles of the uterus had not contracted; bleeding had become excessive, and post-partum haemorrhaging was the cause of her death.

They placed Laurie in a single room, for the moment, tucking her frame beneath the bed-clothes. She looked as though in deep sleep, but Harry knew she could not be awoken.

Standing over her, he was drawn, once again, to the haunting image of her mother, dying in his arms. He wanted to reach out and hold Laurie, but didn't want to disturb her restfulness. Instead, he bent over and placed a loving kiss on her forehead.

Leaving her, he made his way down the hall, where the medical team were now focused on the twins. By the time Harry stopped, to look through the nursery ward's window, all of their assessments regarding vital signs and physical responses had come back clear; both had been given the necessary vitamin injections.

Seeing them lying together, in a warm isolette – wrapped, in caps and surprisingly alert to their new surroundings - he was in no doubt that they were the two most beautiful things he had ever seen, just as their mother had been. Their transition from their mother's body, out into the world, seemed not to have done them any harm.

Other than that now they had no mother to bond with, or feed from, as was usual.

How do we end up where we are?

We often question whether our life is the one we truly wanted. We may search for answers we can never find; sometimes we are just not looking in the right place.

So often we try to plan things well, but we never see the true designs we make for ourselves; not everyone sees the colours before them - just a slight shade of grey.

We are all creatures, each of which serves a purpose, however random or inconsequential; for each of us there is a plan – there is cause and effect. And, through our actions, we all continue the everlasting circle. The actions that we begin - like life - will never stop; they will continue to unravel, layer upon layer. We can never see, or reach, the centre; one dead layer after another, we peel them away, allowing a new skin to grow, continuing to protect the secret buried underneath: the true reason to our life.

Only, this wasn't Harry's circle; he was still here, and Laurie was gone, before him - it wasn't supposed to be that way. He had been the next layer to be peeled away; Laurie had plenty of time left, surely.

Those she had left behind - the newborn - needed her; they needed someone young, fresh and good, to guide them towards a promising future. Not someone like Harry: all he had ever known was pain, which had tormented him into committing vengeful acts - acts which had doomed not just him, but the whole community around him.

With Martin and Laurie now gone, who was left to claim the money?

He cursed himself: how could he even think of money, with these two orphaned infants before him? Orphaned by his actions; his own decisions. Decisions which had cost them the chance at a normal life, and a proper family; he had taken that all away.

Once again, he had failed.

God had shown him that nobody - no mortal - has the power to control life. What we take away can, at any time, be taken from us. Perhaps this was God's justice: the hand of the Lord, come down upon him, in judgement.

But, why take Laurie? Why not take his life? Laurie was an innocent; she was good and had, this very day, brought these two children into the world.

What did this world now offer them, with no mother or father?

He had never considered himself father material. He knew nothing about raising a child; it was a big step in life, and one which he had decided not to accept. Responsibility for Laurie's life he had left to Helena, allowing her to make her own choices and decisions. She had done a better job than he could.

Looking at the twins now, he did not feel shame for staying away, just as Martin felt no shame about abandoning them. Perhaps, on that account, the two men were the same.

They were so small; such very tiny little babies, just as Laurie had been, when he had been to see her at the hospital. Yet, still, he had walked away.

In spite of it, these past few days he had spent with Laurie had been the most precious of his life.

This time, there would be no walking away from his responsibilities.

He would contact social services immediately. He didn't want Laurie's children going to live with strangers, or spending their lives bouncing around in the system; they deserved to be with what remained of their real family.

He was a changed man, and he had again been given the opportunity to rehabilitate his soul, for a worthier cause than himself. It was time he stepped into the light, and stopped hiding in the darkness. There would be no more making deals with the devil.

If Laurie was still here, he was sure she would have approved.

Some believe that our relationships in life can continue, even after death.

But death always seems to come too soon, for those who are left behind. Perhaps not fast enough, to those who live an undeserving life.

What we each choose to believe is our own business.

But, one thing is certain: the gift of life is the greatest any person can bestow. And, even though you may not have lived so long – and been what you could have been – perhaps you have, at least, seized that gift. Made your own contribution; something to leave behind. So that when your time does come, there are no regrets.

Maybe Laurie is better where she is now, than where she has been; if there was nothing for her in this world, maybe there will be in the next. She has not left her children alone: they will be watched over, just as she was.

Only, this time, the time together will be longer; hopefully long enough give an old man peace.

Isn't that all that anyone asks? And, for most, all we can really strive for?

CHAPTER 32

They say that honesty is the key to sustaining any relationship. But, the real challenge is to be honest, and throw in a few omissions, every now and then.

It doesn't matter who pursued who, or who told the most truths, and who told the most lies: in the end, we all hold something back about ourselves.

Perhaps the work we do isn't as great as we make it out to be, or we don't earn as much as we suggest... or fail to mention the fact that it is not totally legitimate!

The fact that we lie to those we care about, in order to protect them, is noble. Unless, of course, they get caught up in our business and it puts their lives in danger.

It is a common scenario in the movies.

What you don't expect is to be working on a contract, when your boyfriend drops by to save your life, by putting bullets in the back of the thug who has a knife at your throat!

Sitting opposite each other, in a booth at a burger bar, as we were right then, I couldn't help but think about people, with all of their own little secrets.

Neither of us had been totally truthful about what we did for a living, a fact which, for most couples, would normally make for quite a conflict. Yet, surprisingly, even then I couldn't look upon him as a total mystery.

As his alias, Mr. X was a well-respected killer, within our unique and selective community, known for his dedication to always putting the interests of the profession before any personal affairs.

Dipping a French-fry into a pot of ketchup, I was now impressed by how cool and relaxed he was about this situation, despite the fact that I had killed his nephew, three days earlier. One would think that he harboured some form of animosity toward me, yet, at that moment, he seemed quite content consuming his fries, as I tucked into my quarter-pounder without cheese. The one thing, at least, that I now knew he hadn't lied about was being a vegetarian.

I used to cherish every moment, sitting at a table in my house with this man, who wasn't crazy for meat - it was a common topic, from breakfast through dinner. Being a butcher, the subject is an important feature in my life, but don't get me wrong: that doesn't mean that I don't find it refreshing to spend time with someone who is more interested in my flesh, than that of an animal.

If I'm starting to weird you out, then try putting yourself in my *position!*

Being a butcher, or a contract killer, leaves little room for socializing... or fucking.

I like sex as much as the next woman.

And, if you don't think that I was just a little bit horny, at that moment, knowing that the guy I had been seeing for the two past months was in fact a contractor, well...

The thing about my business is that you never know who you think you know.

I always thought that it was rare in life, to meet another person with whom you find you share a special connection; someone with whom you can truly relate and communicate, on the same wavelength.

Of course, we had never talked openly about our lives, and our sideline professions; it's not like we can state our occupation on Facebook. Even when we were together, the topics had been pretty normal.

Dating wasn't exactly a regular thing, when I spent most of my career away from home. Him being a Big City guy, it had been a while since we had last got together.

And now, here we were, our masks pulled away; truly face to face.

Yet, even now, neither of us seemed to want to come right out and say anything about this sudden revelation. When all is said and done, and words are not easy, what is there to say but the first thing which comes to mind?

"How did you find me?" I asked.

With deep breathing and dry palms, the guy was as cool as a cucumber. "Simple," he said, finishing his meal: "I just looked up the address of the nearest Lotto Centre."

The statement put me somewhat on edge again, and I began to question his motives for being there.

Normally, to even consider forming any kind of relationship within the fraternity would be considered complex and very risky; we were, after all, death merchants.

"How did you know about Lotto Centre?"

He took a sip from his milkshake, and wiped his fingers on a serviette. "I had a little chat with somebody, who filled me in. I had the impression I was going up against the best, yet you let that guy get close enough to kill you."

I knew now I had to be mindful of his movements. This was a potentially dangerous predicament to be in, despite the fact that we were in a public place; it wasn't exactly neutral ground.

"The way you took out those guys on the train - including my nephew -" he said, dispassionately, "I would have thought you'd be ready for anything."

Rather than patronizing, I found his tone to be slightly teasing.

"I didn't know he was your nephew," I said, noting no discernible change in his mood, at my statement.

Situations like this one could be a powder keg - the dialogue between the two opponents would decide whether it would remain stable, or become volatile. I still wasn't sure whether he had been contracted by Braddock, or whether he was carrying out a personal vendetta; a job was a job, and there could be no strong emotional ties for people in our profession.

There did, however, need to be rules, as in any social structure. We may have worked outside of the law, but even in criminal enterprise, we had to follow certain guidelines, to ensure that business was conducted in a controlled manner. Both of our families had always been devoted to ensuring peace, even in rivalry, or matters of family honour and justice. Whenever peace was threatened, meetings such as this needed to be held, with fairness and open mindedness.

You see, it is even possible for people like us to work out our issues, without the need for violence, despite the fact that death is our business, and is always the underlying topic.

When it comes to matters regarding territorial dispute, or contract pilfering issues, it is usually a simple case of compensation to the injured party. But, in situations where family members have suffered a loss, at the hand of a rival, it is the responsibility of selected members of each side to talk through the circumstances. Difficult as it is, we have to remain professional and, at times, unemotional - which is hard, when you've lost kin by the actions of an intimate acquaintance.

"That's why you and I are still talking," he said, with complete candour. "I'm not here to settle the score, if that's any concern."

There were times to be ruthless and times to be prudent, and I was relieved he was taking this the way he was. But, I was also curious about why he wasn't acting the avenging uncle.

"You were doing your job, so I already know it wasn't personal on your part," he said.

I knew he wasn't lulling me into a false sense of calm: his reputation preceded him, and there weren't many who could remain as civil as Mr. X, even at the most difficult of times.

Peace can only be achieved when people come together and reason, in a civilized manner. When reasonable people find the ground to sit down and talk civilly with each other, reason will usually prevail, over uncontrolled, emotional rage. And sometimes, in order to ensure peace, in a diplomatic and professional manner, we have to find other means of dampening the fury burning within our heart.

Whilst our hearts are not made of stone, nor can we allow them to be poisoned, for fear of losing what humanity we have left.

He could not play the part of an avenging relative. Seeking vengeance required one to be victimized - as a professional, he could never allow himself to feel that way.

Besides, as he looked in my eyes, I could see that there still seemed to be some deep, fiery passion, which made it impossible for him to hold such a deep, dark vendetta against me.

He looked me mischievously in the eye: "I found my answers and the people who were responsible, so I settled up with them - even the man who put out the contract. You took care of business at your end, so I would say this matter is settled."

He had seen me kill Martin! He was very good: I hadn't seen him at all! His nest position must have been a good one, to see me tripping Martin down the stairs, the way I had.

I only wished I had been there when he killed Braddock.

News of Braddock's death would be a relief to many, especially Harry, who was not connected to it in any way.

"I'm partly to blame as well," he said, regretfully: "what we do is never personal; it's always business. My nephew got in with the wrong crowd, despite my offer to take him on… but… it was his choice."

He looked at the watch on my wrist, questioningly. *Souvenir?* his eyebrows seemed to ask. He had never considered me to be the sentimental type.

"I might as well tell you, since this mess is pretty much at an end: the ticket wasn't Martin's; he took it from a dead man's wallet. He even stole this wrist-watch," I said, showing it more clearly to Mr. X. "If possible, I'm hoping to return it to whatever family he has left."

I noticed another raised eyebrow, this time questioning: "It would be so wrong if you didn't?" He was serious, apparently a little cynical in matters of sentimentality.

"Obviously, I'll send it back by post; I'm not offering to hand-deliver it," I said, taking another bite of my burger. "I don't suppose they would just accept that I found it by chance, which would lead to certain questions that I can't answer."

It felt strange to be talking this way, with all now out in the open - not at all as if in the same company as when we had last seen each other. Truthfully, I had suspected that I wasn't the only one of us with secrets, but it was okay then, because I thought I was protecting him - how funny that seemed now.

"How's your sister getting on, by the way?" he tactfully changed the subject.

When it came to matters of my family, I had always been reluctant to mention much; he knew that we worked in a family business, but as butchers – now, he knew the rest.

"Well, in a couple of months, she'll be out of high school. College next and, if she chooses, following in the family business… meat, that is!"

Right then, now there were no more lies, there seemed to be an awkwardness emerging between us. We had seemed to be getting along so well, but it dawned on us both that it was a bad idea to get into too many personal details, too quickly; there were still things we needed to keep private. Secrets were, at times, a small price to pay for a measure of happiness.

"You know, a lot of people wouldn't understand how important a legacy can be. What is left, when we die, allows the lineage to continue," he said, almost uncharacteristically. "People like us will always be needed to maintain order, and ensure that business doesn't get out of hand."

I simply nodded. I couldn't deny that there were many who entered this work without appreciating its complexity, and the commitment to keep it clean. Even though our two families may have done things differently, we all did the same job and served the same purpose: to keep the country free of anarchy.

"Well, I have to make a move: got some family business to attend to," he slid out from the table. "I hope we can get together again sometime; I really enjoy your company, and I think it might get even more interesting now."

I didn't say anything, and he left me sitting there

That's how we ended it.

Disappointed by this outcome?

Perhaps you expected big fisty-cuffs, or a shootout?

Well, we leave that to those guys in the movies. Besides, enough blood has already been spilt for your entertainment.

I did also say that it was probably not going to end as you might not expect.

That's how real life is: unexpected. And, the older I get, the more I find the world changes around me. Nothing really stays the same; each day is new and unique.

If you think it isn't possible for two professionals to sit down and work out their differences, in a civilized manner, then you haven't been paying close enough attention to this story. You have to learn to respect the responsibility that comes with this lifestyle.

At times, things can be worked out civilly, and at other times they can't. At the end of the day, that isn't necessarily the decision of the parties involved.

It would be foolish to have you believe that we always walk away, but those who care enough to maintain peace are more likely to live to a respectable age.

We choose this life. We can quit any time, but then what else is there for us to do? What is the retirement policy for a contract killer? I've never heard of one put in place by a criminal organization. If you're independent, you just quit and hang up your tools.

But, if you don't have someone to whom you can pass on your legacy, what point was there to your life in it? Your work goes unnoticed.

The only other question which remains is: where does it go from here?

If you think I've done all this because I regret my life, or I'm asking you to feel sorry for me, then forget it. I have no regrets; all the choices

I ever made were of my own doing. There were times I made mistakes, sure, but I made good decisions, also.

I would have chosen no other life. Because, for me, there is no other life.

Take a look at yourself and ask: "Is what I am and who I've become what I wanted?" Only you know the answer, and it is only for you to know what to do with it. Stay as you are or change it - your life is yours, to do with whatever you please.

I'm not really interested or care whether you believe this story to be true or bogus. Or whether my, or anyone else's, actions in these pages were right or wrong. The fact is, you don't live in my world, so who are you to judge?

There is more to this tale's ending, as well what you've seen and heard so far.

I manage to track down the old man's family, through the obituary columns. It turned out that he had not actually died of natural causes, as Martin had implied: the article read that he died because of a fatal blow to the head, before all his possessions were stolen.

It just goes to show that anybody is capable of anything, no matter how horrific!

The family received the watch anonymously, in the post, as I promised, along with a kind letter detailing that it had been found in a local pawn shop – which, of course, doesn't really exist.

As for the families in Ravenfall, they got a small portion of the money Martin had wired into Harry's bank account – unfortunately, it wasn't enough to build Harry's mall.

Did he ever get over his daughter's death? you might ask. What parent could? But, he has new purpose now: taking care of the twins - both boys.

I went back to my family, and to the shop; nothing changed for us. It never does and it never will!

Even now, as I sit with them all at the dining table - Mother cutting the roast chicken, as Father pours the wine - I hold my sister's hand, and we say Grace, for the offering we are receiving. There isn't the slightest stain of blood which haunts me, or image which keeps me awake. Today is our family day; what happens out there in the world has nothing to do with what is around this table.

This is what we do, and we're the best, so we don't worry.

Tomorrow, I'll help my father with the meat delivery, after he and my sister come back from one of the lamb suppliers, at one of the neighbouring farms. We get most of our meat that way, helping to support local businesses in the community, and enabling future generations to continue in our way.

So, as I bring this story to a close, just remember that the work of an assassin is not as heartless or as cold-blooded as you might believe it to be, even when the target is a bastard and a thief! Be honest, would you have spared Martin's life? I'll leave you with that question.

Maybe I'll be seeing you again. I could, after all, be in your own home town.

So, next time you go in your local butcher's, for some freshly cut steak, always smile at the young lady serving you - it's only polite!

LAST WORDS

Well, you're still here, which means that you stayed until the end. So, now you know the answer to the same question that everyone else asks.

But, before you go, ask of yourself: *"Why did I not withdraw?" You could have stopped reading at any time, and closed the book, but instead you stayed with me, no matter how dark it got, as I revealed my story. I warned you it wasn't romantic, and it wasn't going to end well, yet you kept on the journey with me - a journey of my past and my present.*

As for my future, well, that is something I will have to wait for, and see for myself.

Maybe you still have questions, looming in the back of your mind? Don't be shy: go ahead and ask - it's no more than I would expect. Unfortunately, I have nothing more to tell; our time together is done.

Not many are as curious as you!

Perhaps you really don't want to know any more, anyway.

Or, do you already have the answers? Well, then you have the advantage over everyone else.

If you have the answers, keep them; those of you who still seek them will have to wait, for the day that the dark shadows vanish and the light of truth shines down on us all.

No matter what happens along the road of life, I, at least, will have no regrets. The journey I chose, I chose of my own free will - what is there to regret?

Call me whatever you want: "murderer"; "cold-blooded killer"; "assassin"...!

Now I know I'm not you, still with your same question; at least I am free of that burden.

How do I do what I do?

Well, if you still don't know the answer to that question, the reason is very, very, simple: you haven't read the book!

ACKNOWLEDGEMENTS

The publishers and authors would like to thank Russell Spencer, Matt Vidler, Susan Woodard, Leonard West and Paul Addison for their work, without which this book would not have been possible.

ABOUT THE PUBLISHER

L.R. Price Publications is dedicated to publishing books by unknown authors.
We use a mixture of both traditional and modern publishing options to bring our authors' words to the wider world.
We print, publish, distribute and market books in a variety of formats including paper and hardback, electronic books, digital audio books and online.

If you are an author interested in getting your book published, or a book retailer interested in selling our books, please contact us.
www.lrpricepublications.com

L.R. Price Publications Ltd,
27 Old Gloucester Street,
London, WC1N 3AX.
020 3051 9572
publishing@lrprice.com

www.ingramcontent.com/pod-product-compliance
Lightning Source LLC
Chambersburg PA
CBHW071443170626
46811CB00007B/2472

* 9 7 8 1 9 1 6 4 6 7 9 4 1 *